The Dark Waves of Winter

Edited by David M. Olsen

Kelp Books, LLC

1491 Cypress Drive #475
Pebble Beach, Ca 93953

"Sometimes They Bite" originally appeared in *Mystery Magazine*. "Room and Board" originally appeared in *Fishy Business*.

ISBN-13: 9798986946207

Cover design by: Polyankakul
Library of Congress Control Number: 2022949603
Printed in the United States of America

Table of Contents

Room and Board Vinnie Hansen 4

Neighbor North Lindsay Jamieson 14

The Dark Watchers Nik Xandir Wolf 38

To Catch a Thief Hilary Davidson 54

Snowman Billy Minshall 67

Thanks People Michael Scott Moore 75

Make Him Suffer JoAnn Chaney 86

Down in Monterey Gar Anthony Haywood 97

November Snow Ewan A. Dougall 108

The Rolex David Zimmerle 123

Undertow Shannon Hollinger 137

Seal Colony Brian Asman 158

Lili's Song Jenny Bhatt 178

The Dead Spot John Palisano 192

Playing Chess Gary Grace........................ 207

Sometimes They Bite Lawrence Block................ 222

Room and Board

Vinnie Hansen

"Dude, I know a way you can pay."

Jayden cracked open a crusty, pink-rimmed eye, his gaze traveling up brown fabric to a blurry figure hovering above the back of the couch. "Huh?" His stomach tumbled. From the meth or from the dawning, Matt had another scheme for him; Jayden wasn't sure.

Matt walked around the couch to face him, swigging a Red Bull breakfast and tossing messy, sun-bleached hair from his eyes. "Yeah, bro, Tasha is sick of this shit." Matt swirled a finger—traces of crystal at the end—to indicate the cheap ballpoint pen on the coffee table and the tiny, empty plastic bag beside it. "You can't keep couch surfing without contributing. Least not here."

Jayden blinked and propped himself onto elbows. Without Matt's assistance, he'd be living in his truck, shooed from place to place by the cops, competing for available toilets with the hordes of homeless in Santa Cruz.

Matt paced back and forth, like he meant to deepen the groove in the worn carpet. "So I have a plan." He drained his drink, crushed the can under his Converse sneakers, and threw the flattened metal onto Jayden's stomach.

Drops of liquid shocked his skin. He'd been sweaty last night and stripped down to his boxers. He brushed the cold metal to the floor and sat up, wrapping his arms around his torso. Epically groggy, he squinted at Matt, trying to follow his words.

"They need a docent at the surf museum."

Jayden rubbed the goose bumps on his arms and scanned the room for a possible cigarette. "What's a docent?"

Matt lit a cigarette, then fished another from the package and lobbed it to Jayden. "Someone who shows people around, answers questions."

Matt had not yet untacked the sheet covering the window, so Jayden peered through the dimness at him. "Why does anyone need to be shown around? That place is like the size of this room."

"I know, huh?" Matt flicked his burned-out match to the floor and resumed pacing. "It's perfect. You just sit there and answer questions about surfing." He pitched the book of matches to Jayden.

"How much does it pay?"

Matt stopped walking. "The thing is, it doesn't."

***

Jayden's flip-flops slapped the concrete floor of the lighthouse, home of the museum. He followed black hair swaying above a tight butt. Peach-colored yoga pants gripped curves so closely that the girl might as well have been naked. *Dude, if you don't stop, you're going to give new meaning to Woodies on the Wharf.*

Biting his chapped lip, Jayden forced his attention to the displays. On a bulletin board beside him, yellowing newspaper articles showed photos of record waves.

What Matt wanted as payment for a place to crash was an early Johnny Rice longboard. According to Matt, it was hanging on the far wall. Surfers lusted after the artistic boards shaped by the dead, local surfing legend. "It'll be epic riding that thing," Matt had said.

Jayden wasn't surprised at Matt's plan. As long as Jayden had known him—since middle school—Matt had survived by posing as a Greek god with Jayden, a useful dark shadow, following his glory.

Problem was, in the little museum, boards leaned and hung everywhere—dozens of them.

The hottie in front of Jayden explained the duties, adding, "The docent gig is really chill."

In front of an exhibit of black-and-white photos of Hawaiian prince surfers in Santa Cruz, the girl turned to face him, all smooth skin and blue eyes. "If you surf Steamer Lane," she burbled, "you can come straight out of the water and be at work."

He hitched up his long shorts, which were sagging off his hips. "Awesome." *Especially if my schedule overlaps yours.* His gaze roved up the brick walls. "Some of these displays are way high," he said, scratching an ear.

She eyed him. "Yeah, it must have been crazy hanging the big boards." She pointed at a board propped in sand behind a cordoned-off area. "That plank weighs ninety-five pounds."

The board reached to the rafters.

"Check this out." She motioned to a surfboard missing a chunk from its bottom. "Shark attack."

"That's dope," he said.

"Totally, huh? Better than a leg, though."

***

Lighting a cigarette, Jayden sank into Matt's couch. Or, to be more accurate, Tasha's couch. "I had to fill out an application," Jayden whined, "*and* interview with the Santa Cruz Surfing Society." He threw the burned match onto the littered coffee table. "I hope you appreciate what I'm going through here."

In front of him, Matt, shirtless, resumed wearing out the carpet. Broad-shouldered and bronzed, Matt attracted babes like a sale at Forever 21. "Another option," Matt offered, "is you could get a real job."

Jayden snorted. This from a guy who'd never worked a day in his life.

After Jayden's parents kicked him out the first time, he'd bagged groceries, but that schedule seriously interfered with surfing. He'd quit to take a night gig at a theater. Leave it to Matt to get him fired for letting him and Tasha sneak in. But what could he do? Just a room in Santa Cruz ran $800. "If I'm gonna go through all this," Jayden said, "you better be sure Tasha will let me stay."

Matt stopped and smirked. "She *loves* me."

Jayden frowned. "If you have that much influence, why do I have to go through all this bullshit?"

Matt leaned over the coffee table and drilled a finger into Jayden's chest. "You're in no position to negotiate." He fished a cigarette from the package in the pocket of Jayden's flannel shirt. "So, how's our plan

6

going?”

“Your plan, you mean.”

“Yeah.”

“Okay, I guess,” Jayden said. “I asked for the least busy day, like maybe I wasn’t sure of myself, you know.”

“You’ll want to park in the spaces beside the lighthouse.”

Anxiety welled up in Jayden. “If I can get one.” This was all easy for Matt. He was taking none of the risk.

“Well, if you can’t, wait until someone leaves and go out during your shift to move your truck. It seems pretty loosey-goosey over there.”

Jayden scratched at his arm, sprinkling himself with cigarette ash. “Damn.” He swiped at the burn, smearing gray along the top of his hand. Matt’s whole scheme depended on the laid-back vibe of the museum, and the idea that with surfboards all over, no one would miss one. At least, not right away.

“Relax, dude,” Matt said. “Even if someone sees you, in that vicinity, lots of people are walking around with boards.”

“Not Johnny Rice longboards.”

“Who’s going to pay attention to that?”

Jayden stubbed out his cigarette in a jar lid and scrubbed his forehead. Tasha’s couch squished under his weight, but at least he could stretch his feet over the armrest and get comfy. There was no way to get comfortable in the cab of his truck. “Seriously, do you have anything better than cigarettes?” he asked.

***

Jayden sagged on a wobbly stool behind the counter, feeling as noodled as if he’d surfed all day. He appreciated the divider between him and the museum visitors. People flowed in and out of the single room—kids on rollerblades, old farts with canes, and foreigners.

These people with their questions: “Is this the original Jack O’Neill wetsuit?” “Which surfboard is worth the most?” “What do you do with Sex Wax?”

In between answering questions and selling keychains and beanies, he’d been busy checking out how he might climb up to reach a surfboard. At least a dozen of them hung from the rafters in rope cradles. He might be able to use the sandwich-board sign that said *SANTA CRUZ*

SURFING MUSEUM T-SHIRTS FOR $20 as a step stool to clamber on top of the postcard display rack.

At ten minutes before four, Jayden pushed upright and used his hands like a megaphone: "The museum closes in ten minutes."

The last few visitors straggled toward the door. A young man with a heavy accent stopped to ask him, "When will there be more surfers?"

"When the surf's up?"

The man blinked at him. "When will that be?"

"Call a surf shop," Jayden said. "They can tell you."

Finally, the place emptied, and he locked the door. He circled the room, reading the labels. *Epic good luck.* A custom Johnny Rice surfboard leaned against a case housing old surfing DVDs.

He hefted the glossy redwood board out of the sand display. He couldn't tip it without banging into stuff, so holding it in a vertical position, he duck walked it across the room. Damn, the thing was heavy. Peering out the exit, he tipped the board to carry it under his arm. The rush of adrenaline was almost as good as meth.

The esplanade veered away in a horseshoe around the lighthouse, so walkers and bikers weren't paying any attention to him. *Just like Matt said.* The ocean vistas, their cell phones, their dogs riveted their attention. Heart racing, Jayden lifted the board into the back of his old Toyota truck.

He trotted back to lock up the building, looked around again to see if anyone was watching, and then drove off. *Piece of cake.*

***

Matt stared into the bed of Jayden's faded-red Toyota. "Dude, this is made of redwood."

Jayden ran his hand over the glossy finish. "Pretty sick, huh?"

"This is the wrong board."

The juice drained out of Jayden. "It's a Johnny Rice longboard. That's what you said."

"There's a balsa wood one. With a trick design of different woods on the fin." Matt clapped Jayden's shoulders and spun him to face him. "It's hanging up. Was this one hanging up?"

Jayden gulped. "What am I supposed to do?"

"Take it back. Get the right board."

"That might be better to do at night."

Matt nodded. "Do you still have the key to the museum?"

"You think I drove to the Surfing Society with that board in my truck?" Jayden said. Matt could be so dense.

"Well, before you turn it in, make a copy." Matt dipped his hand into the pocket of his shorts and fished out a baggie. "We'll celebrate later."

***

Penknife in his pocket, Jayden drove across Santa Cruz, taking surface roads. He was pumped, like Scott Lang in *Ant-Man* traveling into the quantum realm. When the Toyota hit a pothole, the heavy surfboard bounced and whammed precariously against the tailgate.

Even at midnight, the esplanade was not deserted. Moonlight silhouetted a few walkers. In the parking lot, a homeless man rattled by, his supermarket cart piled high. He headed toward the field across the street. Jayden swallowed, sweat gathering in his armpits. Without some luck, he could end up like that guy. At least, he had his truck, though.

He climbed from the cab. The quiet of night amplified the crashing of the waves below the cliffs. In front of him, the lighthouse threw its beam out to the water. How amazing that with the duplicate key, he could just waltz right into this place. His heart hammered with excitement.

Inside the dark interior, Jayden lugged the board back through the clutter, hefted it over the velvet ropes, and propped it in the sand. Using his phone's flashlight, he hoped to spot the Johnny Rice board suspended conveniently above the counter or over the flat, glass-covered display case across the room, but the light-colored board of Matt's wet dream hung above the housing for an old DVD player and monitor.

Jayden lit a cigarette and wiggled the stool from behind the counter, placing it beside the tall housing case. Holding the cigarette between his teeth, Jayden scrambled onto the top of the stool. It rocked beneath him. Jayden yelped, latching on to the display. His cigarette tumbled down like a surfer wiping out.

Jayden gripped the top of the case. The stool leg cracked. His foot slipped into the air, the sudden weight yanking one hand loose. Jayden let himself drop back to the floor. *Damn!*

He scouted around on the floor for the cigarette but couldn't spot it. He couldn't waste time looking for it. Kicking the stool aside, he dragged the sandwich board over, scraping it across the concrete.

He sniffed. *Smoke!* He no sooner smelled it than a displayed newspaper article curled into flame. Jayden slapped at it with his palm.

Holy shit! That hurt.

Sucking a burned finger, Jayden considered. The fire would consume the old newspaper and die. The best idea was to get the board and get out quick.

He lifted himself on top of the sandwich board as the flames licked another article. Glancing at the longboard, Jayden pulled up and belly flopped on top of the case.

Pushing up to all fours, Jayden coughed as smoke drifted upward. With shaking hands, he sliced at the nearest rope around the longboard. *Damn, this knife is puny.*

And dull.

But, if he could cut the first loop, he could probably tug and tip the board out of its cradle.

The flames below him devoured the newspaper clippings, then died back as he'd expected.

Jayden sawed at the last fibers of rope. Black smoke coiled up, worse than before, choking him. He squinted down, eyes burning. The newspapers had been consumed, but the wood-framed corkboard behind them was smoldering. He hacked at the rope.

The final thread gave way.

Pulling the board toward him, Jayden pushed the end downward, but the board was too long. The part remaining in the ropes held it in place.

Leaning precariously from the top of the case, Jayden chopped at the next loop of rope.

The smoke thickened. Closing his eyes, he slashed blindly. When the rope snapped, his body pitched forward. He grabbed at the board for balance. Unsupported, it crashed to the floor. Jayden's body plunged after it. Flinging out a hand, he grabbed a rafter and dangled like a monkey.

His heart raced, but damn, this was fun, like making the drop on a big wave.

He released his hold, bending his knees for impact. His feet landed on the surfboard. The glossy wood skidded on the concrete. Jayden sailed backwards. He threw out a hand to break his fall, but his ass slammed against the concrete. Pain shot through his wrist and hip bone. *A total wipeout.*

Above him, the tail of a Santa Cruz Surf Club T-shirt ignited. The ancient shirt burned well, the blaze shooting toward the ropes. A fire alarm shrieked.

Time to bail!

Dragging the board to the door, Jayden glanced, wide-eyed, over his shoulder as the fire crackled along the rope. A surfboard plummeted, hitting a standing surfboard, which toppled another surfboard to the floor.

Holy shit!

He jammed out the door and tucked the surfboard under his arm, his wrist protesting. Behind him, the alarm was squealing his crime to the world, and through the windows framing the entrance, light flickered.

He pitched the board into the truck bed, scurried to the cab, and would have burned rubber—if there'd been any left on his tires.

As he swerved onto West Cliff Drive, the surfboard slid along the top of the tailgate. He hadn't put it in far enough, but he wasn't going to stop now. Late-night strollers, the people in the houses along West Cliff, everyone could hear that alarm.

Jayden careened onto a side street, the board bumping and hopping. He checked the rearview. The board had slipped around, so it was practically sideways, sticking far out on the passenger's side.

A fire truck wailed. Jayden started at the nearness of it.

He flew around the next corner, the board bouncing, teetering from the bed of the truck. The fire engine shrilled toward him. Jayden swerved to the side of the street and hit a pothole. The end of the board lifted, and the Johnny Rice launched into an aerial ride, its final performance, taking the drop before riding across the pavement into the far lane.

Jayden stomped on his brakes and scrambled from the cab in time to watch the fire truck roll over the fin, crushing wood and hope.

At the side of the road, Jayden stood, arms dangling and mouth agape, staring at the bits of board sprinkled across the road. *Matt's gonna be so pissed.*

Jayden darted into the street and started picking up the bigger pieces—the evidence. If everything in the museum burned, they might never know about the theft. And if the door burned, maybe they wouldn't know he'd left it unlocked behind him.

After collecting and tossing bits of surfboard into the bed of the truck, Jayden climbed in and drove slowly away, his hands shaking on the steering wheel. *Maybe the fire experts will figure it was an accident caused by a smoldering cigarette. Dropped by a tourist.* He hoped they never figured out it was him.

He didn't want to be known as the guy who burned down the surfing museum. Even the surfers he hung with would hate him.

If he didn't end up in a bunk at the county jail, he faced a future of sleeping scrunched up in his truck. For reasons Jayden couldn't explain, he found himself back at the museum, parking on West Cliff Drive. *Returning to the scene of the crime.*

Why did criminals do this?

A few spectators had gathered in the eerie yellow parking lot light. None of them looked in Jayden's direction. Through his windshield, he watched a silhouetted firefighter tug on the hose. The others were inside.

The lighthouse might be gutted, but at least it was going to stand, beaming its signal to save lives. If only it could save him. Jayden pounded the steering wheel. What did he have to show for all this? An epic zero. No board. No room.

*Author's notes: Legendary board shaper Johnny Rice passed away in 2015.

*The Santa Cruz Surf Museum is currently operated by the Santa Cruz Department of Parks & Recreation and has been for a number of years.

Vinnie Hansen is the author of the Carol Sabala mystery series, the novels *Lostart Street* and *One Gun* as well as numerous short works. Still sane(ish) after twenty-seven years of teaching high school English, Vinnie has retired and plays keyboards with ukulele groups in Santa Cruz, California, where she lives with her husband and the requisite cat.

Neighbor North

Lindsay Jamieson

When I turn left onto the crowded eastbound 10, I wonder when the guilt will hit: When I crest the Rockies? While I cross the plains? Or on the endless horizontal of Pennsylvania? My acting dreams didn't come true here in Los Angeles. I don't have a star on the Walk of Fame, and only a few credits on IMDb. But I committed murder. And I'm getting away.

Twenty-five years ago, my then husband, Terry, and I moved here from Philadelphia with our beloved dog, Rowdy, who now rides on the floor of the back seat of this car, her ashes in a brown velvet box. We were in our twenties and full of ideas and adventure. We wanted to be in the movies or make them. We wanted to learn how to surf. So we drove across the country with all our possessions in a U-Haul, our Honda Civic hitched to the back.

Still stuck in the right lane, I watch rows of hundred-year-old palm trees south of the freeway lean across the hazy sky. "That's how you find the old houses," a mom in the St. Francis baby group told me when Terry and I were looking. "The old houses are on the streets with the tallest palms." 203 S. Gower Street had three. Before I left this morning, I had lain in the backyard and watched the waxy fronds rustle and flap, so high over our roof that I couldn't see the sharpness of their thorned edges or consider their weight; when Santa Anas rip out those giant fans, they'll crash to the street, block the sidewalk, dent the roofs of parked cars. But I love those palms. Even on my worst days, they'd wave in the breeze, and I'd feel like I was on vacation. The sound was enough to lull me into a trance. It's time to move on, but I'll miss living under their spell.

At the craft service table, the key grip on the one national commercial I scored, which had earned us (along with what Terry was making in the prop department on TV shows) enough for the down payment and a round of renovations on the Gower House, said something I'll never forget: "You move to Los Angeles, and it's like you dive into a swimming pool. You swim to the deep end and climb out, and twenty years have passed." I had no idea what he meant; I was still in the shallow end.

The traffic opens and I gun the gas and I turn up the music and I think: guilt will never hit, because everyone got what they deserved.

We rented a small bungalow near Paramount, thinking we'd try our luck for a year or two, give it a shot, return to PA if we failed. Terry managed to get into the union in the art department, and I got an agent through a friend from school and scored a few little parts. I thought I had it made when I was hired for that national spot. And we learned to surf.

We started at Surfriders, where everyone learns, on boards we'd bought on Craigslist from a fireman in El Segundo who had a garage full. We'd both spent time as kids on the Jersey Shore, bodysurfing in the warm summer Atlantic, but nothing had prepared us for the thrill of riding a Pacific Ocean wave. Just parking on the PCH and wrestling into our wetsuits was a rush. We were so far from home in so many ways… We paddled out with large groups of beginners and screamed with delight when we caught our first rides.

Terry made a friend on a horror movie, Eddie, who was a native and knew how to surf. On the mornings Terry didn't have work, we'd leave when it was still dark, take Crenshaw south, then speed west on the 10, and up the PCH with our boards strapped to the top of our Honda, blasting Hole, or Nirvana, or the Red Hot Chili Peppers.

It took a while, but we managed to move on to more challenging breaks, and we invested in new boards. Eddie showed us secret spots in places like Point Dume, beaches that required a key. Sitting on the outside together, bobbing in the swells while waiting for a set, we'd marvel at the rugged beauty of the Santa Monica Mountains, the blueness of the sky, the clarity of the water, as if we were somewhere like Greece, a place so foreign, the alphabet wasn't the same. We'd pull off our suits and drive back down the coast, then through the city we'd grown to love—pollution and traffic and all. And where we'd already lasted longer than we'd planned. Hosing off our gear in our Hollywood yard, drinking Pacificos with limes, we were the luckiest people alive. We believed it was only the beginning; our bravery would continue to pay off. But like that key grip warned, time sneaks up on you in LA.

Suddenly I was nearing thirty, and though what I really needed to do was get a new agent, headshots, etc., I was struck with the baby urge. Then I was pregnant. And I hadn't considered all the ways our lives were about to change. In the second trimester, my doctor told me to stop surfing. Yes, I wanted the baby, but that didn't mean I wasn't envious watching from the rocky beach while Terry mastered his bottom turn. Everything happened so fast, it was like it was preordained. The Gower House, which I walked past daily with Rowdy, and then Rowdy and baby Connor strapped to my chest or in a stroller, was the same.

"It's for sale," I told Terry. "I peeked inside. Still has the wood." Connor was less than a year old.

"Painted?" he asked. To be fair, the wood in every house we'd seen—including our rental, which was about a mile north—had been ruined by previous owners, every historical detail painted over with glossy white. But why would I make such a fuss over more of the same?

"No!" Impossible, but true. "Even the ceilings," I said. "Wainscoting might be mahogany."

This was 2004, before the bubble burst. "It's not worth what they're asking," a woman with a tidy silver bob whispered to me at the realtor's open. "I've lived across the street"—she pointed—"since eighty-six." (She gave me a heart attack when she told me what she'd paid.) But the banks were giving away loans, and I'd been watching houses sell since we'd moved, prices steadily rising, and knew Marline—that was her name—was wrong.

Terry, who'd grown up in a small apartment, clutched his gut while we waited for the counteroffer at 7:00 p.m. on a Tuesday; his Astro burger sat, still wrapped on a plate, untouched.

"If we're broke, we can stare at that ceiling for entertainment," I said. It was California redwood, vaulted and beamed. Original art glass sconces shone orange on the walls, and a wood chandelier with the same art glass hung from the ceiling's apex. Terry was now a prop master, working on a marquee show. I figured something would happen for me soon, too. I believed taking risks paid off.

"Renting worked fine for my family." He grabbed the Maker's Mark from the bar cart I'd found at a yard sale. It glug glug glugged into his iceless glass.

"But we'll build equity if we buy. We can stay forever. Raise our family here." I glanced toward Connor's bedroom, where he slept in the glow of a night-light that cast blue ripples across his crib. This new adventure was domestic, which was a radical turn. Work and the baby made it almost impossible for either of us to surf. After a fourteen-hour day, Terry would linger in the garage, admiring his board. And I flooded our son's room with images of waves.

"Or always feel strapped. We could lose everything." He emptied his glass in one gulp, then poured another. "If that happens, it's on you."

"Fair enough," I said while I reached for the bottle. "But if it's a huge win?"

With our glasses raised, we locked eyes. "You get that too."

He might not have offered me a drink, but we were still in it together back then. I grabbed the phone when it rang. "Deal," I said. The offer was better than we'd hoped. Terry clenched his fist for the win.

During the weeks we waited for the inspection and title search, I parked on Gower and Second at different times of day with Connor in his baby seat to see what that sliver of the neighborhood was like. Twice I watched hookers turn tricks on Second, but I didn't tell Terry. The used condoms we'd found on the parkway of our rented house made him curse at Los Angeles as if it were worse than back home. When I was a teenager in Philly, there was so much crime, we carried mug money, so when I watched a naked leg swing back into the passenger's seat, then a condom fly out the window, I wasn't concerned. City crimes were familiar to me.

The property was on the corner, and a decent backyard separated us from the house behind, so all I really had to worry about were the neighbors to the north. They lived in a two-story with Swiss details, like the cottage Hansel and Gretel find after they're abandoned in the woods. The paint was dirty and chipped, but it still made me think of how Grimm's brother-and-sister duo trick the witch and cook her in her own oven, then steal all her gemstones and gold. It's a fantastic twist, the children changing their destiny, escaping not only the witch and the horrible stepmother who turned them loose, but also getting rich.

Our house was more Arts and Crafts than Craftsman—it had curves and a roof that looked like, when it was built in 1913, it might have been thatched. There were so many trees on the property, my contractor referred to it as "Casa de Arbol." I loved that. A split-trunk pine over the garage, a tall cedar out front, a fat (fertile) olive tree in the backyard, ficuses that hugged the Second Street side of the house, those three California fan palms (the only indigenous variety in the state), and a pittosporum privacy hedge beyond the main bedroom, which bloomed white, orange-scented flowers in the spring. That's something I didn't expect about LA—the intoxicating fragrances: night-blooming jasmine, honeysuckle, lavender... All of it tempting us: stay for the magic, don't abandon your dreams.

On move-in day, I met the owners of the run-down fairy tale–inspired house, Mr. and Mrs. Matthews, while they were walking their puppy, some kind of small goldendoodle breed. I'd seen the elderly couple at St. Francis Mass. "They sit in the front row," I said to Terry, who was sweating through his Panavision T-shirt, because, though it was only April, it was ninety-five degrees. Maybe that one-day heat spike was the first sign.

"We raised both our children here," Mrs. Matthews said. Her blue eyes were fogged over and leaky, red rimmed. I wore shorts and a tank top, held Connor on my hip. Mr. Matthews stood next to his wife like he did at Mass, and I overlooked the bad luck of the heat and instead chose to believe in the good luck of neighbors who grew old together, walked their dog in the afternoon holding hands.

"Our daughter, Joan, lives on Gramercy," Mr. Matthews said.

"She's an attorney like their father." Mrs. Matthews glanced at her husband. "JD—"

"That's our son," Mr. Matthews said. "He still lives with us." They both looked up to the small, glass-slatted windows in the attic room I'd seen glow TV blue on those nights I'd scoped out our house. From their frail, spotted wrists to their stooped-over shuffles, I'd guessed these folks couldn't be younger than eighty-five, so Joan and JD had to be older than I was, then.

"No grandchildren," Mrs. Matthews said. She wore her pure-white hair in a bun, and her skin was blue with veins. She smiled at Connor and touched his fat foot. He leaned into my shoulder to follow everyone's gaze to the room where JD lived, then kicked me in the ribs.

"Ouch," I said while Mrs. Matthews frowned. "Boys," I added, as if she were a playground mom and her children were toddlers, and she were deciding if we were worthy of a playdate. I was the one who should have been wary; the threat was her son, not mine.

We first encountered JD when a few months after we'd moved in, he knocked on our door. Terry was home, thank God—by then he was usually on set. "Howdy, neighbors," JD said. He was so thin, his clothes looked empty, and his long, greasy gray hair, '70s era, stuck to the sides of his face. Three feet away, I smelled wine oozing from his pores. I stood behind Terry, curious and afraid. We'd heard JD curse out his father, call him a piece of shit, slam his door—his bedroom was across from ours, separated only by our pittosporum hedge—but I'd never seen his face. "Aren't you gonna invite me in?"

"I don't think so," Terry said. I peeked at Connor, absorbed in his trains in the family room.

"I lost my virginity in your garage," JD said with his mouth hanging open, remembering the moment, it seemed. I almost gagged.

"Why don't you go sleep it off, old man?" Terry said. I'd never heard him talk like that. I held his arm, concerned he might throw a punch. I didn't want to have issues with the neighbors, but I'd be lying if I didn't admit protective-man-of-the-house Terry turned me on.

"Who you calling an old man? You've got that plank-ass longboard that you never even surf. What's the problem, dude? Old lady won't let you ride?" He laughed and stumbled toward the steps, then down the top one, but he managed to throw me a knowing look: I had complained when Terry had left me alone with Connor to go surfing at dawn on his day off. A few times we went together and brought Connor, took turns watching him while the other surfed, but Connor couldn't last, and inevitably one of us would end up catching better waves. When we hired a sitter, seconds in traffic added up to money wasted. That hour was no longer a music-filled quest. And wiping out was more terrifying—what if our selfishness cost Connor a parent? I'd changed. And we'd fought about it. JD must have heard.

"At least she's keeping a kook off the water," JD said while he wobbled. I had a strong urge to shove him down our thirteen-step stoop. "I'm the real deal." He tried to turn back but only made it halfway. He glanced at the sky and swayed, watching the palms. "My uncle had land in Point Dume. Surfed my whole life. Real Californian here." He poked his thumb up like he was hitching a ride to the beach, into his bony chest.

He hadn't laid a hand on Terry or me, but what he'd said hurt. Before JD's insult, Terry stood tall and wide, protecting me from the mean drunk. But after, his shoulders fell, his head drooped. "I'd like you to leave," Terry said.

JD chuckled the whole way home. Terry never spoke of it again. I never felt protected again either. JD had found a wound I hadn't noticed. Or maybe I'd noticed but ignored. That was the end of a big part of our adventure, our foray into the waves; the boards were gone within a month, sold (half of asking) to another thirty-year-old couple from a cold, flat, oceanless state.

Joan, the obvious winner of the two, was a few years older (though clean living made her look a decade younger than JD). She'd visit and walk that doodle, Harley, then chat with her parents in their neglected backyard. On those evenings, JD would blast his TV so loud, I could hear the laugh track. But like Gretel, Joan took care of her brother. One morning, I opened my curtains to find JD lying on the parkway with his head half in the gutter. Terry wasn't home, or I would have called him in to watch JD pull out his flip phone, make a call, then recline again on the filthy curb. A few minutes later, Joan pulled up in her brown Volvo and helped JD back into the house. It wasn't enough to keep us safe.

When Connor was three, he and his buddy Jonah were playing on the front lawn, and JD almost ran Connor over with his white Datsun 280Z. Connor had wandered into the Matthewses' driveway. I heard the annoying loud engine rev and scooped up Connor while JD, lit cigarette dangling from his thin frown, sped up. "Get that kid out of my fucking drive," he yelled through his open window.

"Hey," I yelled back, but he kept going, almost rammed into their garage door. I started for the car but stopped. He was drunk. He was dangerous. And I had my child in my arms. Jonah's mother grabbed her son and fled (and never returned). Instead of confronting JD, I ran crying back into my house and locked the door. I called Terry, but it went straight to voicemail. It's not like he could do anything from a soundstage in Santa Clarita. I held Connor, who, scared by my reaction, clung to my shoulders, and wished for the first time in my life that I had a gun.

I waited for Terry in our wood-ceilinged living room. He'd left before I'd awoken, so he should have been home at a reasonable hour, but it was after midnight when he unlocked the front door. "Go say something to the father," I begged.

"You could snap JD in two with your bare hands," Terry said as if that would make me feel safer when Terry was in New York or Atlanta or right here in LA, not home or answering his phone. I didn't want to touch JD, let alone kill him with my bare hands.

"You want me to fight him? I'm alone here, Terry. I'm scared."

"You're overreacting." He walked past me on his way to the bathroom, threw his bag on the dining room table. I trailed behind, watching his back.

"He almost ran over Connor—why don't you care?"

"I worked a fourteen-hour day. I have to be back on set at six a.m. I can't handle your hysteria now."

"You're being an asshole."

"Nice," he said.

I wanted to break down the door and punch and kick him. I wanted to scream. But that always backfired with Terry. As it was, because I said he was being an asshole, he slept in the guest room and didn't speak to me for a week.

The Matthewses' house quieted too. And the parents stopped going to Mass. I worried one of them was terminally ill, and listened for their names in the prayers. Because the only signs of life were the cigarette butts JD stamped out in the driveway, and the empty gallon wine bottles accumulating in the recycling bin. I hadn't seen Joan for months.

"She died," Marline said one day, when Connor was learning how to ride a bike. It was gray out, as it so often is in Los Angeles in May. May gray...which I always enjoyed. A reprieve from the dry, hot sun. "Stomach cancer." I was sorry it hadn't been JD. It didn't make sense for Joan to go first.

When Connor started kindergarten at the St. Francis Parish school, I thought I'd try to restart my acting career, but my agent blew me off. Terry had been promoted to art director and was chummy with the showrunner of the series he was on; they played golf together, had drinks after work. On the way home from a T-ball game, I asked Terry if he could help get me a walk-on, maybe something with a line or two. I'd read the scripts. "I'm perfect for that medic. Or the mom in the ER."

"I'm not in a position to ask," he said. Connor's team had lost, but he'd managed to hit the ball every at bat, which they don't all do, though it's sitting motionless on top of that plastic stick.

"But you're, like, best friends with the showrunner."

"All those actors have credits, Chelsea. It would be out of line for me to ask."

"I had that commercial," I said. But it sounded even lamer coming from me. I shrunk down, wishing I could melt into the roasting-hot passenger's seat.

"*Network* credits."

We'd promised Connor ice cream, so I couldn't get out of the car at the first red light and run. "What's wrong, Mommy?" Connor asked.

"Nothing," I said. The show aired a few weeks later, but I didn't watch.

Less than a year after Joan died, an ambulance woke me in the middle of the night. Well, Rowdy, who'd become extra sensitive to loud noises since her eyesight had gone, went crazy when it arrived, and made Connor, by whose bed she slept, cry. I held his hand while EMTs wheeled out Mr. Matthews. Marline watched from her lawn.

"Is he dead?" Connor asked. "He looks dead."

I wasn't sad about Mr. Matthews; I was worried about JD, who didn't even wave good-bye to his father's corpse. "I think he might be," I said to my son, who wiped his nose on the leg of the Target yoga pants I'd worn for two days.

"He was ninety-three," Marline said the next day. Together, we stared at the paint-chipped gingerbread house. "Died before they reached the ER. Stroke."

It took me two days to get Terry on the phone. He was working in Chicago, and he never picked up when I called. And he rarely returned my texts—we'd just gotten iPhones; right away he declared texts weren't for him. When I first heard his voice, I was so livid he hadn't checked in—I had a five-year-old child for fuck's sake—I almost forgot why I'd called.

"Mr. Matthews died," I said, but it didn't have the impact I was hoping for—I wanted him to be afraid for us, I wanted him to care, but the old man hadn't been shot by robbers; he had died in his damn sleep.

"What a shame," Terry said, as if he and Mr. Matthews had been friends.

"Why a shame? Only a terrible father would raise a monster like JD."

"The man just passed for Christ's sake. Have a little respect."

"JD almost killed your son." The phone was hot in my hand.

"Is this what was so important that you called me ten times in two days?" Terry said from his hotel room. "You wonder why I don't pick up."

At Saturday Mass, I listened for Mr. Matthews's name in the prayers. "Lord, hear our prayer," I said with everyone while wondering who in the world had called the parish office to add him to the list of the deceased. But there, among the families and coerced teenagers and nurses in scrubs, was Mrs. Matthews in the front pew with a woman who had shown up during the week, a caregiver and housekeeper, I'd assumed. She helped Mrs. Matthews out of church when the closing hymn began.

I was in the middle of that swimming pool that represents life in Los Angeles, or maybe life in general, swimming to the other side. While Connor struggled with homework and played a million sports and I pretty much gave up on my career and ran the school auction instead (turned out I had a knack for extracting cash), I forgot about Mrs. Matthews and JD. Rowdy grew so old, she couldn't climb the stairs. She was sixty pounds, but I carried her up and down like a baby in my arms. When Terry was home, she'd stand in front of him, block his path.

"What's wrong with her?" he asked.

"She's fifteen."

We tried to prolong her life: baby food, medications, soothing baths… But there's no cure for old age. One morning, she walked into the backyard and curled up against the fence we'd built years before, by then already weathered gray and termite holed. I knew what that meant, and I didn't want Connor to find her there dead. I hoisted her into the back seat of the Honda and interrupted Connor's playdate so he could say good-bye. "I love you, Rowdy," he said. Then he collapsed onto his friend's lawn and bawled.

"You should have brought her five days ago," the vet said when I arrived.

"How is that helpful?" I said. "You think I don't know that?" I'd had it with Terry and JD, and I snapped. "You think I don't know that the first love of my life is leaving me as we speak? I know." I swiped at my tears. "I fucking know."

"Well, you're here now," he said, backing down, taking her from me. I followed him into the back.

With the sounds of dogs and cats and birds echoing through the part of the vet office that owners never get to see, I held Rowdy and told her I loved her while her life ended on a cold metal table. "Don't be scared, baby," I said, crying. "I'm here." But Rowdy's eyes had closed. She'd stopped wheezing. No soul rose from her bloated body, no angel appeared, but she was gone.

When Terry returned from his job, he held the box that's in my car now. "I should have been nicer to her at the end," he said. "I'm sorry," he said to the box.

Maybe a year later, or two—memory warps time—during late summer, or what I'd come to accept as fire season (orange sunlight, fallen ash dusting the sidewalk like snow), Connor, who'd been riding his bike over tree roots and broken pavement, seeking the highest jump, ran in with the mangiest dog I'd ever seen.

"Can I keep him?" he said. I didn't immediately say no. I couldn't. Not to him or the skeletal dog who was missing large patches of hair. He wasn't a stray. Connor gave him a bath, and for the first time in all those years, I knocked on the Matthewses' door. The caretaker, whom I'd become accustomed to, answered, wearing an apron over a housedress, and brown orthopedic shoes

"We found Harley," I said. "My son is giving him a bath."

"You have the dog? I couldn't find him all day."

I caught a glimpse of the living room, if you could call it that, piled with newspapers and trash. The rancid smell hit me. I avoided looking, didn't want to spot a pile of dog shit or the tail of a dead rat. I was glad I'd left Connor at home. "Why don't we keep Harley," I said. She looked toward the second floor, where I assumed JD lurked. His mother too. If this was how he treated Harley, what kind of condition was that woman in?

"Who's there?" JD's scratchy voice accosted from above.

"She has Harley, Mr. JD. He got out." She flinched like he might shoot her through the ceiling.

"Go get my mother's fucking dog," he yelled.

I wanted to say no. I wanted to fight. Younger me would have. She would have been righteous. She would have insisted. But I couldn't stand any more acrimony. I was too tired.

Harley was so relieved to be clean and fed, running around, jumping on the sofa. And Connor was so proud. Returning that dog was one of my lowest days. I should have reported JD to animal control.

"I'm Alma. I take care of Mrs. Matthews," she said when I urged Harley back inside. Alma looked at me like she agreed it was sad, like we were in this together, both of us at the mercy of the situation, lacking free will. "Life…" she said. And I wondered if she'd seen Terry parked out front in the middle of the night, talking—and yes, texting! —on his new iPhone.

Then, after three days of record-setting hot winds that yanked frond after frond from my trees, several cop cars, an ambulance, and an ambulance-like bus that read *Coroner* arrived next door.

"It's just as well," Marline said when Mrs. Matthews emerged from the house, already dead on the stretcher, body bag zipped closed. I agreed. Living like that wasn't living at all, locked upstairs all the time. It had probably been a year since I'd last seen Alma help Mrs. Matthews to a chair in the backyard. I'd watched from my bathroom window, afraid exposure would kill the old lady. Or wind. "God be with you," I said that day, and on the day she died, crossing myself both times, praying, as a mother of a son, for her soul. "Rest in peace."

The next day I waved Alma over to Second Street, around the corner, where JD couldn't see. "Let us take Harley. Please."

"He took him to the vet to—" She made the gesture for slitting someone's throat.

"What?" I felt like I'd killed Harley myself, like I'd let it happen— I had. "We need to call the police."

"Oh no, miss, no." She clutched my arm. "No police." She wasn't a citizen. I couldn't call the cops.

I was in the deep end of that metaphorical pool, treading hard, as if I could stop myself from reaching the far side. The only yelling left on the corner was at my house, on the rare occasions when Terry came home. Connor played freshman football and JV baseball at the all-boys Jesuit high school that Terry, who'd gone to St. Joseph's Prep, insisted he attend. So I had games to watch and team meals to arrange. I'd had no idea "snack mom" would still be a thing. But I liked watching the boys play. And the mom jobs took my mind off the acting career I'd once again failed to ignite. Cheering for the team was a respite from my marriage, which had reached the deep end and drowned.

We tried couples therapy, but our love was long past being revived. So Terry, who had moved to a furnished apartment in Los Feliz, wasn't there when I found the entire pittosporum hedge pruned naked, cut down to leafless stubs. I ran down to view the wreckage. I banged on JD's door.

"He cut down my trees!" I said to Alma, wishing I wasn't alone. "They'll never grow back."

"They drop berries on his car," she said, as if she'd stood silent while he sawed off their limbs.

"His fucking Datsun?"

"I know, missus," she said. "He's..." She twirled her finger near her head.

"He can see right into my room now." My fists were so tight, my nails cut into my palms.

"There's nothing to see there," JD yelled down. Alma made a sad face, like she and JD sat around in the swill, gossiping about the sorry state of my life.

The landscaper I called thought I should sue. "They're worth over a hundred K," she said. "Hundred-year-old trees." But I was already in a divorce. It's not like I could hire more lawyers to take on JD. I had the trees cut down and planted a hedge that didn't shed, but it would be years before they reached my windows. God willing, JD would be dead before that. We just had to hold on a little longer. By then, his liver was so enlarged, it protruded over his ancient, flared jeans.

Terry bought Connor a rebounder so he could play catch with

himself in the backyard. "Be careful," I said when he was gearing up for varsity tryouts. "A baseball can crack a skull."

No such luck.

"If another one of those fucking balls lands in my yard, I'll jump over that fence and break your neck," JD yelled one evening while I grilled chicken thighs—which Terry, who only ate white meat—shunned.

"I'd like to see you do that," Connor said. I considered stopping him, but I liked the sound of his now deep voice challenging the small, evil man. I smelled JD's cigarette smoke through the olive tree, but he didn't say another word. Connor smirked like when he struck out a batter for the inning. That all-boys school was teaching him to be kind of a dick.

Alma grew salty too. She'd march up my stoop to complain when sprinklers watered her RAV4 instead of my new trees. And when Connor and his friends sneaked onto the roof (Marline mentioned that too). Single moms, I was learning, were easier to foil.

One afternoon, while I cleaned beer cans and weed detritus off the roof, I stopped to take in the view of Griffith Observatory and the Hollywood sign, both spotlighted by the sun, with snowcapped mountains beyond. The air was extra clear. A stiff, steady breeze hummed through the fronds while bright-green parrots cackled and zoomed in and out of my trees. I should have realized that was a significant moment—all of that beauty in one frame… My life was about to change.

JD's Datsun rolled up the drive, and a young man wearing the same Xavier hoodie Connor always wore climbed out of the driver's seat, then walked around to help JD out of the passenger's side. He looked up at me standing there overwhelmed by the majestic backdrop, and waved. "Hi," the young man said. He had thick black hair and tan skin.

I waved back, empty Coors can in my other hand. Then JD waved too. And smiled. "You be careful up there," JD said, his voice still gruff, but also, sincere. I almost fell off.

The next day, the young man knocked on my door. "I'm Mike." I wanted to run my fingers through that hair, tug on it. In his fresh polo shirt, dark denim jeans, and black Chucks, he moved like a kid—quick eyes, coordinated muscles, irrepressible smile—but he was thirty, at least. Now out on my porch, I stood close enough to smell his aftershave. I was thankful I'd stopped wearing my wedding ring. "I noticed your son goes to Xavier," Mike said. "I love the way he and JD kid around. JD thinks he's cool. They had a chat about football and cars the other day. JD and I both went to Xavier too." I must have been in the kitchen when this bro down occurred, because any interaction between Connor and JD was a surprise to me.

"Men for Others…" I said. The brotherhood. Of course.

"AMDG," Mike said. I laughed and wondered if Terry thought about the meaning of that oath—"for the greater glory of God"—while he was fucking Dana at work. "But I don't drink the Kool-Aid," Mike added. Then we both laughed. And smiled. "But JD does. And he'd like to make amends."

For almost running over my child? For scaring away my friends? For killing his mother and his dog? "He butchered my trees," I said.

"He wasn't sober."

"Oh, that *amends*." I was probably the last person alive he owed.

"He hates to have bad blood with the neighbors. He'd like to call it water under the bridge." Which made me worry that at that very moment, Connor was at Xavier learning clichés.

"Did he send you over to set up a meeting?" I asked with a voice I hadn't used since Terry and I met on a music video; he had been the prop master, and I had been a background dancer, all of us working for free.

"He wanted me to feel it out first—he'll get up the nerve to come by himself soon."

Feel away, I wanted to say. "Sure, okay," I said. "I can play nice for the old man." Mike and I stared at each other, and I bit my lip, trying to fight off the blush I felt rising in my skin.

"What's up with you and JD?" I asked Connor while I was cleaning the kitchen, and Connor was breaking in the new glove Terry had bought him for making the team. JD hadn't come by yet. Neither had Mike. "I hear you're bros."

"He cracks me up," Connor said. "Has a ranch somewhere and a house on Plymouth too." The key part of what he'd said was blocked out by concern about my son fraternizing with the murderer next door.

"He might be sober now, but I'll never trust that man."

But Connor had stopped listening. He folded his glove around a softball and used four industrial-strength rubber bands to force it closed.

Like always, that night he would sleep with it under his pillow. "I never would have guessed he was rich," Connor said.

JD repeated Connor's real estate tale when he hobbled (a few months of sobriety couldn't undo the damage he'd done) over to the fence to make amends while I was picking up the baseballs in my yard. "I've been an asshole to you. I've always been a mean drunk. Forgive me," he said. Mike pulled up in his Subaru WRX STI. ("That's the car I want," Connor had said.)

"It's all good," I said to JD while Mike strode toward us up the drive, the whole time looking at me. "I'd rather get along."

"I just inherited a shit-ton of real estate. Had no idea I'd be the last man standing." JD was one of those lucky Californians who'd inherited priceless land that had been bought for pennies. "I'm putting in a pool," JD said. If it weren't for Mike and his tight white T-shirt, I would have sued JD right then and there for my trees. "You and your boy are welcome to swim whenever you want."

"Unless you're selling." Mike ran his right hand through that hair. "I'm in real estate."

Of course. As if every single person I knew in real estate hadn't called me the minute they heard about Terry and my separation, all of them pretending to be my friend. I felt like I chump, falling for Mike's smile, assuming his flirting was real.

"I'm not selling." I would have to sell eventually, but brother Mike didn't need to know that.

I'd have thought JD was full of shit—and maybe even working with Mike, trying to get my house—but he traded in that Datsun for a Mercedes, and a painting crew arrived and spruced up the exterior of his house. Also, if the money were a lie, Alma and Mike wouldn't have kept hanging around. I spied them arguing in the driveway but was too far away to hear what it was about.

"Smells great, Chelsea," Mike said across the fence one night when dinner was on the grill. "JD would like to invite you over."

"I'll have to check Connor's schedule," I said.

Mike leaned into my yard and waved me closer. "It's you he's inviting."

I felt sick. "Oh God."

"Do it for me," Mike said almost in a whisper. "And bring over a bottle of wine."

"I thought he was sober." The gross thought of JD hitting on me was replaced by the charged sensation of Mike's hand on my arm, his light squeeze.

"But I'm not. Are you?" He tilted his head and raised his thick eyebrows, stared hard at me with those dark-brown eyes. I didn't care if it was part of a con.

"What's this about?" I asked. He handed me a business card with his picture and the words: *Real Estate*, but no affiliation like Coldwell Banker or Sotheby's.

"When you're finished eating, give me a call," he said.

***

We met at a dark, narrow bar on Western called Frank's that didn't make signature cocktails; I wasn't concerned I'd run into a St. Francis or Xavier mom. I felt like I was twenty anyway, pre-marriage, pre-motherhood. I ordered Bulleit Rye on the rocks; Mike, a Jameson and a draft. I hadn't smoked in decades but was desperate to light up. He swiveled toward me and raised his glass. I pressed my knee into his. "How old are you?" I asked.

"Thirty-seven." He told me he played football at Xavier, and we ragged on that for a while, the coltishness, the shaved heads for Hell Week, the bedazzled moms.

"I never knew Catholic school moms were so hoochie," I said, which was true. They showed up in matching white jeans and purple T-shirts, always tight, and high wedge shoes that made climbing the bleachers a spectator sport—I was certain someone would topple over the edge. Their (blonde) hair was perfect, and their diamond rings large.

"Yeah, I was hot for all of them when I played."

I pictured him in the uniform, purple spandex squeezing his quads.

"I knew it," I said. Because I was hot for some of them too. Stunners in school logos, purple panthers across pushed-up boobs, diamond crosses sparkling between. I'd always felt like someone's sister next to them, or someone's aunt. Mike ordered another round.

"Are you getting me drunk?"

"Yes," he said. I could tell from the way his eyes narrowed that if he hadn't actually scored with one of those moms, he'd tried. He touched my arm, my knee, my thigh.

"So how did you and JD become pals?" I asked. Had he been watching the property? Had he listened for the names of the dead at St. Francis Mass?

"He's sweet on you."

"Gross," I said. "He killed his parents. He killed his dog!"

"Shhhhh." Mike raised his finger to his lips.

"Are you an undercover cop? Seems unlikely LAPD would care. City's probably psyched to get more property taxes out of the lot. But you know all about that." I'd stopped whispering, but his ear was still close to my mouth.

"Where's your husband?" Mike had two agendas, but I could only figure out the one.

"What husband?" I still knew how to angle my eyes, and my shoulders, and my hips. "You're too young for me."

"No, I'm not. I'm gonna get me a hot Xavier mom."

I fucked him in the back seat of that Subaru.

"Jesus," he said.

I pulled up my jeans. "I'll want a cut," I said. I'd figured it out.

"What?" Mike said, like he'd been caught stealing candy.

I climbed through the seats to the front, lowered the sun visor to block the streetlight from my eyes. "I know what you're doing."

"What am I doing?" He climbed after me, then buttoned his jeans.

"We're past that," I said. And he kissed me. And I kissed back. Hard.

"If he starts drinking again, he won't stop," Mike said. "I'll get him to sign over the deeds. But I can't get him to drink."

"But if I bring over the wine…"

"There's no way he'll refuse."

We watched an Uber drop off a ride.

"He should have died before Joan. He should have died first," I said.

"But he didn't," Mike said.

While my *friendship* with Mike ramped up, Alma became a real pain in the ass. "That boy was on the roof again," she said after berating me about my sprinklers staining her RAV4. "I worry he'll slip..." She made that slit-throat gesture.

"Alma's been snagging the mail. I caught her going through JD's files," Mike said after we had fucked in my bed. "I think she's after the house." I didn't believe him, but that weekend JD and Mike drove up to the ranch for the day, and Alma brought her whole family over. Several young men Mike's age drank beer in the backyard while a woman, whom I guessed was Alma's daughter, paced with her hands on her hips as if she were the one putting in a pool.

"He doesn't even pay her." We were back at Frank's, and, while we drank whiskey, I rubbed out the knots in Mike's neck. "But she won't leave—she has some idea she's in the will. JD's making the most of that situation."

"Damn."

"I've convinced JD to check his will to make sure—trust me, she's not in it—but that will give me access. I have a notary friend who can help."

I kissed him behind his ear.

"Problem is," Mike continued, "I can't get her out of the house during business hours. She's determined. She's digging in."

"I'll take care of it," I said.

At 10:00 a.m. the next day, I watered her car; at 10:05 a.m. she charged up my stoop. I met her at the door.

"Your sprinklers!" Alma yelled like she was my neighbor.

I cut her off. "I was about to come over and warn you," I said.

"I'm not moving my car," she said.

"Not the sprinklers..."

She pointed at her water-attacked car, tightened her face like an angry squirrel. She was about to explode. "Your—"

"You know that app, Nextdoor? I read there were immigration raids. You should probably stay home for a few days."

Again, like a squirrel, she scurried to that Swiss-themed house of horrors, grabbed her bag, ran back to her RAV4, and sped away. It was fun to act again, and this job was about to pay. While she was hiding, Mike's notary friend arrived, and JD made Mike the executor of his estate.

For our dinner, I chose the short purple and white dress I often wore to Xavier events, grabbed the bottle of white wine I'd purchased for the occasion, made sure Marline wasn't watching, and hurried to JD's. He answered, leaning on a cane. Six months of sobriety wasn't going to cure his cirrhosis; his bulging liver looked like it was about to burst. He was so close to death, I like to think of what we did as an act of mercy.

On the way to the dining room, which though cleaned up, still smelled like death, Mike gave me an appreciative once-over and winked.

"Do you like white?" I said.

"JD doesn't drink," Mike said.

"It's just a little wine." I heard his Datsun heading for my son, saw the ambulance lights, and the expression on Harley's face when I'd relinquished him to Alma.

"How much harm can that one little bottle do?" JD said.

The answer was *a lot*. Because after the one bottle, JD ordered a case delivered from Bogie's.

"What will you do with all that property?" I asked while I sipped my second gin and tonic. He could barely focus on my face.

"I'm selling the house on Plymouth," he said, "but I'm keeping the ranch. Fifty acres... And here..." He gestured to his dead-grass outfield still dotted with baseballs.

"The pool," I said. The Angeleno dream. "Is Mike helping with contracts? He's so smart."

"Xavier boy," JD said. We drank to that.

"Go Panthers," cheered Mike.

We drank to that too. Then JD plunked his head on the table and passed out.

Mike walked me home. "Once I get the deeds signed over, we'll just have to wait."

I attacked him with a kiss.

"You going Friday night?" he asked when I pulled away. My face was red and chapped from his end-of-day stubble.

"Everyone goes to homecoming," I said before running off.

When I reached the lawn, I yelled back, "Second quarter. Behind the gym."

With my bedroom curtains drawn, I dug out the one pair of white jeans I'd bought years before. I tried them with wedges I'd never worn and my official baseball-mom shirt, a tight purple V-neck with Connor's number—in rhinestones—on the sleeve, *Ryan* across the back. In my mirror, I posed as the Chelsea I could have been, the Chelsea I had become.

Friday afternoon, I stopped at the Beverly Center to purchase a Victoria's Secret push-up bra (and matching panties). I blew out my hair like I did for auditions, then pulled it back in a high pony, because the night air always made my hair frizz. I applied three times more makeup than normal, extra eyeliner and mascara, blush. But I wasn't done. I found every piece of Xavier jewelry I owned: the charm bracelet with all the saints, the bracelet that read *AMDG*, the gold panther pin with the amethyst eye, and the 14-karat cubic zirconia cross. It was a good thing Terry had taken Connor fishing for the weekend; he would have accused me of dressing like I was from Manhattan Beach.

It's no wonder those Manhattan Beach moms were always in such good moods, because when I passed through security, I felt sexier than ever. I wasn't sullen or insecure; I was fierce. People noticed me—men noticed me—like they hadn't before. I'd been hiding behind motherhood. My marriage was over; this was my coming out. The baseball moms loved it: "You look hot!" "You should show off that body of yours more."

"Thank you," I said, like a beauty queen accepting her crown. "You're so kind." And also, "You look hot too." Because like always, they did.

We sat at the forty and watched the cheerleaders' (chosen from several all-girls Catholic schools) opening routine beneath the downtown skyline. I'd never experienced Friday Night Lights before Xavier, and this was it: the night sky forever lighter in the west, moon rising over the palm trees, that distinct ocean breeze from the South Bay reminding everyone that LA was, at its core, a beach town. I looked for Mike, but my eyesight was starting to go, and the lights were so bright, and the game made it hard to focus on anything but those boys and the ball. I watched the clock count down. When there was a minute to the end of the first, with great caution in those wedge shoes, I climbed down from my glittery perch.

I tried not to think of Connor, who had a locker behind the gym sophomore year, when I ran my fingers, nails painted purple for the game, across the gray metal.

"Fuck," Mike said when he saw me. He'd worn a tight Xavier polo that showed off his youth, those muscles in his neck and arms, his velvet skin.

"Fuck me, Xavier boy," I said. "Fuck me hard." I grabbed onto his shoulders. The locks rattled when we crashed into the lockers. The horn blew and the cheerleaders cheered and the bleachers roared when the first Xavier touchdown was scored.

Alma returned Monday. JD was back on the sauce, hard. Mike didn't know how to get rid of Alma again so soon, but I did.

At a quarter to two, the next day, Alma ran screaming from JD's house. "My car's been stolen."

I opened my door, stood at the top of my stoop. "Oh no!" I said. "Shit."

She looked up and down the street, stopped at my house. "This place is cursed," she said. "This corner, where you live. Everything falls apart here."

"Why don't you leave?" I said.

"There's money," she said, right there in front of Marline and the new couple two houses up the street who'd run out when they'd heard screams. She climbed up the bottom half of my stoop and lowered her voice. "Mike thinks he's taking the house. No way! Mrs. Matthews put me in the will." Alma outed herself. Fucking beautiful. "It's mine."

I had the number of the lead officer at the Olympic station. He was a good guy; we'd met at the neighborhood association meeting Marline hosted the year before. "He won't ask you about your status," I said. Alma called from my kitchen phone, then she ate the lunch I had made. Meanwhile, Mike, who'd parked the RAV4 around the corner, had his notary friend back to transfer the deeds.

"What happens now?" I asked Mike in a hotel room up by the 101 with a city view. I'd made him my real estate agent (in exchange for half of the commission), and we were celebrating the sale of my house. We'd gotten several offers over asking; the whole thing had taken three days. On the eighteenth floor, we couldn't hear sirens or cars honking. It was all just pretty lights, red and white stripes, candy canes stretching south across the endless grid.

"When he dies, I inherit everything." Mike opened the second bottle of Veuve we'd picked up at Pavillion's on our way to the hotel. "The house on Plymouth goes on the market this week. I'm asking three. JD's house should sell easily for two point five. I couldn't have done it without you."

"Cheers," I said.

It had been twenty-five years since Terry and I had driven from Philly, taken the Crenshaw exit north to this little neighborhood where we had a family in the house of the trees. I looked at the glittering sprawl like it was the last shot of a movie and the credits were about to roll. Soon the music would start, and the lights would come up, and the audience would exit the theater, most leaving their trash on the floor for the cleanup crew. Mike refilled my glass.

"How much for me?" I asked. I was too young to live the rest of my life off my half of the payout from my house. "What do I get? Besides hotel sex for a night." Mike pulled me on top.

"Two million." Which, considering the ranch, was maybe twenty percent. "And a fresh start."

It took fifty-two days total. Which wasn't a day too soon. He'd started luring Connor over for drinks. "What the hell?" I said one Sunday afternoon when Connor stumbled in drunk.

"What? You've been over there drinking with the dude too."

Which was the truth. Mike and I had shared bottles of wine and gin and whatever with JD while he tore into his parents, and Joan. "Crooked lawyer like the old man. Acting like a fucking queen. Who's royalty now? Karma's a bitch." Indeed.

Alma had no idea about the contracts or the deeds. Whenever Mike wasn't there, her family and friends filled the place. JD never paid her, and Mike had been right—she wasn't included in the will, but she didn't know that yet. A few days before the end, I heard JD yell down at her: "Get out of my fucking house." I ran to my window to watch. The daughter I'd seen grabbed a gallon bottle of wine and ran it upstairs while Alma used that same slit-throat sign to explain what she was plotting to the rest of her clan. She was killing JD too.

I'd expected an ambulance like when JD's parents died, but instead, the news came from Connor, who'd gone over there to do God knows what. "Mom! Call 911! It's JD!" He ran into the kitchen, where I was listening to a podcast and baking cookies for the baseball team.

While I explained to the 911 operator, I thought about Rowdy. I hadn't wanted Connor to find her in the yard, but that's exactly where he found JD, who'd probably bent over to pick up a baseball and fallen. For all those years, I'd worried one would hit him in the head.

Mike and I met one final time at Frank's, then enjoyed a night at my place when Connor was on his prospect weekend at Lehigh. Both the Plymouth house and JD's sold within a week. Alma raised hell when she found out she was not in the will, but she wasn't a relative; there was nothing she could do. Oh well. The money was already mine. We'd deducted Mike's slice of my sale, funneled $300K into a 529 for Connor, and Mike wired the rest directly into my checking account as four years of back salary—he'd made me an employee of his LLC. "I won't forget you," Mike said. "My hot Xavier mom."

"You have to," I said. "We have to forget that we ever met."

Then I savored the kisses I knew were the last.

The temperature in my Mazda reads 112 degrees when I pass the wind turbines on the 60. I turn up my AC. The cool air brings me back to that swimming pool, except now when I picture it, it's got lane lines and colorful flags, and I'm wearing a gold medal because I've won. Terry and I followed our dreams here, and I acted mine right into the driver's seat of this luxury (hybrid) car. I won't grow old on Gower or drink myself into a dead heap for my son to find in the backyard. In PA, I'll be set for life.

"So long, Golden State."

Lindsay Jamieson published her first novel, *Beautiful Girl*, with Paper Lantern Lit/The Studio (now Glasstown Entertainment), under pen name Lida James. Her fiction and nonfiction have appeared in several online publications. Her next novel, a collaboration with actress and writer Krysten Ritter, is scheduled to be published by Harper Collins in 2023.

The Dark Watchers

Nik Xandir Wolf

"Did you see them?" I said, staring into the cracked screen of my iPhone.

"See who?" my ex-wife said.

"The Dark Watchers. It was them. I finally believe my mom."

"It's dark and you're trapped in the mountains, your mind is playing tricks," she said.

I looked around, surrounded by thick moss and dense ferns, and redwoods towering over, hiding me, sheltering me. My ex-wife was right; when you were in the woods, in the dark, even the most absurd fairy tales seemed not just plausible—they became real. I looked around. The moonlight slicing through the branches made the low mist glow like a breathing enchantment just off this abandoned stretch of Highway 1 in Big Sur.

"My therapist from when I was a kid would have called them a projection." I laughed. It seemed impossible to me that I was ever anywhere but here. With the sound of foghorns playing in the distance over the soft crashing waves. My reality warped by solitude, fatigue, and blood loss.

"Maybe they represent something to you. Like death," she said. "You were always obsessed with death."

"It's hard not to think about death when you're dying," I said. I pulled my hand away from the wound on my side, and it was oily with dark blood. The bullet had gone clean through. I thought about when I'd spread Mom's ashes out here all those years ago.

***

Two days ago I slept on my little sailboat, *Orielle*, in the B dock in Moss Landing. I was wide awake with the early morning sound of seals and seagulls, and the low thunder of commercial fishing vessels starting. In the distance, the soft hum of twin foghorns groaned at even intervals, marking the two rock jetties at the entrance to the marina. A cold, exhausted feeling trickled up my legs. I stepped off my boat and checked the time on my watch. It was 5:15 a.m. I took a quick look out at the cold blue of the Pacific stretching out ahead, the U shape of the Monterey Bay just visible in the pink light creeping over the mountains to the east, and started walking.

I hadn't slept well with the jittery nerves and strung-out tension regarding the meeting I had that morning. My whole life to this point rested on this one thing. I needed access to a bigger ship, the *Maître D*. Without it, my last fraying thread in life would snap, and I was sure I didn't have the guts or the stamina to start over again with a new idea. I was thirty-five and had given everything I had to this. To becoming a writer. I would rather die than go groveling back to the corporate dicks at Big Lizard Insurance. The only thing I missed about my old life in Monterey was my daughter, Olive. My ex-wife, Evelyn, either allowed it or forgot I had access to it, but I tuned in every night to watch the little angel sleep through the monitor app. I also cried—dry heaving sobs that soaked my chest in real pain—that I couldn't be there every night to put her to bed. She was eleven months old now, and I'd been gone for half of it. I had missed her first steps.

I stepped into the Moss Landing Café right at 5:30 a.m. and started toward the counter when one of them grabbed my arm. It was busy inside with fishermen and boat dwellers getting coffee and three-dollar plates of pancakes, so they had blended in.

"Nick, sit. We've been waiting for you," he said.

It was Marco Tallini, the owner of the *Maître D*, and his savagely obese partner, Rocky—last name I didn't know. Marco was lean, dark, with black-and-grey, deeply receding hair and thick eyebrows. He had good genes that, at forty-nine, offered him a youthful frame and still-boyish good looks.

Rocky motioned to sit down, removing my ability to decide for myself. Seeing the two guys here gave me *Goodfellas* flashbacks and sent a spike of fear into my belly. "We have coffee for you," he said, his voice quick, but deep and resonant.

It didn't matter how scared I was of the guys, or their reputation around here, I needed a larger boat, and they were the only ones offering. My Catalina 22' didn't pass Coast Guard inspection and was really just a day sailer anyway, without the bathroom and storage for overnight travel on the sea. Plus it had no radio or GPS. Or lights. I was dead if I tried to go down the Big Sur coast in that thing.

I sat next to Rocky and across from Marco, who slid a mug over and filled it from a carafe of steaming coffee. "Rocky and I have decided to accept your offer," he said.

I wondered if I appeared as confused as I felt. I'd finally—after nearly a decade of writing classes, an MFA and three unsold novels— landed the biggest story of my career. It was for *Outside Magazine*. A five-thousand-word feature at a dollar a word, finding hidden barrels that nobody had ever surfed on the untouched miles of cliff-drop coastline down Big Sur. It was dangerous, but it was my big break. If the story got some traction and national attention, it would be that much harder for editors to reject my current novel.

I'd been shooting my mouth off about selling the story every night at the Undertow—gangsters, drug runners, and psychologically unstable boat dwellers had called Moss Landing their home for the better part of a century, and the Undertow was their bar. And the bartender, Maggie Chavez, took it upon herself to put the word out.

Everyone with a boat in Moss Landing drank there, and she knew them all by name. At first, I was greeted by laughing and pointing from the corners of the room when I came in at noon each day to start drinking. It made sense; the cost of gas for most of these big fishing trawlers would run ten or twenty grand to get down to San Simeon and back. And the sailboat captains wanted a thousand a day. I thought I was going to have to steal a boat, but then she had come through with a lead. She told me she found a boat, but to be careful because Marco had spent some time up at San Quentin. All I had to do was meet them here, Sunday at 5:30 a.m. sharp.

"I'm sorry?" I said. My heart fluttered in my chest, and my instincts were telling me to bail.

"What, am I not enunciate clearly? You're the writer, right? You have to go surf a few waves down the coast, take some pictures. We also have business down the coast. We can use an extra deckhand. It's win-

win." Marco's protuberant black eyes glared hard, bored into me, and shook my confidence down to the studs. "We go down that way all the time, we can show you the beaches you can only get to by boat."

I felt sick, and the hot coffee made it worse. "What kind of business?"

I heard a seat adjust behind me and turned just enough to see a third guy, Tony, I believe, pivoted in his seat and leaning over so he could listen in on the conversation.

"The business," Marco said, leaning closer, "is none of your goddamn business." He leaned back, looked around, and laughed lightly, as if to settle the tension out. It didn't help. "But if you have to know, it is a simple pickup. We are loading up some imported product and bringing it to port."

"What if," I said, "I already found other arrangements?"

All three laughed, and Rocky clubbed me on the back with his fat hand, nearly knocking the wind out of me. "Listen, guy," Rocky said, "you need a boat, we need another deckhand. It's a deal nobody else is going to give you in a million years. Say yes, say no. But if you say no, you just better watch your fucking ass." They all laughed hard again, and I caught another club on the back.

"You look so scared. Christ, Rocky is fucking with you," Marco said, smiling wide. Then he leaned in again. "I'm sure you've heard that I spent time in the pen. People talk. You know what I did? Involuntary manslaughter. A bar fight. When I was twenty-two years old up in Oakland. It's ancient history." Marco stood. "We're honest businessmen picking up some fresh langostino from Mexico. All legal and imported here at Moss Landing. You see all the Coast Guard and Department of Fish and Game around. Nothing goes on here anymore. It isn't like it used to be. You think about it, and you let me know. We set out Friday."

I moved to stand, and Rocky pushed me back down and leaned in. "That means we'll see you Friday. Four a.m., C dock. We know where you live." He smiled, and the three of them stood and left the restaurant. I sat there and watched them leave, my stomach knots starting to unravel slightly. I took a sip of the coffee; it was cool now. I drank it down anyway and tried to steady my nerves.

***

"You're not hangin' overboard chucking stones yet. You must have been out on the boats a few times," Marco said, taking a seat near me at the rear of the ship while Rocky, at the helm, kept us full speed up and down the massive ten-foot seas. The whole bay was a blanket of fog, and I kept having a flash of terror that we might hit another boat. Or worse, get T-boned by a bigger ship.

"Can he see where we're going?" I asked.

"He's got the GPS on. He's got this. You good, kid?"

"I'm fine," I said, though I was thoroughly nauseous and felt like if I moved too quickly, I might puke. I wasn't seasick. Seasick was a fate so close to death, you wished it would just come and finish you. "I worked on the fishing boats in undergrad at Cal State Monterey Bay. Paid my tuition in cash each year."

"I like that. Some initiative. Most of those college boys have soft hands. You know. Pencil pusher hands. Figured you for one of them when I heard you were a writer."

"Hell, my dad is a carpenter," I said. Though my father owned a small general contracting firm, I didn't think it was necessary to elaborate. With the Moss Landing boating community, the more blue-collar I appeared, the better. "If it wasn't the boats, it was swinging hammers at construction sites all over the Bay Area."

"A college boy who can work with his hands. But I bet you went through all those jobs thinking you were smarter than that. Am I right? Like you knew it was temporary."

I had thought exactly that, and the fact that this man saw right through me like this was both unnerving and comforting. I didn't have to pretend. Also, he wasn't exactly as he appeared either. He was more insightful and self-aware than I had given him credit. "I just knew it wasn't for me. The same way anyone knows anything in life."

"You were too good for that kind of work, is that it?"

"That—that's not it at all," I said, stuttering on my words.

"I'm just fucking with you, kid. I have two sons a little younger than you. Neither one wants do this type of work."

I nodded, wondering how old his kids were. I was always judged as being in my late twenties, since I could barely grow facial hair and had somewhat of a baby face that was a mismatch for my six-two, two-hundred size. My old boss at Big Lizard called me Baby Huey, and I had wanted to beat the shit out of him with his own hands every time he did. Or maybe Marco thought I was younger because I was chasing dreams. "I liked construction okay. And I like being out on the water, that's why I love to surf even though I'm not the best. I just knew, since I was a kid really, that I wanted to write."

"How the hell does a kid know something like that?"

"I don't know. But it's like how you said, but not quite. Like I did go through life and my jobs knowing it wasn't for me, sure, but also, I felt like a spy. Like I was supposed to go through all of this shit so that I could catalog it. Write about it. Make sense of it at some point in the future."

"That's what you were thinking while you were gutting a thousand salmon?"

"Yeah. I mean, some of the time."

"But was there like one thing, one big moment where you knew that you were going to do it? Spend your life on it no matter what?"

"My mom used to do some writing. She would send off stories to literary magazines and get rejections back. She liked to write when she was cleaned up. Maybe seeing her do it was that one thing. I don't know for sure." I always felt guilty bringing up my mom's addiction. It felt like a betrayal to her memory. But there was no way to glorify heroin addiction. Even though it started with prescribed Oxy. It had turned her into a living, breathing zombie, capable of anything.

"But there's no money in it, right? Like a bestseller is like winning the lottery, it seems to me."

"Yeah, you're not wrong. Hell, I've been writing for damn near ten years, and this is the first paying gig I've gotten."

"Hard way to make a living, kid."

"What about you? Is being a fishing boat captain your dream?"

Marco let that statement settle in; he looked out at the sea, the fog so thick, our voices were muted by it. Everything felt soft and fake, like a stage.

"I always wanted to be—nah. You know what. It doesn't fucking matter what I wanted to be, because there are dreams, and there is reality. No offense to you, but ninety-nine percent of the world has to wake up and realize there is work to be done, a family to be fed, and find a steady paycheck."

"I quit my job to do this," I said, but all I could think about now was Olive's tiny, beautiful face and shock of black hair in the monitor app. I would make it. I would be the one percent that never gave up on that dream. "I have a daughter."

"Don't worry, kid. There are easier ways to make a living than gutting fish and swinging hammers. This writing shit doesn't work out, you come to work for me. Import, export. It's so much easier than doing all that work. You just drive the goddamn boat around. The open sea and your own goddamn schedule. Especially when the fish is frozen. It's a great fucking living."

I didn't respond, though if I did, I would have told him being out here wasn't bad at all. In fact, if I could shake this nausea away, it was a pretty damn good day. I couldn't wait to dig into the first surf spot. Get some photography, use the small drone I brought. It was an easy assignment now that I had a boat and a captain that knew what the hell he was doing. Now all I had to do was pray there were some decent waves to surf and shoot. This time of year in the fall, there were usually consistent swells.

Marco stood. "We're going straight through to our meeting around Lucia Lodge. Then we'll head back up the coast and let you get your surfing footage or whatever. We'll just need your help with loading the langostinos."

"And we can hit the spots on the map I gave you?" I had sent Marco a list of pins of all the beaches along the coast that looked approachable from the sea; I figured we could scout them and only stop at a few of the best ones.

"Oh yeah. We'll check your spots. Don't you worry. Just don't forget to change our names in your little story."

I nodded, knowing that I would have, but also thinking if this were a legitimate operation, wouldn't he want the exposure? Free advertising?

***

It was close to 7:00 p.m. when Rocky finally started to power down the motors. It was still bright and clear now, though the sun was dazzling us low on the horizon to the west with orange and blue and red shimmering off the scalloped surface. I could just see it out ahead, but there it was. We were finally approaching another boat after fifteen hours getting tossed around by the great Pacific Ocean with nothing but cliffs on the starboard, and open sea on the port. We had pulled into a little alcove and were so close to the shore, I could hear the waves crashing.

When we approached the boat, Rocky slowed to a stop and kept the engine idling. Marco threw the bumpers over the side in case we touched the other ship. The other boat was bigger and a lot nicer. It was a small pleasure yacht with long, sleek tinted windows and a pearl-white hull. I could just make out the figures on the other ship; there were three of them. Marco stepped beside me at the rear of the ship.

"All right, kid. Anything goes wrong, hit the deck and let Rocky handle the dirty business. He was holding a leather shoulder bag by the handle that he slipped over his neck so it hung at his side.

"I thought I was going to load langostinos?"

"You are, but you're going to wait for my all clear. Then you can come and take the boxes and load them into the big refrigerator below." He pulled a snub-nosed revolver from the bag, checked the bullets, then slid it into the small of his back, covering it with his Pebble Beach windbreaker.

My pulse kicked so hard, the rush of blood in my ears was louder than the diesel engine. We pulled alongside the other ship; the two captains backed them up, rear to rear, so Marco and I faced the three people that I had seen from a distance. As we neared, their faces became clearer and clearer.

Two women stood at the helm; tall, professional, emotionless behind dark sunglasses. They had on slightly different versions of the same upscale yacht wear. A tall, Eastern European–looking blonde with wide shoulders and a thick neck. And a Latina with her arms crossed in a blue blazer and hair bobbed short with bangs falling in her eyes.

"These two run the show up from Mexico. Keep an eye out," Marco said.

Our boats got close, and just before they bumped, Marco sprang forward, gently guiding the two rear platforms so they rested against the bumpers, and looped our ships together.

"Drop anchor," the Latina said. I wasn't sure who was controlling the ship, because I couldn't see the captain up on the next level at the helm. "Come aboard, Marco. Let's have a drink."

***

"You having fun yet, writer boy?" Rocky said. We were sitting in the cockpit at the rear of the ship, waiting for Marco's signal. It actually made sense why he wanted me when I thought about Rocky's sheer girth. The guy was far too large to do any moving of boxes. They needed a younger back for this shit.

"I like being on boats. What's keeping them so long?" I asked. I kept waiting for gunfire to break out, since deals like this always seemed to go bad in the movies. But that's movie magic for you. In real life, deals like this probably went off without a hitch the vast majority of the time. Assuming we weren't just buying langostinos based on the fact that Marco had brought a goddamn gun with him. And these women didn't look like your typical seafood purveyors.

"He's just checking them out. If there are too many dead ones, it lowers the price. Just get ready to earn your keep. They're coming."

As if on cue, Marco emerged from a rear cabin door, smiling wide, and motioned me on board. I followed him through the fiberglass palace and down into the cooler in the cabin. I kept my focus and stayed professional by going straight over and picking up four boxes marked langostino, straightening, and walking back out the way I had come. It took me twenty trips to remove the full load, and I was tired and sweating by the end. On my last trip, the tall blonde asked me if I wanted a beer and to relax a minute. Her voice was a deep baritone. I politely declined and picked up the last stack of langostinos and exited the ship. Marco said some parting words and followed closely behind me.

Once we stepped back onto our ship, he untied us.

"Not as easy as you thought it would be, right? That's a lot of seafood."

"Christ. I haven't carried that many fish since I was twenty-two."

"You did good. Let's go get you some waves, huh?"

I nodded and continued down below with the final load. I opened the big refrigerator door and walked them inside, then dropped them down to the floor. When I did, the wet bottom of the middle box split open, and a plastic bag bulged out that didn't look like any langostino. I tugged at the bag, and the box split more, and a vacuum-sealed baggie the size of a fist came through that was full of little blue pills marked M30. I knew what they were.

They were fentanyl, a synthetic version of the drugs that had killed my mom. I fucking hated, hated this drug. I shoved the bag back inside, and I stood, feeling faint when I did. I put my hand over my thundering heart. I slowly backed up, trying to think through my options. Trying to understand if this was how Marco really made his money or if this was a big misunderstanding. Maybe he didn't know what was in there, and he was just the delivery person. One who didn't ask questions. But I doubted it, and I wanted off this ship. Now.

I took another step back and expected to hit the inside of the cold door, but it was already open, and I fell. But instead of landing hard on my ass, I was snatched from the air by shockingly strong hands. It was Rocky breathing heavily and holding me firmly around my chest.

"You okay, writer boy?" he said, standing me up and spinning me around with incredible strength. "You don't look so good." He slapped my face with his massive hand, and it stung.

"I—I'm good. Just got a little dizzy from all the lifting."

He laughed. "Sure, writer boy. You need to get out from behind that computer more. Stay here." Rocky nudged me aside and went into the refrigerator, shuffled some boxes around, and stepped out. He closed the refrigerator door, placing a thick padlock on it. "Let's go topside."

I stayed at the rear of the ship while Rocky went back up to the helm, and Marco met him up there. The other ship was already almost gone from view. Rocky and Marco started the *Maître D* and huddled close, talking low about something that I figured had to do with me and the fact that Rocky was suspicious as fuck after our little encounter down below. It didn't matter; I could find a way back without them, and I wasn't going to let that fat asshole decide my fate. I was here to surf anyway.

I slipped below and put on my wetsuit and booties as quickly as I could, tucking my cell phone inside a waterproof pocket. I took my shortboard from its case and tucked it under my arm. When I got topside, Rocky and Marco were still arguing. I jumped straight off the back, got my chest on the board, and started to paddle hard for the shore. I could hear Rocky shouting from the boat. "Get the fuck back here, writer boy!"

Despite not being in the greatest box-lifting shape, I did have surfing shoulders, and I could paddle hard and fast. By the time Rocky got a hold of Marco's gun, or perhaps his own, I was already fifty yards off. Standing on a moving boat, trying to hit a moving target on the ocean surface at fifty yards was impossible. Unless you got really fucking lucky. So the first two shots missed by a lot, but then the sadistic fuck got lucky and tagged me right in the side. I screamed and looked back. I could barely see them in the fading evening light, but I was sure he was smiling.

I belly rode a wave into shore and ditched my board. There were too many exposed rocks for them to run the ship onto the shore, so if they were coming for me, someone, meaning Marco, would have to swim for it.

I ran hard even though it felt like a red-hot spear was lodged in my side. I pushed through the sand and all the way to where the cliff started. I sat there a moment to catch my breath. I checked the gunshot, and it had gone clean through. I ripped the neoprene from my left arm and shoved it into my wetsuit to keep pressure on both sides of the wound and close the holes and stem the blood loss.

I had done some bouldering and rock climbing in undergrad. I needed distance from these assholes, and I needed help, so I started up the cliff. One hand placement here, and a foot placement there. While blood leaked from my body. I was lucky, since it was only about two hundred feet up to the road from here, and it was over a thousand in some parts of Big Sur.

I got to the top, exhausted and faint, and I rolled over on my back to look the way I had come. The ship was still there in the little bay with its lights on. With the road close to the cliff line, I wondered why there were no cars, but then I remembered the mudslide. The only way in or out of this place was on foot or helicopter. I thought about whether Marco would come for me or not. He liked me. But that was before Rocky shot me. He probably thought he could flip me, make me a regular part of their crew. I was broke, desperate; a writer. But now I was shot, and if I made it to a hospital, it would get reported. They needed me dead and buried at sea.

It was dark now, and I wondered if they would wait until

morning with the clouds blocking out the moonlight. There was no way to be sure, but I was so tired, I couldn't keep my eyes open. I got up and walked stiffly for a few hundred yards and collapsed under a redwood tree. My eyes fluttered shut.

***

I was in and out of sleep and hallucinating. Or at least I thought I was hallucinating because at one point, a mountain lion as big as a Shetland pony came prowling out from the dense forest across the street. I knew mountain lions were common in these mountains, but I'd never even heard of one this big. He stopped and watched me, pacing back and forth, lapping at a pool of water in a deep tire mark in the mud.

Then, later, when he was still there, watching, waiting, perched low with his tail back, the low rumble of foghorns sounded off. Only this time, they weren't in the distance. There were right here next to me. Inside of me. I closed my eyes hard, and when I opened them, three massive black figures as big as oak trees rose from the shadows behind the mountain lion.

Faceless, eyes like starbursts in the darkness of their cloaked heads. Their mouths opened, white light spilling from them; a deep foghorn sounded off, and it was so loud, it felt like my chest would burst. The mountain lion ran into the underbrush, and when I looked up, the Dark Watchers were gone. Blended back into the shadows of the tall, thick redwoods. The clouds disappeared, and the forest came alive in the dim glow of the moon and stars.

***

"Your mom believed in the Watchers, right?" my ex-wife said from somewhere inside the cracked, black screen of my cell phone. "And she died young."

"They always were just old Native folklore to me. I know Steinbeck wrote about them. But Mom, when she was back from rehab, she would come down to Big Sur and leave them gifts. Baskets full of flowers, stuff like that. She liked to write about them like she knew them. She used to say they only revealed themselves to certain people, special people. Sometimes hundreds of years apart. I spread her ashes down here."

"I—how did she die again?"

"Jesus, we were married for three years." *Before you asked me to leave.*

"You never talked about it like that. Like how it happened."

"Would you?" I sighed and lifted my head to check the cliff's edge, still nobody. Maybe Marco had decided I wasn't worth it. Or figured I was as good as dead. "Stabbed thirty-seven times. Some fiend she owed money diced her up in Chinatown, in Salinas. She was trying to get clean at the time and help with the community gardens there."

"And that's why you started drinking? Her death stuck inside you?"

With my ex, it always came back to my drinking. I pushed hard against my wound to stanch the bleeding and sobbed softly.

"Christ, Evelyn, I didn't start drinking at eight. And everyone has a goddamn vice."

"I don't understand why you won't give it up to get her back. Whisky doesn't even seem to make you happy. You cry when you black out."

"Bullshit. I feel better inside—I like the way the whisky works through my body like a poison. I like feeling close to death."

"You like being haunted by it."

"Maybe. Some people try and forget death is coming for them, I used it for motivation. Three books with the same sick feeling in my guts that I will die, and no one will ever read them or even know I tried. That my existence won't have mattered."

"I think, beyond that, you're afraid you'll die alone like your mom."

I sobbed into my hands. "I am alone! Look around!" I spat and lifted my hand to look at the wound again. If the bullet had clipped my intestines, I was going to die of sepsis before I could walk another mile. "Nobody gave a shit when my mom died. Just another junkie off the streets to them with nothing to her name. Not a cent. Only thing she had was a letter for me."

"What did the letter say?"

"That she loved me. People make mistakes. And to spread her ashes down here."

"Did you leave your daughter a letter?"

"I did not. Probably so the universe would make sure I came back."

"If you don't get up now, your daughter will never even know you existed, and nobody will ever read your stories. Is that what you want?"

"No. God no. I want to live. I *have* to live."

"To see us again?"

"Of course to see you again. I have too much to do, everything I have put off my entire goddamn life. I can't die. Not before. Not like this. *Goddamnit!*"

Just then, I heard a gunshot in the distance and saw a spark where a bullet ricocheted off the road beside me. I grabbed my cell phone and rolled behind the trunk of the redwood. Marco was coming to make sure I was dead.

I pushed my broken phone into my wetsuit pocket. Not like there was reception out here even if it did work. The fact, though, that I could really hear her voice meant I had lost too much blood. I stood and began to run, feeling a stiffness in my legs and feeling the sloshing around of hot blood inside my wetsuit. I held as much pressure on my side as I could, and it now felt hard and numb where the bullet had gone through.

I followed the tree line along the road, wishing for a car. But since the mudslide a month earlier, this whole section had been carved out of existence. No cars would be coming. I ran north toward Big Sur. There were people there. I could get medical help. Maybe. It was my only chance.

It hurt to run. Marco had made it up the cliff, and I could see his light, boyish build running toward me. He was much faster than me and was gaining on me on this stretch of shiny, wet road. His Pebble Beach windbreaker shimmered in the moonlight. It was bright now. And cold, but the wind felt good on my hot face. The wetsuit was filling with sweat and hot blood. I tried to run faster and heard another gunshot. A searing pain ripped through my right shoulder; I fell hard and spun onto my back to face the bastard.

"You fuck," Marco said. He was in good shape, but he was panting for breath. "You fucking make me scale a goddamn cliff and run you down in the street? Christ, kid. I liked you. I'm so sorry. It wasn't meant to go down like this."

He leveled the gun at my head.

"Wait," I said.

I looked across the road again, and there he was. That impossibly large mountain lion pacing just inside the tree line. He crouched low, moving closer, about to pounce.

"You never finished the story," I said, and coughed hard, wiping from my face blood from the impact with the street. "What you wanted to do when you were a kid."

He laughed. "Yeah. You're right. Fuck it. I wanted to be a pro surfer. You happy? I was pretty good at it too. Why do you think I agreed to take you? Shit, I was going to bring you in and help you make the real money. Goddamnit!" He cocked the hammer.

My chest felt heavy now, like an elephant was sitting on it. I struggled to breathe. "My dad told me to get a real job instead of writing. I guess he was right."

"My dad beat the shit out of me when I told him I wanted to surf. You, well, never really know. Maybe all that shit you wrote in the past will become something once you disappear. At least that thought will give you something nice to dream about, huh? Good night, kid, I—"

Marco never finished his sentence, because the mountain lion, which I had thought might have been part of my hallucinations, leapt from the undergrowth and tackled Marco, sinking his huge fangs into the side of Marco's head. Marco managed to fire another shot before the sound of teeth ripping through flesh silenced Marco's screams. The mountain lion dragged the mangled corpse across the road and into the trees.

I stood and limped north, holding the wound on my side and shoulder, toward Big Sur. There were people out here. Campgrounds. Mansions down driveways. The Esalen Institute was only a few miles north. All I had to do to see my little girl again was stay conscious and keep walking.

The distant sound of the foghorns grew louder again with each step. I kept walking. My chest heavy again, full, about to explode, and around me, in all directions, dark figures rose from the trees. Eyes like starbursts, mouths gaping open, light spilling into the road, the asphalt rippling and trees shaking around me.

I kept walking, and a Watcher rose in front of me in the street.

I knew I was dying, and it felt different than I had imagined. I wasn't afraid of it. But there were two thoughts that kept circling my fading consciousness like water down a drain.

My daughter.

My words.

My daughter.

My words.

Then another thought. My mom's letter. Her fixation on the Dark Watchers. Was it possible she knew I would need her here, on this day, seventeen years later? Her ashes summoning this thing in front of me. To save me? Was this all a dream? A hallucination?

I kept walking.

The foghorns guiding me. Protecting me.

Singing me home.

My daughter.

My daughter.

When I approached the Dark figure in the street, a light breeze blew a swirl of fog away, and the night cleared. The creature was gone. And ahead, only a few hundred yards, was a small inn with the lights on.

When I reached the door, I turned around, and the forest grew still and quiet. I shivered and pushed the door open.

Nik Xandir Wolf has been published in various magazines and publications. His debut novel, *Shadow Valley*, was released in November 2022 and quickly became #1 bestseller. He lives in Pacific Grove, California, where he surfs regularly.

To Catch a Thief

Hilary Davidson

"I know what you're thinking," the elderly woman said, the crimson slash of her mouth quivering as a flush rose on her pale cheeks. "But I am not confused, or discombobulated, or mentally incompetent."

"Of course, Madame Flemming," Phillippe LeClerc answered reflexively.

"I am eighty years old and as sharp as anyone half my age. I'm the victim of a crime." She paused to blow her nose. Her eyes were red from weeping.

"Yes, yes, of course." LeClerc nodded reassuringly. He had nodded just like that, his attractive head tilted just so, to comfort many wealthy American tourists in his five years at the Hotel Belle Claire. When you worked in hospitality on the French Riviera, that was an essential skill.

"Someone snuck into my room early this morning and stole my jewelry."

"Your maid told the desk staff that you saw the man," LeClerc said. "Could you describe him to me?"

"I didn't get a good look at him at all," Flemming answered. "I left the hotel before sunrise to walk by the water. My husband and I used to come here together every few years, before he passed…" She paused, wiping her eyes and taking several half-choked breaths. "He died of cancer three years ago. That's when everything in my life went wrong."

LeClerc stared out the window impassively. It was late morning, and the winter sun was shining on the water, creating the illusion of dancing lights. Even in January, Cap Martin dazzled.

"Perhaps you should lie down," LeClerc said. "You've had a painful experience."

"No, I need to do this. While it's still fresh in my mind. On my walk back, I saw a man, all in black. He was on a balcony, and he leapt over to the next one. Like a cat, a black cat. I didn't realize until later that he'd been on *my* balcony."

"Where did he go after that?"

"I'm…I'm not sure. A wave rolled in and…well, it caught me by surprise. It was cold and I tripped and fell. It took me a minute to right myself again. When I looked at the hotel again, the man was gone."

"What happened when you came back to your suite?"

"I opened the door and everything was quiet. Annette—that's my assistant—Annette was still asleep. I went to my room and realized the balcony door was open. The jewelry on my bedside table was gone."

"Was the safe open?"

"No. He took the jewelry from the night table."

"*Crime d'opportunité*," LeClerc murmured.

"Yes, exactly." Flemming gazed at him with her watery pale blue eyes.

"Gangs, the organized criminals, they attack the jewelry shows at the big hotels, and they take the contents of the safes. This sounds like an amateur, a copycat."

She nodded in agreement.

"Tell me what is missing," he urged.

"My watch—it's Cartier, platinum and diamonds, worth a fortune. It was a gift from my husband for our fortieth wedding anniversary. It was inscribed 'To Dodo, Love, Todo'—Dodo is me, Dorothy. Todo was a silly name I had for Howard." She wiped her eyes. Her grief was a palpable thing, sitting in the room with them like a pet. "Also a bracelet made of platinum and diamonds. Another gift from my husband. I'll never see it again."

"Please do not give up hope," LeClerc said. "Is that everything that's missing? If there's more, I would need an itemized list."

"My heart," she said. "It feels like someone ripped that out."

"Could you retrace your steps for me since you arrived? I know you checked into the Hotel Belle Claire two days ago."

"I haven't done much of anything," she said. "My husband used to have friends here who we met up with. But they're dead now. That life is gone." She twisted her wedding ring around. "No one tells you that. How, as you get older, all you do is miss things. Everybody leaves. Everything vanishes. Sometimes it feels like I'm the last one at the party."

LeClerc let that poignant sentiment linger in the air for a moment. The woman's pain was tangible to him. "What brought you back here, since your friends are gone?"

"Nostalgia, which I've found to be a powerful drug," she admitted. "And my grandson. He's living in Monaco this year. I saw him last night. He took me out to a wonderful place for dinner. I forget the name of the restaurant, but it was lovely. The first good evening I've had since my husband passed."

LeClerc made a mental note. There was a particular type of young man who lived in Monaco, and that type frequently accrued gambling debts. "What's your grandson's name?"

"Trevor. He's a darling boy. He'll be brokenhearted when I tell him what happened to me." She wiped her eyes again.

"What kind of work does Trevor do?"

"Oh, I don't really know. A lot of this technological realm is beyond me."

That was strike two against Trevor, LeClerc thought. A shiftless gambler without a job? One who knew exactly where his grandmother was staying and what jewels she traveled with? His list of suspects was already laser focused.

"I never imagined I would encounter a cat burglar in real life," Flemming mused. "I remember watching *To Catch a Thief* when I was a teenager. Alfred Hitchcock, you know."

"Yes, I know."

"I thought it was all so romantic," she went on. "But a real-life cat burglar is nothing like Cary Grant, is it?"

"Madame, there are more films and stories about cat burglars on the Riviera than actual cat burglars," LeClerc said.

"It's very real. I read about that diamond show—one man with a handgun making off with millions in jewelry. That would never happen in America."

Her superior tone was hard to bear quietly, but he smiled. He had experience with high-strung guests.

"Where is your grandson staying?"

"At the Hotel de Paris in Monaco. Why?"

"I'll need to speak with him."

She stared at him. "I don't understand. What would Trevor have to do with this? Shouldn't you be questioning the staff?"

LeClerc had a fleeting vision of stomping around the Hotel Belle Claire, demanding that the staff turn out their pockets. Perhaps that was what an American investigator would do, but that wasn't good form in Cap Martin. "It's just standard procedure. I am certain I will be speaking with many people," he answered, aware that details would only feed her anger.

Her mouth quivered. "When are the real police getting here?"

"I am the real police, madame," LeClerc assured her. "You cannot imagine that a small, medieval town like Roquebrune-Cap-Martin has a police force like an American city?"

"You're just a hotel detective. I want the real police. They need to take my report."

"I was on the police force in Paris for a decade. I promise you, I will investigate, and I will liaise with the municipal police as necessary. But no one is coming here from Cannes or Marseilles to look for your missing watch. That is the job of the house detective. I will need to speak with your assistant now."

Dorothy Flemming folded her arms and glared at him. "Let me save you some time with your investigation. My bracelet and watch were stolen. My assistant doesn't know anything about it. Annette was asleep. I already asked her."

"American efficiency, I appreciate that." LeClerc smiled. "I will have to speak to this assistant all the same."

She grumbled something under her breath but called for the other woman and retreated to her bedroom, slamming the door behind her. The assistant was a tall Black woman in her forties. She was powerfully built, but the feature LeClerc noticed most keenly was the extensive scarring over one of her forearms, which rendered the flesh puckered and pink.

"Annette Jackson," she said, extending her hand to shake. "I'm Mrs. Flemming's healthcare aide."

"She described you as an assistant."

"She hates having a healthcare aide," Annette confided in a soft voice. "I only met her after her husband passed, but she's had a few bad falls. She injured her wrist, and she can't pick up anything heavy. She's very independent, but she needs help with a few things."

"I have to ask if you heard anyone come into the suite this morning."

"No, I didn't hear a thing," Annette said. "I was up late with Mrs. Flemming. She was so happy to see her grandson, but she got very weepy after that. We were up until two, having tea."

"Why?"

"She said she'd been cheated."

LeClerc's pulse shot up. "By her grandson?"

"I don't think so. I mean, she loves Trevor. She says the rest of her family only wants her money when she dies."

"But someone cheated her out of money?"

"She was crying and saying how she'd been cheated over and over. I tried to comfort her. It's not easy when she gets like that."

"Have you met this Trevor?"

"When he picked Mrs. Flemming up last night, and then he came in for a bit when he brought her back here."

LeClerc's mind was bubbling over with suspicion of the grandson, but he needed to pay attention to other possibilities. Lowering his voice to a whisper, he asked, "Has Madame Flemming misplaced her jewelry before?"

"No, she's a very meticulous person," Annette said. "The most surprising part of the story, to me, was that she hadn't put her watch in the safe. It's a Cartier, so you know it's expensive. But I know she loved it because it was a gift from her husband. It's inscribed 'To Dodo, Love, Todo.' It makes me think they must've been pretty cute together."

"What about the bracelet?"

"What bracelet?"

"The one that was stolen?"

Annette looked puzzled. "Mrs. Flemming was crying about the watch. It was hard to make out everything she said, but I don't remember her mentioning a bracelet."

LeClerc filed that away. It wasn't unusual for a guest who was genuinely the victim of a theft to embellish their list of losses. But that was the insurance company's concern, not his.

"Did you notice anything out of place in the suite this morning?" he asked.

She shook her head. "No. Whoever came in, they went for the master suite, I guess."

"Your arm that is injured…that didn't happen here, did it?"

"Oh, no, that was from a kitchen fire last year." Her eyes shifted to the carpet.

"Was that at your employer's home?" he asked, sensing her discomfort.

"I'd rather not discuss it," she said. "Mrs. Flemming has had some bad luck, generally. Sometimes I think she doesn't pay attention to what she's doing, because she's so angry at the world. She's very focused on what she's lost."

LeClerc considered that on his way downstairs to his office on the ground floor. He'd requested the video footage from the hotel's security cameras from the past twenty-four hours, and it was waiting for him in his virtual inbox. It didn't take long for him to find the footage of Madame Flemming, and he slowed it down to a crawl: There she was, walking out of the hotel with a trim, elegant man—presumably her grandson—at a quarter to eight, and there she was, returning with the same man just after eleven thirty. They both appeared to be laughing and having a fine time. Whatever jewelry she was wearing was subtle, certainly not the kinds of pieces that caught the eyes of jaded Riviera-based thieves.

He paused the film and zeroed in on the grandson, Trevor Flemming. He captured a clear image and sent it to a friend on the municipal police force in Nice with the details he had and a request for any information.

Then he looked at the video from that morning. There Madame Flemming was, going out well before sunrise, and there she was an hour later. He paused on her image and enlarged it. The elderly woman's eyes were wide, as if she were frantic or terrified. Her distress was clear.

He didn't believe she'd actually seen a cat burglar, but he was willing to believe that she was certain she had spotted one. Something had frightened her when she was out, if only a glimpse of a shadow moving across the building as the sun came up.

On his way out, he stopped at the staffing office. His co-worker, Florence, glanced up at him. She was a thirtyish woman with her hair styled in a glamorous updo and cat's-eye glasses.

"Do you know Cary Grant's ghost is still haunting us?" he asked.

"Forget Grant. *Lupin* is the hot ticket now."

"I haven't seen it yet."

"It's on Netflix. You can catch it anytime."

"Maybe I will." He paused. "I take it there haven't been any other reports of pilfered jewels this morning?"

"None. I mean, it's January, so we're pretty empty, and it's not the season for galas and tiaras, you know?"

"Okay, thanks," LeClerc said. "I'm off to find the errant grandson. Wish me luck. I have a feeling this guy is down on his."

***

Trevor Flemming was not at all what LeClerc expected. LeClerc had formed a picture of a deadbeat, high-rolling casino gambler with a drug habit, a lowlife who was willing to rip off his own grandmother. But when he asked for Trevor Flemming at the desk of Monaco's legendary Hotel de Paris, he earned a cold stare.

"Just a moment," the desk clerk said. But instead of picking up the phone, she retreated to a doorway behind the reception desk.

A moment later a man in an expensive navy blue suit appeared before him. Behind him, a large man loomed like an exaggerated shadow.

"What's you interest in Trevor Flemming?" the first man asked.

LeClerc explained who he was and where he worked, and added that Trevor's poor grandmother Dorothy Flemming had been robbed that morning. That changed the dynamic quickly, though it still took another half hour for Trevor to appear. In that time, LeClerc learned that Trevor was a security expert staying at the hotel to improve its systems. Background checks upon background checks had been performed. The young man was clean as the proverbial whistle.

When the frantic-looking young man appeared, LeClerc recognized him immediately from the video footage.

"What happened? Is she hurt?" Trevor asked him, his face flushed.

"Your grandmother is physically safe. Emotionally, she is not doing so well."

"What happened?"

"Someone took a few things while she walked on the beach this morning," LeClerc said.

Trevor looked pained. "That's awful. Nana's had such a bad run of luck the past few years."

"What do you mean?"

"My grandfather was killed three years ago," Trevor said. "Nana's had several falls since then. Last year, she had a kitchen fire. Oh, and her car was stolen. It's been one awful thing after another." He sighed. "I'm glad Annette stays with her, but if she ever quits, my parents say they'll put Nana in a home."

"I'm sorry, perhaps I misunderstood," LeClerc said. "Your grandmother told me that your grandfather died of cancer."

"He was diagnosed with an inoperable brain tumor," Trevor said. "About a year after that, he had the car accident. It was awful, basically a head-on collision with a truck. But he had always been such a good driver. The accident only happened because of the tumor. He was confused."

"Your grandmother wasn't with him?"

"No. We're all grateful for that."

To LeClerc's mind, it sounded as if, perhaps, the grandfather had chosen to end his own life, but those were not words he could give voice to. Suggesting such a thing would do far more harm than good.

***

There was a heaviness in LeClerc's heart when he returned to the Hotel Belle Claire, and it worsened when he discovered Madame Flemming waiting in the lobby for him.

"I wanted to set the record straight about a couple of things," she said quickly. "I feel bad about suggesting the staff here could be involved. I'm not accusing anyone of anything. It could be that a man broke into the hotel or else climbed up from the street"—

"Of course, madame," he said. "Those are possibilities indeed."

"Everyone at the hotel was always so good to Howard and me," she continued. "We came here for our twenty-fifth wedding anniversary, then for our thirtieth, and somehow it became another of our special things."

"That sounds very lovely."

"It was while it lasted." Her words were seeped in bitterness.

"Thank you for telling me. You should know that our staff is very loyal, and they go through a lot of security checks."

She nodded. "The other thing that I wanted to mention is that a pair of my diamond earrings is also missing."

"Earrings? They disappeared since this morning?"

"No, they were on the night table, too, I guess," she said. "The funny thing is, I thought I put them in the safe, but I must've forgotten. I don't know how, except that I was very emotional last night. Poor Annette had to sit up with me."

"This is very interesting," he said. "You didn't notice them missing this morning?"

"No. I thought I had put them away. I guess I got confused." She shrugged. "I mention it because my insurance company needs a police report. Not a hotel-cop report."

Before he could answer that, she turned and headed for the elevator.

It wasn't unusual for an American tourist to immediately want to file an insurance claim, LeClerc reminded himself as he walked into his office. But, in light of Madame Flemming's many troubles, it seemed to him like she might be attempting to milk the insurer for all she could. LeClerc had no particular sympathy for large corporations, but people who committed insurance fraud seldom thought about how payments really paid out: if the insurer had to pay a large sum to Madame Flemming, that same insurer would turn around and sue the Hotel Belle Claire.

When he sat down at his computer, he discovered he'd left it frozen on the image of Madame Flemming's horrified face. He stared at it for a moment, frowning in concentration. What was it she had said to him? *I didn't realize until later that he'd been on my balcony.* There was no reason for her to be so upset by what she'd seen. It wasn't as if she'd told the front desk that she'd spotted a man on a balcony. It was only later that she realized that she was a victim.

LeClerc played the video again and again. Upon closer inspection, her face was tear stained on her return to the hotel. But it was only when he rewatched the earlier section of video that he realized the most important detail: When Madame Flemming went out of the hotel before dawn, she'd been wearing her watch. When she came back to the hotel, her wrist was bare.

***

"I appreciate you coming here," LeClerc told his friend from Nice. Inspector Maron was a Paris veteran as well, but the Riviera was her birthplace. She was darkly tanned, with silver hair and expressive green eyes.

"It's not a problem," Maron said. "When you explained the situation, it was clear it is necessary."

They went upstairs to Madame Flemming's room together. Annette answered the door and ushered them inside. The elderly woman was perched on the sofa. There was a tray of vanilla-scented candles on the table in front of her, and they cast a strange, brooding light on her face. She was sipping a martini with an olive. There were two glasses— empty except for their olives—on another tray.

"I have brought a real police officer," LeClerc announced. "Madame Flemming, this is Inspector Maron. She has some questions for you."

"Finally," Flemming said. "I've been waiting all day for this. My jewelry has been stolen, and I need to file a report—"

"Just one moment, madame," Maron said. "There is a question about your Cartier watch. Hotel security cameras show you wearing it when you walked out of the hotel this morning. It was not on your wrist when   you   returned."

The older woman stared at her incredulously. "You don't know what you are talking about."

"Madame Flemming, we have the video." LeClerc brandished a tablet. "You can watch it." When she didn't answer, he queued it up.

They watched in silence. Annette edged around the sofa so that she could see as well.

"This is insane," Flemming muttered. "My watch was stolen. It's worth a fortune. It—"

"Was it stolen by someone on the beach?" Maron asked.

"No! The beach was virtually empty."

"So, no one accosted you. No one took your watch off your wrist." Maron's voice was cautiously neutral.

"No! I told you, it was stolen. You probably confused the footage from the day before. I went out to the beach then, too."

"Madame Flemming, this morning you told me that you fell when a wave came in," LeClerc said. "Is it possible that the wave carried away your watch?"

Her face was a mask of shock and sadness. "Howard gave me that watch for our anniversary," she whispered. "It's priceless."

"But that's what happened, isn't it?" Maron asked. "The water, it carried your priceless watch away."

Annette tapped on LeClerc's shoulder. When he looked around, she gestured with her head for him to follow her.

"Excuse me, I need to make a call," he murmured.

"I'll let you out," Annette said.

Once they were out of sight in the front hallway, Annette let out a long sigh. "Look, I only started working for Mrs. Flemming after her husband passed, but I can tell you about her never-ending battle with the insurance company," she whispered.

"What do you mean?"

"Mr. Flemming had inoperable cancer, a brain tumor. When he had his accident…well, the insurance company decided that was suicide," Annette said. "Which meant they refused to pay out his multimillion-dollar insurance policy. Mrs. Flemming took them to court, but she lost."

"You're saying she has no money?"

"No, she has money, but she wakes up every day believing she was robbed," Annette said. "She's had some bad things happen to her, and she's bitter. I wondered what was going on when she kept adding to her claim today. I believed the watch was stolen, but then it was also a bracelet, and also earrings, and everything is worth zillions."

"I see. I appreciate you telling me this."

"Can you cut her a break?" Annette asked. "She's so bitter about everything she's lost. Even if you're just playing along for a bit. Let the insurance company back home be the bad guy."

"Are you aware of her committing insurance fraud?"

"No, but her car went missing the one week I took off. I have questions."

"Thank you for your honesty," he said.

When he walked back into the sitting room, Maron was discussing insurance with the elderly woman. "You will have to see if your policy covers accidental loss," Maron said. "Most do, from what I've seen."

"They will cheat me, just like they've cheated me before," Flemming said. "They can't do that if there's been a robbery."

"And I cannot write this report up as a robbery," Maron said. "That would be fraud. That would be a crime."

"All right," Flemming said coldly. "I understand. You can go."

Maron shot LeClerc a glance, as if to say, "Who does this old lady think she is?" But LeClerc shrugged and they exited the suite.

"Thank you for coming by," LeClerc said.

"It was you who solved the case of the missing watch," Maron answered.

After they said good-bye, LeClerc retreated to his office to finish up for the day. He was interrupted by the front desk clerk. "Galyna from housekeeping found this on the beach," the young man said, holding out a platinum watch.

"Galyna from housekeeping deserves a raise," LeClerc answered, examining the watch. It wasn't the diamond-encrusted timepiece Madame Flemming had described, but it was a Cartier Tank watch. Inside was inscribed *To Dodo, Love, Todo.*

It was undeniably the missing watch.

LeClerc tapped it to his heart. "What are the odds?" he asked. "The waves take, and the waves give back."

He took the elevator up, suddenly elated to be able to give Madame Flemming her watch. Perhaps her spirit was broken, but to have this treasured keepsake back would be a balm. Maron hadn't even mentioned the issue of filing a fraudulent police report. What could they do with an eighty-year-old woman?

He knocked on the door and waited. No one answered, so he knocked again. Perhaps the older woman was tearing up again, and her aide was comforting her. The watch could wait until tomorrow, he thought.

But he put his hand on the doorknob, and it was hot to the touch.

LeClerc ran back to the elevator and pulled the fire alarm. Then he ran back to Flemming's door and hit it with his body. It budged, but it didn't break. He threw himself at it again, and it splintered.

The sitting room was on fire. Flames, guided by the curtains, climbed up the wall. The sofa was on fire. Black smoke clustered in the air. Annette lay on the ground, unconscious.

"Everyone cheats me," Madame Flemming said. She was on the carpet, one leg twisted under her at a strange angle.

"What did you do?" he shouted.

"I won't be cheated again," she snapped. "Help me up!"

LeClerc grabbed Annette under her arms and dragged her out of the suite and down the hallway. When he went back to the suite, more black smoke was billowing out.

"Help me!" Her voice was weaker now, but just as insistent.

For the first time in his career as a hotel detective, LeClerc suppressed the voice that told him to accommodate the guest. He remembered the burns on Annette's arm and understood why her eyes had flickered dangerously at the mention of the kitchen fire. He backed away from the heat and the flame and scuttled down the hallway, finding Annette and dragging her down the stairs to safety.

Hilary Davidson has won two Anthony Awards, a Derringer Award, and a host of other accolades. Her novels include the Lily Moore series: *The Damage Done, The Next One to Fall,* and *Evil in All Its Disguises*; the Shadows of New York series: *One Small Sacrifice* and *Don't Look Down*; and the stand-alone novels: *Blood Always Tells* and *Her Last Breath*. She is also the author of some fifty short stories; a few of the earliest have been gathered in a collection called *The Black Widow Club*. Visit Hilary online at www.hilarydavidson.com.

Snowman

Billy Minshall

Seven-year-old Brandon McHenry played the cherubic snowman in the school Christmas pageant and made the audience laugh, then cry when he melted. The stage was the only place where the pale, fair, and fat little boy felt loved. He wanted that feeling to go on forever.

Years later, when he was thirteen, first love bloomed when Brandon watched his friend Martin Salazar play the lead in *Godspell.* Watching Martin perform, Brandon felt something new. A closeness, but not the way that boys were close when they played sports. Here was an unidentifiable longing that troubled Brandon. He wrestled with it, pushed against it.

Two years later, at the age of fifteen, chubby Brandon McHenry found that his feelings for other boys had intensified. These were the days that predated gender fluidity, when sexuality was fixed; before the internet. At that time, what someone desired couldn't be readily identified, couldn't be clicked on. Certain words, finite labels, existed. *Gay, bi, lesbian,* even *trans*. But there was not a way to access an immediate community where Brandon could connect and create an instant family with people like himself. Instead, there was unbearable silence. Brandon's watchful eye searched his surroundings for a glimpse of someone who might be like him. But assuming that he identified that someone, he still had to muster up the courage to approach them. *What if they laugh at me? Then what? What if they tell everyone? They might beat me up. They might kill me.* Brandon was restless and terrified, and at school the other boys called him fat and asked him if he was a fag.

The summer before tenth grade, Brandon and his parents, William and Lorelei, went to Florida for summer vacation. The family drove twenty-one hours to a small motel in Daytona Beach called the Beacon by the Sea. The three of them shared a single room with two double beds. The mattresses sagged in the center. A run-down kitchenette included an olive-colored, half-size electric stove with one working burner. The bathroom smelled like mold and ancient sewage. When they ran the bath, water flooded the floor through the bottom of the rusty claw-foot tub. The soggy, weeping mess of a room had a sad, patchy peach paint job, which might have been coral at one time, or maybe eggshell.

"We're not here to stay in the room. We're here for the sun," William explained to his family.

"I can't read in this light," Lorelei said.

"This is vacation time, not reading time," William said.

"I enjoy reading, Bill. I know you don't get that, but it brings me pleasure. For me, it's not a chore."

"You can read on the beach. There's plenty of light there," William offered in earnest.

"It's not the same thing. The beach is hot and noisy! Jesus. You know what? Never mind. It's lovely. The room is absolutely perfect!" Lorelei began to unpack.

Brandon watched his father process failure. William McHenry tried, always tried, but nothing he did was enough to please Lorelei or Brandon. Brandon knew that his dad was content to leave his family in the Beacon by the Sea and head out before dawn each day with a full tackle box. Shiny lures that were sure to catch him a swordfish, a shark.

"Well the beach is right there if you want it," William said.

"Who goes to Florida in the summer? It's so humid," Brandon said.

"Honey, go take a swim and cool off. I want to talk to your father," Lorelei said.

Brandon left the room and headed to the white sands of Daytona Beach. The immaculate shoreline was stained with locals and tourists sporting mullets. Leather-skinned, bleach-blonde women smoked while they carried their infants. Motorcycles parked on the sand, and white teenaged boys in Speedos wore half shirts adorned with Confederate flags. Men chewed spearmint Skoal; Mötley Crüe howled on giant boomboxes. Brandon knew that he didn't belong here. He felt inferior. He felt like a mistake.

In the distance, a Ferris wheel and a pier. The beach stretched out forever. Brandon trudged through a wasteland of people who might have been forty but were already gruesome and unsalvageable. A swath of potbellied, sexless masses lolling in the sunshine, choking on corn dogs and Budweiser.

On the pier, Brandon passed the arcades, overcome by the aroma of cotton candy and funnel cakes. He salivated, which made him feel even worse about himself. Still, the sun was nice. The sounds of life and the oceanic landscape were different than his landlocked existence on the Great Plains. Here, the sea moved in and out and crested and was beautiful and cold and violent and nourishing. Water gave life.

He wandered into a neon-covered souvenir shop. A pitiful bell rattled when he closed the door behind him. Brandon scanned the shop with its fluorescent pinks and yellows and oranges. He saw postcards on a lime-green rack. Images of half-naked men greeted him. "Brad" said, *Welcome to Sunny Florida!* These guys looked beautiful in Speedos. The men on the postcards were tan and blonde with hairy chests and white teeth. Brandon studied them. He thought they looked perfect. Next to the postcards, keychains. One that read, *Silly faggot, dicks are for chicks.* Brandon hurried out of the store.

His eyes stung from the salt air, and Brandon blinked back tears so he could stare at the guys that passed by. None were quite as handsome as the models on the postcards, still they intrigued him in their Metallica T-shirts with their pentagram tattoos. Brandon wondered how they smelled. He wished that he was confident enough to take off his shirt and roam freely along the boardwalk or ride the Tilt-A-Whirl in jean shorts and nothing else. Brandon's loneliness was unbearable; shame enveloped him. Why did he feel this way? A handsome young man passed by, and Brandon stared, but this time the passerby stared back. At first, Brandon thought nothing of it. Then the man looked back once more and smiled. Brandon's dick moved. Not because he was turned on, but because he felt seen. The man had beautiful bleach-blonde hair with black roots, and he wore white Guess jean shorts and a white T-shirt. *Like an angel.* Brandon followed him.

The angel looked back, then stopped next to the pier that led to the Ferris wheel. "Dr. Feelgood" played from one of the nearby arcades.

"Hi," the angel said.

Brandon didn't know if he should run. He choked. He felt like crying.

"I'm Thomas." The angel Thomas extended his hand.

"Brandon." They shook hands.

"How old are you?"

"Fifteen," Brandon said. Then quickly, "I'll be sixteen in September though."

Thomas nodded.

"How old are you?" Brandon asked.

"Nineteen. So, what are you looking for?"

"What?"

"You got any money? We can get a room," Thomas said.

"I have some money," Brandon said. His mom had given him sixty dollars to spend.

He followed Thomas along the boardwalk.

"Where you from?" Thomas asked.

"Kansas."

"I'm from South Carolina. I came here a couple of months ago. I'm a model," Thomas said.

"Really?"

"I was in a Montgomery Ward catalog" Thomas said with a smile. "In my underwear."

"Wow."

"I surf, too. Used to surf all the time in Myrtle Beach. But the waves in the gulf aren't nothing. Even the waves here on the Atlantic suck. California, though, is just awesome. Yeah, the Pacific is freezing, but the waves are bigger, they're just, like, higher. It's so different than Florida or South Carolina. Nothing compares to the Pacific Ocean and California."

"I've never been to California," Brandon said.

"Me neither, but I know it's so much better."

Thomas lured Brandon away from the busy boardwalk, to a motel window. He asked the clerk for a room. The sun was setting.

"Forty bucks," the guy behind the bulletproof glass said.

"You got the money?" Thomas asked Brandon.

Brandon handed over forty dollars.

***

The air-conditioned room was freezing and reeked of stale cigarette smoke. Thomas sat close to Brandon. The queen-size bed was covered with a rotting, scratchy comforter.

"You ever done this before?" he asked.

"No," Brandon said. Then, "Do you have a condom?"

"I can do it better without it," Thomas said.

"Okay," Brandon said.

"Give me your other twenty," Thomas said. Brandon did.

Thomas pulled a small baggie out of his pocket and smashed up a little rock on the glass-topped nightstand. He took out his pocketknife and sculpted the crushed ice into a line. Thomas rolled up the last of Brandon's vacation money, then snorted the line up his right nostril.

"You like to party?" he asked Brandon.

"I don't know," Brandon said.

"Try it," Thomas said.

"What is it?"

Thomas laughed and cut up another thin white line that glistened like snow. Brandon looked at the perfect suntanned man with soft skin, who smelled like banana and coconut, but also like decay, like rusting metal. Thomas put his arm around Brandon and brought him in close, protective.

"Go on. You're gonna love it," Thomas said.

Brandon leaned over and snorted the ice the same way that Thomas had. Instantly, Brandon's face was on fire and his right eye cried. Then, his head lightened and the world widened and nothing mattered and the angel Thomas got naked and mounted Brandon and entered him without a condom. Brandon squirmed beneath Thomas, afraid and ashamed. He wanted to retract, to take himself back.

"Rub your dick, it'll help with the pain," Thomas said.

Brandon did and it helped. And after that, Brandon didn't really feel anything other than the violent bedding beneath him. After a couple minutes, Thomas made a face and grunted and went limp. He pushed himself up and off Brandon and grabbed his bag of drugs and the rolled-up twenty-dollar bill. He dressed quickly, and if he said good-bye, Brandon didn't hear it. Thomas vanished and left the motel room door open behind him. The sticky summer dusk lurked outside the motel door, unable to penetrate the freezing room.

Brandon was left alone, high and freaked out. His face was on fire from the drugs. Frantically, he gathered his Ocean Pacific swim trunks and Coca-Cola T-shirt, put them on, and left the room and sped back down the beach, edgy and terrified; tweaking. He decided that he'd probably die from an awful disease.

He made it back to the family's room at Beacon by the Sea, where his mom read and his dad watched the news.

"How was the beach?" William asked.

"It was fine," Brandon said.

He clenched his jaw and was hyperaware of every move he made. Crippling self-consciousness. *They know. It's over. Be calm. You're fucked. You suck.*

"Are you all right?" Lorelei asked, looking up from her book.

"Yes, I said I was fine!" Brandon snapped.

"You know," William told his son, "I was a teenager once upon a time, but I never talked to my mother like that. So, get it together and watch your tone!"

Lorelei returned to Jane Austen, and her husband to CNN's *Crossfire*, and Brandon to his shame spiral.

***

The rest of the vacation was a blur of salt water and sun, of drowning and emerging then wanting to drown once again and forever. Brandon barely ate for the rest of the trip, and if his parents noticed, they didn't say a thing. He was sickened by himself. After a week, the three of them piled back into their butter-yellow Buick. They ascended through Jacksonville, then Atlanta, then Birmingham. At one point, Brandon's dad, William, informed his family that they were approaching Memphis, and said that now would be the time to stop for barbecue. Lorelei barked at her husband and told him to keep his eyes on the road. They didn't stop. Then more unremarkable highway, to Tulsa. Two hours north toward nowhere and finally, home. For the rest of the summer, Brandon didn't really eat, and he couldn't really sleep.

***

Brandon was fifteen pounds lighter by the time school started. His skin was bronze and his hair was Ken-doll blonde. He was beautiful and unreal and began his sophomore year of high school with an onslaught of compliments from the people who used to torment him.

"You're so tan! Oh my god, how did you lose all of that weight?"

"You literally look like a surfer! You're so lucky that you got to go to Florida. Was it fun?"

"So much fun," he told them.

Two weeks into his sophomore year, Brandon was cast as Johnny in the school's production of *The Outsiders*. He hung out with the popular kids because they insisted, because he was just that handsome now. He went to parties, he drank, and he made people laugh. He became the class clown, which suited him and saved him from questions about why he didn't have a girlfriend. Because he was funny, people thought of Brandon as a friend but not someone you would date. It was perfect.

***

When his parents were asleep, Brandon sneaked out of the house and wandered the lonely gravel streets of their neighborhood, an enclave of lower-middle-class white people whose only worldly power was the color of their skin. The stench of sulfur from the nearby sewage plant hung in the air. Brandon gagged, his pace quickened, his shoulders and jaw tense. He didn't belong here any more than he belonged to that hateful stretch of Florida shoreline. Brandon bit the inside of his cheek, and when the metallic blood flooded his mouth, he remembered the angel Thomas and his skin that smelled like rusting metal. Thomas, who had left him alone in a freezing motel room, high on crystal meth. Thomas, who'd vanished without saying good-bye, without saying anything. Brandon had been so frightened that day, so confused and agitated. But he'd also experienced a miraculous detachment. When he'd snorted that fine line of snow, Brandon hadn't cared that he might die an awful death from an incurable illness, and he had felt no shame about who he was. He liked guys. Guys in Speedos, guys in boxers, in sweat pants, in surf gear. Hang-ten guys. When he was fucked up, Brandon could want them freely. And when he graduated high school, maybe he would move to California. Thomas had said that the surf was better there, and Brandon already knew that the waves were bigger on the West Coast, which meant that the surfers themselves were greater. And certainly, there must have been guys in California more beautiful than Thomas. Kinder, smarter, more loving guys who wouldn't leave him hanging. In California, at America's end, Brandon McHenry was sure to begin.

But now a Doberman barked behind a chain link fence. American flags and yard art adorned the front lawns. A breeze picked up and carried the sewage smell south. Brandon's pace slowed. He trudged the miserable road, past a wasted cream-colored Winnebago, an El Camino on cinder blocks, an old hearse coated with primer, and finally past the next-door neighbor who kept Christmas decorations up all year, including a solitary plastic snowman set apart from Santa and his reindeer, hat and scarf faded from the seasons, holding a sign that used to say *To Noel.*

Billy Minshall is a writer and actor based in Southern California. His book reviews and personal essays have been appeared in the *Kelp Journal* blog and *Gay Chicago* magazine. His short story "Big in Japan" was published by *The Coachella Review.* As an actor, Billy has appeared in several commercials and on multiple television shows, including *Chicago PD.* He had a small but pivotal role in the indie film *Tom of Your Life,* which film critic Richard Roeper called "one of his favorite films of 2020." Billy completed his bachelor of science in English from Northwestern University's School of Professional Studies, and earned his graduate degree in fiction writing from the Low-Residency MFA program at UC Riverside at Palm Desert. He is working on his first novel.

Thanks People

Michael Scott Moore

2006

The cardboard sign on the soft hat by his feet said, *Thanks people—anything helps. Me and my ferret are hungry*, and the ferret, a nervous creature with off-white fur, snaked and scratched the sides of its cloth-mesh bag. Darren lit a cigarette. He sat just inside a Metro entrance in downtown LA, and from this position he could watch people's knees.

The western sky had thick swipes of orange, like a furnace glow. Glass-globe streetlights flickered on. People hurried from sighing buses to the coffee shops, the restaurant-bars, the sandwich and noodle joints preparing to shut. They hurried past Darren in stressful herds to the underground trains. Leaning against the wall, he watched them all from his encampment, which consisted of a rolled-out sleeping bag, his soft top, and an overstuffed field pack.

"What's his name?" said a stranger, meaning the ferret, and Darren said, "Murphy," just to watch this old guy scratch at the cloth screen and croon, "Hey, Murphy, how's it going, Murphy," even though the ferret's name wasn't Murphy.

"Where'd you get him?" said the man.

"Bought him in front of a supermarket."

"Really? An animal like this?"

The man kept his gray hair tied in a little tail. A thin chain dangled from a pair of half-glasses on his beaky, womanish face. An old hippie. Darren mistrusted him. He thought he sensed a certain queer interest, and he let cigarette smoke drift into the stranger's eyes.

"Well, good luck," said the man at last, still smiling, with a dollar dropping into the soft top.

"Yup."

Darren's hair flowed in dark waves over his ears, but his beard grew out fringy and thin. His dark eyes regarded strangers with a mixture of professional readiness and suspicion. He kept part of his body at all times against his field pack, against the bulge of a disassembled M16.

The ferret bag trembled, and Darren rooted in his pockets for a stick of jerky. He pulled his combat folder from another pocket and thumbed it open to carve a piece. The pink ferret nose sniffed; the sharp teeth pulled it away.

A cop strolled up with one hand on his holster, and Darren's heart quickened at the sight of the Glock.

"You bedding down for the night?" said the cop.

"Just sitting."

"Well, we got some calls about an armed vagrant, and I'm just guessing, but someone might've noticed your weapon there."

The cop eyed the field pack. Darren could be reasonable. He wrapped the rest of his jerky and folded up his knife.

"Where'd you serve?" said the cop in a mild voice.

"Iraq. One Five."

Darren was curious as to the cop's reply.

"Three One."

"Oorah."

"Oorah. Where's your home?"

Darren kept quiet.

"Look, I'm gonna have to ask you to leave," the cop said at last. "I know you and your ferret are just having dinner, but you can't sleep here."

Darren shrugged while the cop scribbled on a piece of paper. "Here's the address of a shelter on Seventh. You could walk over there."

Darren's brain was prone to cramps, just like his chest. White-hot rage gripped him sometimes. He didn't like shelters, so he wrapped his arms around his knees and let his heart race. He rocked back and forth while a sentence drifted through his brain without completing itself, something from a college class. His brain fell into an endless loop while he grasped and grasped at the line.

History is a nightmare—

What was the rest of it?

History is a nightmare—

The cop watched him.

At last Darren rolled up his sleeping bag, tied it to the pack, and slung everything on, including the ferret. He gave a loose, joking salute and faded into the Metro station.

***

The underground hall smelled like warm bodies and steel. Digital signs ran messages over the heads of commuters, words moving in silent unison with the trains clanging up like giant hydraulic snakes. People made way for Darren. Gritting his teeth, looking for bomb belts, holster bulges—anything—he sat by the window of a southbound car.

An old woman in the next seat blurted, "Peace on Earth!" and Darren cackled.

There were bankers in suits, dads with goatees, and beautiful women. Mexicans in long flannel shirts, Black kids in baseball caps. Gangbangers didn't rush, he thought. They moved with stoned circumspection compared to the businessmen and civil servants. They thought they were tough. But all civilians looked soft to Darren.

"Whaddya got there, a rat?" said one Mexican guy in a bandanna.

"It's a ferret."

The guy leaned over to look. "Keeps moving around, huh."

"Doesn't like the subway."

Darren spoke real slow. He tried not to slur his words.

"You in the wars?"

"Yup."

"Some shit, huh."

History is a nightmare.

The Mexican looked him up and down with quick flat eyes under the blue bandanna.

"You homeless now?"

Darren nodded.

"How come?" said the man.

Darren wondered that himself. He gritted his teeth and listened to the screeching wheels. The reason related to Humvee rides through

Baghdad and Ramadi, where any bundle of garbage was a potential roadside bomb. Darren had learned a sick fear of street trash in Iraq. One night, on the 5 near San Clemente, when a phantomlike plastic bag blew into his headlights, he slammed the brakes. There was a pileup on the freeway and a considerable measure of civilian consternation. Strangers demanded insurance details. Darren was happy to oblige. He retrieved his ferret and his things from the Suburban and found that sleeping outdoors—in the scrub around Pendleton, on the beach at Trestles, in the parks of LA—suited him just fine.

He'd left home by then, but he wasn't homeless, not really. He slept in his truck, or with various friends. Sometimes he drove to Jimmy McAteer's in Oceanside and left with a collection of "go pills" in a plastic bag. His platoon used to pop them on night patrols, and Darren found dextroamphetamine to be a worthy substitute for battlefield adrenaline.

He'd left his father's house because his father had pissed him off. Too much self-contradiction. Ron DiMartini loved pleasure more than physical valor, even if he claimed to value freedom. People in Calaveras Beach knew him as the easygoing manager of a Chase bank, a large, bluff Italian with bovine eyes and hairy forearms who padded around in penny loafers and cotton slacks. His corner office was airy and bright, hung with paintings of bulls. The bank itself was a cube with glass windows built into a concrete parking structure at the base of Calaveras Boulevard. But on weekends his lightness and humor evaporated, and he prowled the house and yard in an alcoholic mist, never sodden drunk but faintly and pleasantly sozzled. He snapped orders; he growled at the news. His frustrations from the week before became everyone else's problem. He was a former hippie who had long ago discovered Ayn Rand, so when a bunch of actual hippies moved in next door to run some kind of food charity, Ron DiMartini traded insults with them across the backyard fence, like a man bickering with his past.

Darren was in third grade then. The next-door house "Seahorse House" became a notorious rat's nest with a shifting population of scruffy drifters who came to populate his nightmares as a child. Darren referred to it as the "Seahorse House" because of some decorations on the front. But he learned to hate hippies, like his dad. Hippies belonged to an era of personal and public history that Ron DiMartini preferred to forget. He was an absolutist, a man who never faced up to being wrong. He had to be right from *A* to *Z*. So after Darren joined the corps in 2000, his father became a patriot, and when the hideous explosions against a blue sky in 2001 flashed across American TV screens, he became a jingoist and a hawk before Darren had a chance to think things through. Ron argued with friends over dinner. He belittled his opponents in the comments of a dozen blogs. He swore up and down about Iraqi stockpiles of chemical weapons and dirty nukes as if he had intel straight from Saddam. Darren thought of himself as a loyal Marine more than a persuaded, confident hawk: he learned to hump a pack through the scrubby hills of Camp Pendleton while his father thumped a tub for war.

Now those debates haunted his mind like the laugh track to a horror film. Darren was prone to silent fits of rage. What should have been regular memories arrived in a blast of heat that seemed to weld his mind to the past. He remembered the waterfall of blood from Ismael's lifted body, the sudden dark color. Or the first man killed in the Mazda, the spray of his skull.

"Where you going now?" said the Mexican.

The question startled Darren.

"To the beach." He straightened up and spoke with resolve, although he'd boarded the train with no destination in mind. "I can go home," he informed the Mexican, "any day of the week."

"Oh, I gotchya."

Home didn't feel like home anymore; that was the problem. His father's girlfriend lived there now with her perfumes and photographs and her own sense of interior design. His mom lived in Pasadena. Darren had paid her a visit. She lived with a new husband in a tree-shaded house where the light filtered through poplars onto polished teak furniture and plush carpet. When she asked about the war, he went into some detail— he tried to be honest—but the way her eyes wrinkled with concern, then searched his face in bewilderment surprised him. She poured a glass of wine and fixed a stare on his wrist, looking, he realized, for an old playground scar. At last she took the wrist in her fingers and turned it.

"The scar's right here, Mom."

"I see it."

"Were you trying to ID me?"

"No, I was just—"

"You wanted proof it was me."

"Peace on Earth!" cried the old woman.

The subway screeched through the tunnel. The yellowish light of the car was nervous; Darren watched the reflection of his face in the black window, flickering in and out.

***

A stream of headlights wavered through the fog on the Pacific Coast Highway. Darren passed an old motel with a neon *VACANCY* sign and an old, familiar Taco Bell. There were new buildings, too—a two-story Jiffy Lube had a pastel paint job and a flourish of empress palms. Which pissed Darren off. Who needed two stories of a fucking Jiffy Lube?

He turned down Eighth Street and paused in front of the DiMartini house. He hadn't seen his father for a year. The light of a wide-screen TV flickered on the drapes. The hippie house next door, with pastel seahorses, waited in the fog. A country ballad played from inside.

Willie Nelson?

There is a train
That races through the night
On rails of steel
That reach the soul

The tune reminded him of a checkpoint in Baghdad, just after the invasion. He remembered the burning car, the boy Ismael's severed leg, and a pair of soccer balls covered in gore.

Fueled by fire
As soft as candlelight

He retreated across the street. The Korneckis' place, a squat brick saltbox hedged in juniper, was fortified against home invasion. Each window had a fancy grate of iron bars. Mrs. Kornecki used to spy on the sidewalk through these bars when Darren was a kid. She would stand with the lace curtains parted, collecting neighborhood gossip.

Darren used the iron grate to lever himself up to the roof. He squatted for a while and listened. When no one came out, he stepped across the gravel to a chimney, unrolled his sleeping bag, and sat. He poured the ferret water from his canteen. He'd started to carve more jerky when he heard the front door unlock and footsteps shuffle on the porch.

Mr. Kornecki's gruff voice asked, "Who's there?"

Darren lay flat and listened to the footsteps move to the edge of the lawn.

"Anybody up there?"

"Who do you see?" said Mrs. Kornecki from inside.

The old man squinted up at the sky. "It's nothing."

"Hah?"

"I say it's nothing."

"Come to *bed*."

The night was clear. The stars reminded Darren of stargazing through night vision goggles with his platoon from ranger graves dug on the highway shoulder. Awesome way to pass the time. With NVGs you could make out which stars were gas clouds or galaxies. Streaks of dust painted the darkness around the thick belt of the Milky Way; shooting stars were brilliant and sudden, and low-flying satellites looked plodding and flat. The difference was obvious—you could distinguish cosmic fires from man-made tin. All of it was tinted green.

"What's that thing in the middle of Orion's sword?" Schmidt had said. "That's not a star."

"It's a nebula," Darren said.

"What's a nebula?" said Schmidt, because Lance Corporal Schmidt was kind of dumb.

"It's a cloud of dust and gas."

Schmidt took the opportunity to fart.

"Like that, Lieutenant?"

"Fuckin' wiseguy," Gonzales had said.

Darren unzipped his pack on the Korneckis' roof. He assembled his rifle and peered up through his night vision scope at the sky. It wasn't as strong as a pair of goggles, but it brought dimension and depth to the field of stars, which stood out like shaded, greenish clumps of lichen. He found Orion and remembered Schmidt asking:

"Who was Orion, anyway? A warrior?"

"Old hunter from ancient Greece," Darren had said. "The Babylonians knew about him, too."

"No shit?"

"They gave him a different name, but they saw the same shape up there," Darren said. "Thousands of years ago. From right where we are now."

"How do you know all that, Lieutenant?" asked Gonzales.

The real answer, thought Darren, was his sister Robyn, who'd taught him about the stars and the myths and the sea. But he missed Robyn so much in the war, it hurt his blood.

"Studied history in school," he said.

"That's a funny thing to study, sir."

"It got me where I am today."

Gonzales chuckled. Schmidt moaned a little in his ranger grave.

"Thousands of years," he muttered. "I have trouble thinkin' up to next Thursday."

Darren would *kill* to bring Schmidt back. Along with whole sections of his old life that seemed to have burned away. Darren could remember bright, polished-blue skies and sparkling sunshine off the waves when he was a kid—beautiful, pure summer days. How could that feel so real? But war had reduced his ecstatic urges to cinders, or dry wings, waving on the edge of his mind.

History is a nightmare.

Darren's teeth gnashed, and he remembered the afternoon Schmidt had died in a rain of bullets from an upper floor of a house in Ramadi, one of those blocky Saddam-era homes with marble-composite stairs. It had been a hot morning, and desert sun flooded through windows on the white landing. They had to clear the house and search it for chemical weapons.

"What if we find something, Lieutenant?" said Schmidt.

"Then we send it straight to the president," answered Gonzales. "Wrapped up all pretty."

"No, Corporal, first we put on MOPP suits," Darren said.

"Shouldn't we be wearing those now?" wondered Gonzalez.

"Just relax."

They cleared rooms on the ground floor. No sign of bad guys. Not a whisper from overhead. Darren told Schmidt to check upstairs with a fire team. Schmidt was an apple-faced kid from West Texas, who shouldered his rifle and led four others up the stairs. These searches came up clean most of the time, so Darren had been on autopilot. But now the memory could lift him out of a dark and peaceful sleep, because it was the last known glimpse of Lance Corporal Schmidt testing the imperceptible boundary between life and death, which, for an officer like Darren, was also the frontier between right and wrong. If he rewound his memory to that point, when you could still see the sweat on Schmidt's face and the blush in his cheeks, you could hold him there, looking curious and unafraid, treading that awful border with his helmet off-kilter in a flood of light so mottled and thick, it made you think of gently falling snow.

Darren lay flat and aimed his rifle at the nighttime sky. The ferret lost interest in the water. It slipped from the bag and hurried to the roof's edge, where it jumped to a branch of the sycamore. The bough shook, and Darren flipped to his stomach. Through the scope he saw the ferret's green apparition curled in a crotch of the tree, and he watched in mute fascination until it jumped down to the Korneckis' lawn. Darren scanned the neighborhood for threats to the ferret, and under an olive tree in his father's yard, he spotted the shape of a cat.

"Oscar."

He snickered. The cat reared up on his haunches, holding his tail in a curl.

"Oh fuck," Darren said.

Oscar pounced. There was a horrible noise. Darren watched them struggle. The target bead from his rifle played on the animals' fur. His finger felt clammy. A voice hollered, "*Oscar!*" and Darren moved his weapon to see the spectral, barrel-bellied shape of his father on the porch.

"Oscar!" he shouted again. "Bad kitty! Get away from that!"

Ron DiMartini hurried across the street. Darren tracked him. He wore an open robe and boxers, and he didn't notice the red bead on his chest.

"Get away from that thing! Jesus," Ron said.

Why shouldn't I? Darren wondered. The old chicken hawk lurched and stamped the ground with his slipper, driving Oscar away. At last he scooped him up, and Darren watched them return to the house. *Why shouldn't I?* Aiming the rifle sharpened his mind and calmed the nervous buzz. His father padded up the walkway, and before the porch went dark, Darren saw Melissa in a wash of light from the door.

His finger was sweaty. He felt ill.

At last he stretched on his back again, covered his face with one arm, and lay still for a long time.

***

In the morning he watched thick fog creep over the rooftops, on the white gravel and clay Spanish tiles. He noticed the smell of lawns and eucalyptus, the steady drip of moisture from the Korneckis' TV aerial, and the rude odor of the sea.

The Korneckis would still have their hearing aids on the nightstand. He disassembled his rifle and rolled up the sleeping bag, slung everything over his shoulders, and clambered down the side of the house, making no noise except for a dull tone on the window bars. He went over to the ferret. The little cadaver jolted him. "Oh Jesus," he whispered. The sharp buckteeth, the strained look in its eyes, the stiff legs, and mess of blood left him with a sense of waste.

"*Murphy.* Fucking hell, man."

He couldn't miss the ferret now. He'd avoided giving it a name for some very good reasons. If he started with the ferret, he might never stop. He nudged the limp animal into the gutter with his shoe.

But the strain of this ceremony flooded his head with adrenaline, and in his first clear moment of the morning, he remembered with a shock that he'd almost shot his father, almost dispatched him to that spirit country where Schmidt and the ferret abided.

History is a nightmare.

The source of the line came back to him, too. It wasn't from one of his textbooks. It was from *Ulysses*, which he'd read as a senior. James fucking Joyce.

His dad liked to talk about history, the grand sweep of it from the Revolutionary War through the end of Communism, the march of freedom and the fight for American values around the globe. Old Ron was a real history buff. But for Darren, even college now seemed like a frothy, irrelevant period of time. He'd been a good student, but now college was a ghost of fluorescent-lit classrooms and graceful, alluring women, part of an adolescent dream he'd reveled in before the war.

History is a nightmare, the line went, *from which I am trying to awake.*

Darren snorted.

Two hippies came out of the Seahorse House, wearing boots and gloves, ready to start their trucks. One had glasses and a blonde ponytail. The other had bent shoulders and a thin goatee. They regarded him with a look of recognition, maybe related to his hair.

"Morning," they said.

"Morning," said Darren.

"You hungry?" one of them said after a minute. "We got breakfast inside."

Darren blinked. Hippies? The idea was so stupid, it almost made him smile. But maybe he could sleep in there. Maybe a hot breakfast would let him ease back in. The idea grew on him until he smirked and gave an unearnest look toward the door—a moment of acting for these newcomers, strangers who must have considered Eighth Street their home.

"Sure!" he said. "Where do I go? Right in here?"

"Right in there, man. Just knock on the door."

Darren adjusted the field pack and felt the rifle stock in his ribs. He was still in a shit-talking mood.

"Aw, thanks a lot," he said.

Michael Scott Moore is an American journalist and novelist. He is the author of *Too Much of Nothing*, a comic novel about L.A., and *Sweetness and Blood*, a travelogue about surfing. His most recent book, *The Desert and the Sea*, is a memoir about his 32 months as a hostage in Somalia.

Make Him Suffer

JoAnn Chaney

A woman needs a man like a fish needs a bicycle.

You've heard this feminist saying, right? It's an oldie but goodie, words that've been true since the day they were first spoken and continue to be so. Maybe even *more* so, nowadays. Take me, for example. I work for the police department—the *ultimate* boy's club, if you ask me—and I've made it all the way to homicide detective. But it's been a hard-fought scrabble against men. I've had to be tougher and smarter than any man around, and I've come out on top. I've learned that I don't need a man.

But I've also learned that a man can come in handy, sometimes.

***

There's a dead man on the beach.

The call comes in through dispatch at five in the morning, and we pull up twenty minutes later. A moist cloud of low-hanging fog makes the scene hazy and soft, as if one of those camera filters had been slapped on the view, rounding out the sharp edges. There are several squad cars already here, and a smallish crowd gathered together near the water. Paramedics and the responding officers. The coroner's van pulls up as I get out of the car.

"Must be slow at the office to get everyone out here so quick," Ashley comments. Brent Ashley, my partner for the last three years. Trustworthy, brave, loyal. Became a cop because he's a good guy. Check marks in all the right boxes. And he's *big*—six seven, nothing but muscle—and when I first laid eyes on him, it gave me all sorts of ideas. His size is probably why he was paired up with me. I barely clear the five-foot mark, which has always concerned the higher-ups, until I reminded them that there's no height requirement to pull a trigger.

We walk down the sand to join the gathering. Ashley took smaller steps so I could keep up with him, and held out his arm when he thought I might trip. My partner has been in love with me since we first met. I'm not being egotistical; I just know it's the truth. When a woman knows, she *knows*. I sometimes wonder what I can get Ashley to do for me, how far I can get him to go.

Down on the beach we are told a simple story. The victim was discovered by a couple out for a morning run. At first they'd thought he was a frat boy who'd pounded one too many Rolling Rocks and passed out on the sand—it'd happened plenty of times before, and it'll definitely happen again. But as the couple got closer, it was plain to see that this wasn't someone sleeping off a late-night bender.

The victim is nude and facedown, nose planted firmly in the sand. There are long tendrils of seaweed wrapped around his legs and trash caught in his hair, and the flesh on his bare back is shredded and bruised. Blunt force trauma, the coroner later confirms. The back of his skull is crushed in. No water in the lungs. Dead before he went in the water, but he's been submerged long enough that fish had nibbled away the most delicate bits. We wouldn't be able to get fingerprints off him—there wasn't much left of his extremities.

I squat beside the victim. The man's skin has gone grayish, waterlogged. On his right shoulder I notice a spot where it looked as though the skin had been scooped right out, leaving behind a sunken crater of a scar. The wind picks up and blows my hair across my face. My lips taste salty. I can hear my own heart pounding, or maybe it's the just the ocean. I hate the dead, even after so many years of this work.

"Probably got caught cheating," the coroner jokes. There's laughter from a few of the men. "Wife bashed his brains in and dumped him in the water. You know what they say. 'Hell hath no fury—'"

"If his wife did catch him at that, I hope she made him suffer first," I say grimly. "Made him regret ever breaking his vows."

There's a beat of stunned silence at my vitriol.

"That's enough," Ashley says. He looks at me, then quickly away again. "We should focus on what's in front of us."

"Oh, yes," I say sarcastically. I wouldn't have thought it possible, but the coroner looks both embarrassed and amused. Most of the officers gathered there do, and they were all cutting side-glances my way. We're a small team and gossip travels fast, and they all know I'd caught my husband cheating a few weeks before and tossed him out on his ass. "Sorry about that."

"You hear from your husband lately?" one of the uniformed officers asks me. He's trying to be funny about a situation where absolutely *nothing* is funny. "Just want to make sure that—ah, that *this* one's not your man."

"She's *pocket sized*," another says. "She doesn't have the strength to kill a full-grown man and dump his body into the ocean."

"You're all either very brave or very stupid," Ashley says. "Either way, shut your traps and get to work. Let's get this guy bagged up and hauled off. The summer crowds'll start showing up soon, and no one needs to see this."

Everyone is suddenly busy following orders, but I keep catching them looking at me from the corners of their eyes, wondering if I'm a woman scorned, if I'd made my husband suffer first.

***

I know exactly what the group of men *and* you are thinking, but let me tell you the whole truth and nothing but: I didn't murder my husband. Maybe I should've, and I've thought about it plenty, but I didn't do it.

And if you're sitting there thinking I'm lying through my teeth, consider this: Why would I bother? Especially to you. It's a lot of work to create a lie and then maintain it, and I have no interest in putting forth that much effort. Not about *that*, anyway.

But it's like those guys said: I'm little. I don't have either the size or strength needed to murder an adult male and dispose of his body.

If I ever want my husband dead, I'll need someone else to do the job for me.

***

"The water must've been rough," the coroner says. We're gathered around the metal table where the victim has been laid out and covered with a white sheet. "Body's in pretty bad shape. Can't pull a good print off him, and his teeth are all shattered, so we can't get dental records. I'm gonna run his DNA through the system but that could takes weeks to get back, and we might not even get a match. And he's been in the water long enough it's impossible for me to even guess how long he's been deceased.

At least a week, probably more."

"All right, we'll start asking around," I say. "Any chance I can take a look? See his face?"

"Sure," the coroner says. "But it's not pretty."

"She should pass," Ashley says quickly, before the coroner can pull back the sheet. "She's got a weak stomach. I've already seen him. White male, over six feet tall, well-fed and in good shape, probably in his midthirties? Someone's gotta be missing him. I'm sure we'll get word."

Once we leave the coroner's office, I sit in the car while my partner stands outside and smokes. I'm watching him while I take out my phone and call my husband. It rings in my ear, and at the same time there's a ringing from the pocket on the driver's door. I think about that. When I hang up, the phone in the door stops ringing, too.

"You okay?" I ask when Ashley finally gets in the car.

"Yeah, why?"

"You're smoking again. I thought you'd quit."

He shrugs and throws the car into reverse. I decide not to press the issue. Ashley has never been big on sharing, even at the *best* of times. He'd never been a great *talker,* but he'd always been an excellent listener. That's why he's a great detective. An active listener is a hard thing to find, and he'd listened to plenty of what I've had to say over the years.

"You hear anything from Jeremy lately?" he asks. I take off my sunglasses and use my shirt to polish a fingerprint off the lens.

"He's called a few times, but I send him straight to voicemail," I say, sighing. "He hasn't left any messages, thank god. I don't want to ever hear his voice again."

"Good," Ashley says shortly. He'd never really liked my husband. "I'm glad to hear you're done with him."

***

I didn't kill my husband. I swear it. I had nothing to do with it.

***

Long story short: I discovered my husband was cheating through social media. Cops aren't supposed to have those accounts, but we *all* do—only we put them under fake names and don't use our own photos. That's the thing about life: If rules exist, they are definitely going to be broken. Especially by the ones in charge of enforcing those rules.

I was scrolling when I couldn't sleep one night, and the app suggested a new friend for me. I didn't know this woman, didn't have any common friends, *nothing*. At first glance I couldn't figure out why she'd popped up in my feed at all, so I decided to do a bit of investigating. I'm not a detective by accident, after all. Curiosity runs through my veins.

But it's like the saying goes: curiosity killed the cat.

I've got to hand it to those developers behind social media sites—they know how to write the algorithms to connect people who might not otherwise find each other. People who maybe aren't *supposed to* find each other. For example, I'm sure no one could've guessed that this seemingly random woman would be suggested to me as a friend, and that I would look at her profile and see pictures of her in *my* home, sitting on *my* couch, eating a meal at *my* kitchen table. There was one of them kissing in our garden, and they looked like such a happy couple that I had to look at the photos for several minutes to make sure I wasn't imagining things. It felt like the breath had been knocked from me; there was an empty hole left where my heart had once been.

"You drove me to it," Jeremy said when I confronted him with the photos. He didn't even try to deny the cheating. "You're always working. You never pay attention to me. If I couldn't get it from you, I had to get it somewhere."

I didn't know what to say. I hadn't expected him to blame *me* for his infidelity. I could've killed him then. Instead, I told him he needed to pack his things and leave. Jeremy refused. This was *his* home, he said—even though he never paid any bills or cleaned—and he didn't intend on going anywhere. Half of everything was his, he reminded me with a smug little smile.

"California's a community property state," he said, "I'll get everything that's mine."

"Oh, I'm going to make sure you get everything you deserve," I said. Every single bit.

***

My husband deserved to die.

***

One morning, not long after I found out about the cheating, I came into work with a black eye. I tried to style my hair and use makeup to cover it up but couldn't quite manage it.

"What the hell happened to your face?" Ashley demanded.

I hesitated, tried to brush him off and ignore the questions, but in the end I told him everything. I told him what I knew about my husband, and the things that'd happened over the years. He already had an idea about some of it, of course. You can't work with someone in such close quarters for so many years without having some sense of their life, even if a word is never spoken.

"Isn't it funny how a person learns to accept certain things from their spouse?" I asked Ashley. We'd left the station and gone to the diner across the street, sat in our usual booth all the way in the back. I had a cup of tea I wasn't drinking. Instead, I just dunked the tea bag into the hot water and pulled it back out again. "I accepted that Jeremy will never put his dirty socks into the laundry basket, and he'll never rinse his dinner plate. And he'll always watch those stupid crime dramas on TV and try to tell me how to do my job."

"How bad has his drinking been?"

"It's been getting worse. First thing he does is crack a beer. Doesn't matter if it's five in the morning, his first stop is the fridge."

"Is he working?"

"He's waiting on a management position." I laughed, but the sound caught in my throat and almost turned into a sob. "Waiting for two years now."

Ashley was staring at me, hard.

"Has he hurt you before this?" he asked. Quietly, so no one in the other booths would hear. "Hit you? Choked you?"

I stared into my tea. Lifted the bag, dropped it again.

"I'm going to assume that's a yes," Ashley said roughly. Angrily. "I've seen the bruises on you before, but I thought it was because you're clumsy. Took a fall, had an accident. I never thought it would be *this*."

"I can explain——"

"Goddamnit, all those women we've seen over the years, beat to shit by a man—you've had to ask them these same questions and told them to leave. That it wasn't safe for them. How could you live like this?"

I was crying openly then. Not even bothering to cover my face.

"I thought I loved him," I wept. "I never thought he'd hurt me, and then he hurt me every way he possibly could. I asked him to stop, and he wouldn't. I asked him to leave, and he wouldn't. I wish he would die. Or that I would."

Everyone—and I mean *everyone*—has a relationship deal breaker. It sends you sailing over the edge, makes you do and say things you'd never thought possible. But you'll never really know what your deal breaker is until you're staring at it in the face. For me, it turns out I was willing to put up with just about anything from my husband.

Until I wasn't.

***

"You can stay at my place tonight," Ashley told me. "Or a hotel. Wherever. Just don't go home. I'll go talk to Jeremy and get him to leave. He shouldn't be there. That's your house."

I agreed. I didn't want to be anywhere near the house then. I knew both my husband and my partner well enough that I had an idea of how their discussion would go. Both men with tempers, and me in the middle. I didn't go to a hotel or Ashley's place that night. Instead, I went to the beach. I was alone once the sun set, sitting and watching the tide come in, and I squished the sand between my bare toes. The air blowing in off the sea was warmer than usual, heavy with the smells of salt and fish.

I wondered if Ashley had actually gotten Jeremy to pack up and leave. I thought about my husband and all the horrible things I'd put up with over the years from him. I'd let him do whatever he want; I'd supported and adored him. I'd thought I could love him into being a better man, but he'd betrayed me anyway. Broke my heart without a thought. I gingerly touched the raw, bruised skin around my eye and thought of everything I'd been through, everything I'd done for love.

I'd loved my husband more than I loved myself.

No longer.

My cell phone rang. It was Ashley.

"Jeremy packed a few things and left," he said. "I'm pretty sure he won't be back."

"Did anything happen?"

He paused. It was over so quickly, it might not have happened at all, but it did.

"We didn't see eye to eye on the situation, exactly," he said. "But we agreed in the end."

***

I took the day off from work and went home. Jeremy hadn't taken much when he'd left, if anything at all. His car was gone, and so was he. The house was quieter than it'd been in a long time. I walked from room to room, and when I was done, I cleaned. Gathered up all the empty beer cans and tossed them into recycling. Loaded the dishwasher and started a load of laundry and ran the vacuum. Sprayed everything down with disinfectant and got down on my hands and knees and scrubbed at a stain on the rug. It was new; I'd never seen it before.

It was blood.

I kept scrubbing until it was gone.

I slept twelve hours that night, and when I woke up, I saw I'd missed two calls. My husband. I didn't call back. I went to work. I went home. I ate meals and ironed my clothes and watched TV. I ignored Jeremy's calls. He texted a few times—things like *hey* or *call me*. I left messages with divorce lawyers. I was sometimes bored and lonely, but I tried to stay busy.

A week passed in this way.

Then that dead man washed up on the beach.

There were no reports of any men missing from the surrounding areas, no suspicious activity. No one called the station, concerned that their husband or brother hadn't come home after a night out drinking. It seemed that every man around was safe and accounted for. So the question remained: Who was this man who'd been found face down on the shore, sand stuck to his skin and seaweed wrapped around his legs?

You hear from your husband lately?

Jeremy was an only child, and both his parents were dead. I was his emergency contact, his next of kin, his sole beneficiary. I was the only person who'd bother to report him missing, but he *wasn't* missing, was he? I was still getting calls and texts from his phone, after all. So he was out there, somewhere.

I received one other interesting phone call in the weeks after I had thrown my husband out.

"I'm worried. He isn't answering any of my calls." It was the girl whom my husband had been screwing behind my back. A young, silly thing. "I need to know where he is. We're in love."

That made me laugh, because the man I'd married didn't know a thing about love. But maybe I don't, either.

"Why are you calling me?" I asked.

"He told me everything. He said you knew about me from the beginning, that you'd agreed to let us be together. I've waited three years for him—"

"Please stop calling Jeremy," I said. "He's come home, we've decided to work on our marriage. I'm afraid he was never in love with you."

I was lying, but what was the harm? This young woman and my husband had lied to me; I was just returning the favor.

"I know him better than anyone," she cried. "He wouldn't leave me."

But this girl was wrong, because it's impossible to really *know* anyone. It doesn't matter if you're married to the person or sleeping in the same bed with them or making promises of faithfulness and loyalty or working forty hours a week beside them—when it comes down to it, everyone is a stranger.

***

I didn't kill my husband. But he is dead.

***

Time passed, as it does. No one came forward to identify the man on the beach, so his body was cremated. No one claimed the ashes, so I took them. I tucked the unmarked cardboard box under my arm and walked out to my car, but I wasn't more than halfway across the parking lot when Ashley pulled up beside me.

"What're you doing here?" he asked. As if he didn't know. He didn't look well. Peaked and wan.

"I don't know him, but I didn't want to leave him here," I said. I touched my face as I spoke. My black eye had nearly healed, although the skin was still tender. It'd hurt, badly. Many people would shy away from hitting their own face on a table corner, but I'd done it. And I'd do it again. Sometimes you have to go big to get the job done. Really commit.

"That's kind of you," Ashley said distractedly. Over the last few weeks he'd become distant, strange. But this is what happens when a good, honest man goes against his conscience and does wrong. "I wanted to tell you that I put in for a transfer. I'm heading north, up to Stockton."

"I already heard," I said. I tried to touch his arm, but he pulled away before I could. He was looking away from me, in the direction of the beach. I knew he was thinking of the dead man. My husband. They were one and the same, you see. My husband had been killed and dumped in the ocean. And now he's ashes in a box.

I didn't kill him, though. I had no part in that. I had just wanted him to leave. I never asked anyone to do anything. I'd swear that on a stack of Bibles.

"You know, Jeremy said he'd never hit you," Ashley said.

"I never said he did."

He made a harsh sound in the back of his throat. He *had* seen bruises on me over the years. I'd hit myself plenty, pinched my skin and twisted it. I'd wanted my partner to see those things. I'd made sure he did.

"Are you sure you don't know that man?" Ashley asked. He was speaking of the ashes, but more, as well. A conversation can be like walking through a field scattered with hidden bombs—one wrong step and you're blown to pieces.

"I don't know him," I said. Then paused. "I never really did."

My partner opened his mouth, seeming to struggle over what to say next, but didn't say a word.

"Thank you for everything you've done for me," I said. Ashley knew the meaning behind my words. I'd never asked him for anything, but he'd done it anyway. He'd seen the bruises, he'd seen my tears—and his love for me had turned him into a killer.

But the act had changed him. He could barely stand to look at me now. Murder has a way of changing a man, even changing his heart.

My partner drove away, and I went to the beach with the box of ashes, very near where the man had washed up. I sat on a bench alone. But I wasn't *really* alone, because I had that box beside me.

"I told you you'd get everything you deserve," I whispered. "Took a few years, but it finally happened."

I opened the box, considered the ocean in front of me. My husband had loved the ocean. He would've loved to have been spread across the breaking waves.

I tipped the ashes into the trash can beside the bench, box and all.

I've known about my husband for years, you see. His lying and his cheating, his unfaithfulness. I've said that I don't know who my husband was, that he was a stranger to me—but that's only partially true. I knew him well enough to know that my dear, sweet husband wasn't going to just pack up and leave easily. If I'd filed for divorce, it would've been bad. He would've bled me dry, left me with nothing. And the law was on his side—he'd walk away with everything I'd worked so hard for. Not only did he break my heart, but he'd break everything else in my life as well.

I couldn't let that happen. I wouldn't.

But I couldn't force my husband out. I'm too small. Like my co-workers said, I'm pocket-sized.

The day after I had realized what sort of man I'd married, Ashley became my partner. And I realized what had to be done, how I could do it. I feel a little bad for what had happened—not for Jeremy, but for Ashley. I made him suffer—made him love me, made him want to protect me—and he is suffering now. But I am free, and that's all that matters.

I learned that a man can come in handy, sometimes.

JoAnn Chaney is a graduate of UC Riverside's Palm Desert MFA program. She lives in Colorado with her family. Her debut novel, *What You Don't Know*, was longlisted for the Crime Writers' Association's New Blood Dagger Award and was one of Book Riot's Best Mysteries of the Year. *As Long as We Both Shall Live* is her second novel.

Down in Monterey

Gar Anthony Haywood

I took a photograph. That's all I did.

A beautiful woman lying on a beach, naked and asleep. Crimson haired, full-bodied, face turned toward the overcast sky. Her clothes and mine are strewn about the sand surrounding her, a signal of our desperation to conjoin. Her mouth is set in the wisp of a smile, something I like to think our lovemaking left her with before she slipped into unconsciousness. Monterey, California, two weeks ago.

The woman is dead now. Her killer used a knife. Not to slash or cut, but to puncture her heart with a single strike, the blade buried deep in her chest. The police thought I put it there, but they no longer do. They found someone else to blame and let me go.

I suppose I should feel relieved, but I don't.

Some days, I feel guilty as hell instead.

***

A man meets a woman like Farah Lang once, maybe twice in his lifetime, and only if he's either ridiculously lucky or cursed by the devil himself. I guess I was a little of both.

Four years before I took her photo on the beach, I met Farah at an outdoor jazz concert at the Los Angeles County Museum of Art. She was sitting on a blanket on the grass with a female friend, somewhere between my beach chair and the quartet playing "But Not for Me," where I had no chance of missing her. She was wearing a yellow sundress, the kind of dress that draws a man's eyes not to itself but all the tan, freckled skin it leaves exposed. Legs, arms, breasts. Her red hair was tied back with a single white band, and her feet were bare, sandals kicked to one side. I hadn't come to the concert looking for her kind of trouble, but once it was there, I knew I couldn't leave without it. When she got up to go to the bar, I jumped up to do the same.

I won't bore you with our opening banter. Whatever I chose as a first line would have only been memorable for its effectiveness, because it led to introductions and culminated, a few hours later, in the exchange of phone numbers. This was nothing new to me; I'd done this sort of thing before and was fairly good at it. I have my charms. But I left the museum grounds that night knowing I'd done something special, turned a corner that would take me somewhere I'd had no plans to go.

I was right. The journey Farah took me on over the next year and a half was as unexpected as it was breathtaking. After all the first dates and exploratory small talk were over—I was a software security consultant and she was a YA book illustrator, neither of us married or otherwise engaged—we fell in love like two people hurtling down a mine shaft. Sex fueled our descent, oh yes, a white-hot flare that blinded us to everything else when ignited, but there was more to our hunger for each other than that. Or so I told myself. Because the idea that I might be in this thing alone—that what Farah felt for me did not run nearly as deep as what I felt for her—was terrifying. No one could be that cruel.

She moved into my Venice townhouse three weeks after we met. We were together for sixteen months and change. We had more good times than bad, but the bad only got worse as time went on, the same wounds being torn open wider and wider. I had never thought of myself as a jealous man before Farah; I'd never been with anyone whose flirtations could really bother me that much. But Farah taught me what if feels like to need a woman to be faithful who can't be. She loved the attention of men and received it in droves. Asking her to shut down every suitor she met when they came at her so frequently was too much. Eventually, I came to understand that I was just Farah's latest failed experiment in monogamy.

When I finally broke things off, it was like performing a self-amputation with a rusty blade. The cut was clean but the wound was dirty. It hurt to open my eyes in the morning, and it hurt to close them again at night. Farah's absence from my life left me with ghost sensations that lingered for months. As for Farah herself, our parting seemed more an insult than an injury. She gave me up with little fight, sad and angry but far short of devastated. Her relative calm was one last blow to my pride to add to all the others.

In the months immediately following our breakup, I saw her only once more, about a year later, at a child's birthday party in Eagle Rock. The child's father was a former client of mine, whose brother-in-law turned out to be Farah's date for the afternoon. I had come solo, which either made our meeting more awkward or less—I've never been able to decide one way or the other.

"How have you been?" she asked me after we'd managed to muddle through introductions.

"Good. And you?"

It was a pointless question. If she'd looked any better, she would have been escorted out by the party's hostess as a threat to every wife in attendance.

"I'm doing well, thanks."

And that was it. Our exchange was short and civilized; tense but entirely devoid of animosity. The only indication of friction, if I wasn't imagining it, came from the man on Farah's arm. Jeff Greene. He was a big man with a wide grin who seemed friendly enough, but I thought I'd seen something shift on his face, only for a second, when he discovered what kind of old acquaintance to Farah I was. I'd never seen that same look on my own face back when she and I had been together, of course, but I had to wonder if I hadn't worn it more than once.

Especially near the end.

***

Cut to three weeks ago, three years and a couple months after that little girl's birthday party in Eagle Rock. A crowded bar on the Central Coast where I was working a contract job for a software start-up. She slipped alongside me to take the stool on my right and said, "Kev."

Nobody had ever called me "Kev" but Farah. It was a privilege I allowed her grudgingly. When I turned, she was smiling like she had never been happier to see anyone in her life. She'd cut her hair and gained a few pounds, but neither had blunted her God-given beauty in the least. She was dressed for a date, but she appeared to be alone.

"Farah. Where'd you come from?" I asked, magically conjuring cool from sudden shock.

"That table over there." She pointed at an empty table for two in the back. "Why don't you join me?"

I considered politely declining. It wouldn't have been that hard. But following her over with drink in hand was the path of least resistance, and before I knew it, I was there, sitting across from her. Just like old times.

We brought each other up to speed. What we'd been doing, with whom and without, and what had brought us here, now, to Monterey. I told her about my contract job, and she told me about the local writer she was working with on a new book. I was supposed to recognize the author's name, because her last Young Adult trilogy had been an international sensation, but I just shook my head.

"Sorry."

She laughed. My cluelessness about some things had always amused her, and her laugh had always touched my heart. Apparently, it still did.

To hear her tell it, she wasn't seeing anyone now and hadn't been for a long time. She'd finally seen the light I had once been waiting to come on for her, regarding the folly of collecting romantic partners like coins in a jar, and she was taking a break from the exercise. She wasn't ready to get married and start having kids, nothing as traditional and boring as all that, but she was done spending time with a man simply because the next one hadn't yet come along. "That life wasn't sustainable," she said, just as I'd always warned her it couldn't be.

She made it all sound quite believable. I found myself wondering why it shouldn't be true, and what she could possibly have to gain by saying it if it was nothing but a lie. Because we both knew I would wind up in her bed that night regardless. She didn't have to feed me any fairy tales of newfound maturity and restraint to put me back on the hook.

The only question was, how long would I stay on it this time?

***

A fly won't re-ensnare itself in the same spider web twice, but the same cannot be said about a man. Lured by the proper bait, a man will walk into the fire again and again. The moment I moved my drink from the bar to Farah's table that night, my choice was made to revisit all the old familiar pain she'd left me with. Nobody forced me; I went willingly.

For the next three weeks, the two of us were inseparable. We fell into our old rhythm as if we'd never fallen out of it. We made love indoors and outdoors, in safe places and places fraught with the risk of discovery: parking structures, the aquarium, on the beach that day I took her photograph. And all the while, we talked like this time would be different, that this time we could make it work because she was better prepared to appreciate what one man, *this* man, had to offer her, and I was less inclined to demand more from her than was possible. Nothing happened to make either of us doubt it was true. But secretly, I was dubious. Experience had taught me to withhold my trust until the very last minute, no matter how convincing the evidence was that my trust was warranted.

And the evidence was considerable that Farah was no longer the woman I had known in Los Angeles. More than once during our rekindled romance, I saw her deflect admirers she would have at least parried with playfully in the past. Her draw on strangers was as powerful as ever, but she seemed to no longer revel in it. She had learned how to smile politely and send a man on his way as quickly and cleanly as an angler demonstrating catch and release. If it wasn't all an act—an extended show of modified behavior put on day after day, night after night, strictly for my benefit—I had every reason to be thankful. Because it meant that I could love Farah without fear and go on loving her. I never again had to look for warning signs of things that weren't there.

I wanted to believe her. I needed to believe her.

But I needed to be sure more than anything else.

***

Farah's place in Monterey was a friend's studio apartment on Glenwood Circle. I came by one afternoon, while she was out at a meeting with the author she was working with, to retrieve a jacket I'd forgotten there the night before. I had my own key and was getting out of the car to let myself in when I saw someone storming away from her door.

He had his head down as he hurried over to his own parked car and sped off, oblivious to my presence, but I'd caught enough of his face to recognize both it and the expression painted on it. The last time I'd seen Jeff Greene, accompanying his date to the birthday party of a six-year-old girl, he'd worn that same look of irritation only briefly, but I had the sense now it was more the rule for him than the exception.

I left right after he did, forgetting my jacket entirely.

***

"You saw Jeff? Where?"

"At your place. How did he know you were here?"

"I have no idea. Are you sure it was him?"

I told her I was sure. She told me she had broken things off with Greene not long after I had met him at the party, and she had only spoken to him twice since. Over the phone, she sounded surprised to hear he was here in Monterey, but she didn't seem particularly shaken up about it.

"I know what you're thinking," she said, "but it's not true. I haven't seen Jeff in years. I don't know how he found out I was here, unless..."

"Yes?"

"Unless he paid someone to find me. I wouldn't put it past him. Jeff is a little crazy."

"Crazy like I was, you mean?"

She understood my inference and fell silent for a moment. "You don't believe me, do you?"

"No. I don't think I do, Farah."

And just saying the words nearly buckled my knees. It was all bullshit. The new Farah Lang was nothing but the old one with a better story to tell and a greater skill for selling it. She might indeed have reached the place where she no longer needed regular conquests to feel complete, but she still required the attention of more than one man at a time. Greene hadn't come to Monterey as a ghost from her past; he'd come as a lover who thought himself a part of her present.

"Kev," Farah said.

"My name is Kevin. And you can go fuck yourself."

***

There is a form of emotional suffering that words cannot do justice. No adjective can accurately describe it, no metaphor or simile can come close enough to touch it. Loving someone who cannot love you back, in kind, is a pain like no other. Wider, deeper, colder, darker. It moves you through other sensations like a churning sea; anger gives way to regret, regret turns into shame, shame morphs into hatred. Hatred of self, hatred of the one who has damaged you. To endure this injury once and survive is a miracle; to know it twice is a nightmare.

I was in this place for two full days after I ended my phone call to Farah. Where I went and what I did in that space of time is a combination of vague recollections and voids I've never cared to fill with memory. I was lost for those two days, untethered from the world by an opaque cloud of drink and depression, and I had no reason to wish I would ever find myself again.

And then things got even worse for me.

"Kevin Tennyson?"

I'd found him and his friend standing at the door of my hotel room after his incessant knocking had roused me from my bed, a little after 11:00 a.m., Wednesday morning. If they weren't cops, they were dressed too poorly for their actual profession.

"Yes?"

The one who'd done the knocking badged me. "I'm Detective William Burst with Monterey PD and this is Detective Mike Shue. Mind if we come in?"

"What's this about?"

"We'd prefer to explain that inside, if that's okay."

I wasn't sure if it was okay or not, but I let them in. I took a seat on the bed and ran a hand through my hair, knowing I had to look like shit because I felt like nothing less.

"Well?"

"Mr. Tennyson, do you know a woman by the name of Farah Lang?"

I flinched. "Yes. We're good friends. Why? What's happened?"

"What's happened is, she was murdered two nights ago," Burst's partner, Shue, said, displaying an amazing alacrity for subtlety. "And we were hoping you could tell us what you might know about it."

"Me?"

I don't know how I got the question out. I couldn't breathe. My heart was somewhere near the pit of my stomach, and a sense of nausea was beginning to overwhelm me.

"Well, as you say, the two of you were good friends," Burst said. "In fact, from what we've been able to gather, you and Ms. Lang were actually somewhat closer than that."

I was working hard to keep the scene in focus. Panic hadn't yet set in, but it was coming.

"Oh my God. Farah."

"Is it fair to say you and Ms. Lang were romantically involved, Mr. Tennyson?"

"Yes. I suppose so. And if we were?"

"We'd like to know the last time you saw her. If you can recall."

"It would have been Sunday night. Late. Look—"

"You didn't see her at all Monday?" Shue asked, taking his turn.

"No. We spoke on the phone a couple times, but that was it. You don't think *I* killed her?"

"Well, you could do a lot to remove the thought from our minds if you can tell us where you were Monday night between the hours of eleven p.m. and two a.m.," Burst said.

I knew exactly where I was. "I was here. And before you ask, I was alone, so no-nobody can vouch for that."

Their interrogation continued for several more minutes. I answered their questions the best I knew how, shifting from one state of distress to another. I was shaving not so much as a sliver off their conviction that I was their man until I blurted out a name: "Jeff Greene."

"Jeff Greene?" Burst asked. "And who is that?"

"An ex-boyfriend of Farah's. I saw him Monday at her place. Jesus, it had to be him."

I told them all about Greene. The look I'd seen on his face at the party in Eagle Rock four years earlier and the one I saw on it Monday afternoon as he fled Farah's apartment like a bison in heat. I told them about my last phone call with Farah and how she'd suggested Greene might be stalking her and why: "Jeff is a little crazy," she'd said.

"Any idea where this Jeff Greene might be now?" Shue asked, sounding only slightly less skeptical of my innocence.

"No. I only saw him here that one time."

"And you say he lives in Los Angeles?"

"Yes. I mean, I imagine he still does. At least, that's where he was living when I first met him. He may have relocated since then."

Both cops gave me a long look. Like I'd somehow slipped up and said something incriminating. I waited them out.

"I think maybe we should continue this conversation down at the station," Burst finally said. "Any objections to that?"

I thought about declining or asking if I could have a lawyer hold my hand. But I was afraid to appear uncooperative or like someone who had something to hide. Farah was dead, and I was supposed to want to see her killer found as badly as these detectives did.

I let them take me down to the station.

In the seven hours that followed, I only managed to further establish myself as the person most likely to have murdered Farah Lang.

I had motive. I'd seen an old boyfriend leaving my lover's place and called her in a jealous rage. I had no alibi for her time of death and hence had opportunity to commit the crime. As time wore on and the questions Burst and Shue posed to me became increasingly repetitive, I behaved more and more like a guilty man. Fear had me in its grip, and I could feel it filling the room along with the scent of my sweat. Someone had beaten Farah to death in her friend's apartment on Glenwood Circle, an apartment to which I had a key, and no one fit the role of prime suspect better than I did.

Except for Jeff Greene.

It took them a while, but eventually Burst and Shue found it more likely that Greene had murdered Farah than I. For all their reasons to believe that I had killed her instead, evidence wasn't one of them. They'd found no bloody clothes in my hotel room, nor a knife bearing my fingerprints. No witnesses or security camera video could place me at or near Farah's apartment at any time Monday night. Computer logs at my hotel seemed to indicate I'd been online when Farah's death occurred.

But Jeff Greene had indeed flown into Monterey from Los Angeles early Monday morning, just as I'd suggested, and flown right back the next day. Traces of blood had been found both in his rental car and in the bathroom of his motel room, and a bloodstained shirt turned up in the dumpster behind that very same motel. A neighbor of Farah's friend to whom the apartment on Glenwood Circle was leased remembered seeing Greene park his car at the curb out in front of the building Monday night, somewhere around 1:00 a.m.

He never did confess, but he didn't have to. DNA ultimately identified the shirt in the dumpster as his, and the blood discovered in the car and the bathroom as Farah's. She'd told me he was crazy, and she'd been right. I wondered if she'd known exactly how crazy he was.

I certainly hadn't.

***

Cops don't apologize profusely. No matter how egregious their error, they offer you the bare minimum of remorse and send you on your way. In that sense, I suppose what I finally got from Detectives Burst and Shue of the Monterey PD was more than fair. Or the best they could do, in any case.

In their eyes, I'm an innocent man. I'm not the one who stabbed Farah Lang to death; Jeff Greene is. He was brought back to Monterey, tried and convicted of murder in the second degree. The jury in his case deliberated for all of three hours, and the judge sentenced him a week later to life with a possibility of parole. I was in the clear.

But I find no joy in being in the clear. Farah is gone, and there is no getting her back. I never had a drop of her blood on my hands, but I can feel it there all the same, and I probably will for the rest of my life.

If only I could have found the faith somewhere to believe that she had really changed. That everything my eyes and ears were telling me about her commitment to being with me and only with me this time around could be taken at face value. But I couldn't. I had suffered too much the first time. I had to know all her latest promises were real and that I wasn't setting myself up to get destroyed all over again.

I had to be sure.

So one night at her apartment, the night before she was killed, in fact, I got hold of her cell phone and pulled a number from it. Jeff Greene's number. I'd snatched the phone up right after she'd taken a call and then moved to the kitchen without it. All I had time to do before she returned to the couch was look for a familiar name in her list of contacts and, finding one, put the phone back where she'd left it. I repeated Greene's number in my head until it was practically emblazoned there.

Hours later, back in my hotel room, I used my own phone to send

Greene a text that was just an attachment, no message included.

I didn't know how he would respond. All I was looking for was a reaction, and all I was hoping for—*praying* for, really—was no reaction at all. If he and Farah were ancient history as she had promised, a photo of her naked on the beach would have little effect on him. He might reply with a *WTF?* and nothing more. He certainly wouldn't show up unannounced in Monterey, because he'd have no reason to know that's where she was. But if my greatest fears were justified—if the connection between him and Farah was still in force, despite the distance currently between them—he would likely react much differently. He would blow up my phone with questions and threats and treat Farah's phone in kind. Farah would call me to demand an explanation, and I'd extract a confession from her after I'd issued one my own.

But that's not what happened. Greene didn't bother with any angry texts or phone calls. He just got on a plane and came to see Farah in Monterey, where he knew she was because they were in fact still seeing each other. Where jealousy merely crippled me, it energized Jeff Greene. And the fire I'd set under him this time turned out to be larger and more demanding than all the rest.

She'd said he was crazy, and crazy was what he looked like that Monday afternoon when I saw him leaving Farah's friend's apartment. But crazy enough to commit murder? No. I was the one who felt that crazy then. Or so I thought.

Now Greene must live with his guilt, and I must live with my relative innocence. I didn't kill Farah Lang. Jeff Greene did. I took a photograph.

That's all I did.

Gar Anthony Haywood is an American author of crime fiction. He was born in Los Angeles in 1954 and worked as a computer technician for over a decade before he started publishing novels. *Fear of the Dark* won the Shamus Award for best first private investigator novel.

November Snow

Ewan A. Dougall

The San Adiutor ferry is as cheery as the graveyard shift on the Styx.

Condemned souls bury their noses in newspapers, ignoring the mist-shrouded island and postcard beaches stretching to the pewter sea. Nothing frightens tourists more than bedbugs and murders. Lucky, then, that the island's police chief, Chuck Edwards, waited until the off-season to get himself iced.

That was November 8, four days ago.

Yesterday, the island's mayor requested help from the city PD. I knew Chuck from years back and haven't taken any vacation time this century. Makes sense that the department sent me.

The wizened Charon bounces us through a reef of jetties to an empty berth beside a shark's tooth of a yacht. *Faithfulness* sparkles in gold against the white hull. A squat geek watches us disembark, his shirt loud enough to cause tinnitus. The reek from the working end of the harbor—where gulls cavort and screech over scraps flung from fishing boats—chases me inland. I light a cigarette to freshen the air.

A prowler sits in a gravel lot beside the marina. In front, a wad of cookie dough stuffed into a deputy's uniform holds a placard with my name.

"I'm Matthew Rivers." I offer him a hand.

The opening of a town car door steals his reply. A rangy, snowcapped man in a pale suit unfolds himself from the driver's seat. "Are you the city detective?" He doesn't wait for an answer. "I'm Henry Bleeker, mayor of San Adiutor. This is Deputy Collins."

"Call me Walter," the other says, setting his lip caterpillar quivering.

I take a long drag. "So what happened to Edwards?"

Bleeker's eyes are flint. "I'm hoping you can tell us, Detective. We don't have much experience with…this. Do we, Walter?"

"Homicides ain't exactly our thing here." The deputy strokes his mustache like he would a cat. "Got the details in the car. You want to look over them on the way to the hotel?"

The mayor points at a wooden fortress a few blocks away. "There's a room for you in the Franklin. For as long as you need." His gaze strays to the harbor behind me, a fleeting storm creasing his brow.

Footsteps crunch. The geek in the Hawaiian shirt advances on us in a cloud of cloying aftershave. Dark hair, slicker than oil, sweeps back from a sniper's dream of a forehead.

"Henry. Walter," he rasps before sizing me up. "You the mainland bull?"

Bleeker finds his politician's smile. "Detective Matthew Rivers, William MacArthur. He owns the marina."

"And a hell of a lot more besides," MacArthur says as we shake. "How long you staying, Rivers?"

"Only until the boredom sets in."

Laughter like a drowning man's last breath. "That shouldn't take long. There's not much to do in the off-season." His face grows serious. "Henry, we need to talk. Privately."

I'm not here for local politics. I finish my smoke, grind the butt into the gravel, and toss my suitcase in the back of the prowler. "We should get started anyway," I say to Collins.

The mayor offers me another handshake. MacArthur sighs and follows suit. "Enjoy your stay, Rivers."

A manila envelope waits on the passenger's seat. I open it as Collins heads into town. Edwards's murder falls into my lap like an obscene jigsaw. The black-and-whites show a bloody and twisted ruin on hard-packed sand at the bottom of a cliff. A wide shot reveals a steep path above the corpse.

"Fairfield Point," Collins says. "Nothing out there except the lighthouse."

"Forget the hotel. Take me there."

As we follow the curve of the bay, I find a photograph of a dilapidated tower. The fall might have been fatal by itself, but Edwards had been pumped with enough lead to sink a liner. More photographs detail the injuries. Bullet holes hold less interest for me than the powder coating Edwards's hands. Not sand. Could be chalk, but no police ever got scrubbed over school supplies. He was discovered some time after dawn by a local fisherman, Philip Jamieson.

"Any other witnesses?"

A shake of the head.

"I'll want to talk to him." I fall silent for a moment, mesmerized by the shuttered shops and darkened windows. "And Edwards's family." A vague memory of meeting his wife years ago bubbles up.

Houses fall away as the land rises. Secluded beaches and sheer cliffs whip past in the early afternoon. Bright surfboards slice through water the color of cold ash.

My driver's eyes flick to the seascape. "The kid on the blue board is Chase, Chuck's son. He and his friends are on a different beach every day." His face twists into a sneer. "His old man's been murdered, and he's out there riding waves like nothing's changed."

Grief is a snowflake, individual and unique. I don't think Walter Collins would understand that, so I ask instead, "How long do they stay out there?"

"Until the light's gone. It's stupid and dangerous, but Chuck used to stop by, watch over them." He glances in the rearview as if expecting to see his dead chief. "He was a good man."

We lapse in funereal silence. I spark another cigarette for something to do. It's a memory by the time Collins turns us down a rough track, past a hand-painted sign declaring:

KEEP OUT

by order of

SAN ADIUTOR PD

Ahead, the crumbling lighthouse points at the slate sky. Graffiti coats the exposed brickwork. Windows spiral up toward the domed glasshouse, their panes opaque with layers of sand and dirt.

Sea air slaps me the instant I step out the car. Old tire ruts mark the loose ground in front of the boarded lighthouse entrance.

"Anyone been up here recently?" I ask as I tug at the wooden panel.

From the car, Collins calls, "Not since Chuck's death. The sign would've kept them away."

Childlike innocence is only endearing in children.

The board lifts from the doorway without much coercion. Ignoring the deputy's startled squawk, I slip inside. Furniture litters the vaulted room, half hidden in the dappled light from a high window. More artistic endeavors cover the walls like modern cave paintings. My pen torch follows a jumble of footprints in the accumulated dust. No impression on the stone staircase hugging the wall.

I begin a thorough search, working from the center of the room out. At some point, Collins's muffled cursing falls silent.

A sideboard blocks the cupboard under the stairs. My flashlight plays over dried blood on the wall. Not fresh, but fresh is relative in a place like this: the stain is days old, not millennia.

Minutes later, I'm hunched in a cramped storage space that's devoid of anything save my own labored breathing. So much for the idea. I start to leave, but a loose floorboard gives me pause. The crawl space beneath is a flour explosion in a blizzard. The packaged bricks are long gone, but the tingling behind my eyes tells me all I need to know.

Outside, I light a cigarette to clear my lungs. "You've got a snow problem."

"Snow?" The pudgy uniform makes a show of looking skyward.

"Cocaine. Coke. Blow." I emphasize the last by aiming a jet of smoke at him. "My bet is Edwards found out and got plugged for his troubles."

I leave him with that thought and head to the bluff. A narrow path slithers beachward. In my mind, a bloodied and terrified Edwards stumbles, loses his footing, and pitches to the rocks below. Vertigo threatens to throw me after him. Swallowing my heart, I complete the descent on hands and knees.

Boulders stick from the sand like uneven tombstones. Did Edwards die on impact, or did he fade into nothingness to the sound of lapping waves? I scour the beach, searching the flat expanse for what I can't say: a message in Edwards's blood maybe, or a signed confession.

All the beach offers is a picturesque view sullied by memory of violence.

Heavy breathing signals Collins's arrival. Lumbering onto the beach like an asthmatic walrus, he ignores the rocks as he passes. Painful, I imagine. Instead, he follows me to the kelp line and stares at the darkening horizon until his face loses some of the redness.

"I used to like coming here as a kid."

I pass him a cigarette. "Seems a nice spot. Peaceful." *And a lonely place to die.*

"Good fishing, too." He uses the lit end to point at a bedrock promontory about half a mile away.

"Let's go talk to our witness." I turn my back on the sea and start the climb back to the car.

***

From Fairfield Point, the coast road scribbles its way west. The sinking sun turns the sky to a charcoal smudge as Collins swings onto a dirt trail. We bump along, skeletal scrub bleached of color in the headlights. The winding path ends at a darkened shack on the shore.

Collins parks beside the wrecks of a battered truck and a fishing boat. The sound of our slamming doors goes for a jaunt around the bay. We mount creaking steps. Collins rattles the door with a meaty fist. "Phil? Phil Jamieson, you in there?"

Except for the sea, the silence is absolute. The deputy glances over his shoulder at me, taking my shrug as permission to try again.

Misgivings tug at my thoughts. I walk a lap, feet sinking into the wet sand, and shine my flashlight through a cracked window. Driftwood furniture and fishing nets instead of wallpaper. An overturned end table draws my attention to a threadbare chair and the figure in it. The torch beam puts a sparkle back in sightless eyes above a bloody hole in the chest. Fishing waders offer little protection against a shotgun.

Covering my mouth with a handkerchief, I head back to Collins. "Open it," I croak.

The stench of days-old tobacco smoke and blood wafts around us into the gathering gloom. Kitchen, living space, and sleeping quarters sit in each other's laps with no distinction between. A potbellied stove stands in the corner, its furnace colder than the room's occupant.

I point my flashlight into the bloodless face. "Jamieson?"

Collins nods, eyes wide.

"I guess he saw more than you thought. Better call the coroner."

As we wait for the whitecoat, I poke my nose around the hut some more but find nothing. Collins stays in the car. I can't blame him: Jamieson's plenty ripe. A gambler would put money on his murder happening within hours of him discovering Edwards. Even in November, four days is time enough to fester.

Screeching brakes pull me outside. Collins, sitting in his car, doesn't look up at the bearded raisin stepping out a meat wagon. He glances at the deputy with professional disinterest. I keep my mouth shut: not having the stomach for the scene inside isn't something he should be ashamed of. I bring the coroner up to speed and step aside to let him into the shack.

"I still need to talk to Edwards's widow," I say, leaning into the prowler and blinking against the interior light's wan glow.

My voice snaps Collins back to reality. "I…I can't. Maryann shouldn't see me like this. Not so soon after Chuck." His sunken eyes are those of a whipped dog.

"Tell me where she lives, and I'll go myself. I'll leave your wheels at the hotel." I jerk a thumb at the whitecoat's heap. "You can hitch a ride back to town when he's through."

A thousand emotions flit across his mug before settling on something like gratitude. He works himself loose from behind the steering wheel, gesturing for me to take his place. I settle in, listening to his directions.

"See you in the morning, Walter."

As I start back to the coast road, I glance in the rearview. The prowler's brake lights coat Collins in shifting red, like a curtain of blood. Then the scene is lost behind a bend, and I focus on what lies ahead.

***

The Edwards house crests a hill above the lights of San Adiutor. A low wall surrounds the two-story structure, the driveway flanked by stone lanterns. I park between a Chrysler and a pickup. The bright-blue surfboard lies hostage in the bed, still dripping salt water.

A slender woman in jeans and checked shirt stands on the porch in a wedge of light. Her piercing gaze flits from my face to the badge in my hand and back. I met Maryann Edwards five or six years ago, and while the silver veins threading her dark hair and the redness of her eyes are new, the determined set of her jaw is unchanged.

"You're the detective Bleeker promised me."

Not a question. "That's right, ma'am. I'm Matthew—"

"Rivers. I remember." She gestures for me to follow her inside.

We walk past a shadowed lounge, down a hallway lined with framed photographs of the laughing family. Music, modern and jarring, drifts from upstairs. She leads me into the kitchen at the rear of the house and leans against the worktop. Dried floodplains discolor her cheeks.

"Coffee?"

I shake my head, tap a cigarette into my palm, and slide her the pack. After a round of condolences, I start in with the questions. "Do you know why Chuck was at Fairfield Point?"

Maryann lets the cigarette smolder inches from her mouth as she disappears into her memories. "From the start of the last tourist season, he patrolled the island at night. Sometimes he stayed out until dawn. I don't know where he went or why."

Putting distance between his family and danger. "Did Collins know?"

"Walter? You've met him: Would you trust him with something you kept hidden from your own wife?" Lemons aren't as bitter as her words.

Again, I shake my head.

Sneakers squeak in the hall. A young man haunts the doorway. "I heard voices. I thought it was Walter." His nose is flatter than Edwards's, and he's got his mother's coloration, but there's no mistaking the resemblance to the dead man.

I offer a hand. "Chase, isn't it?" Then, realizing what he said, I ask, "Does Collins stop by often?"

The corners of his mouth curl downward. "Every night since…I think he misses Dad as much as we do. Are you here to catch the bastard who killed him?"

"Chase!" Maryann yelps like she's been burned. "Language!"

I try not to smile. "That's the idea, kid." Then, meeting Maryann's eye, I ask, "Did Chuck leave any notes?"

Maryann and Chase share a significant glance. "Walter couldn't make sense of them," she says.

My sense of surprise rolls over in its sleep. "Have you still got them?"

"Chase, could you—"

The youth disappears before she finishes speaking. He returns a few minutes later with a small notebook, which he passes to his mother. She opens it, leafs through it, and hands it to me. "This was in Chuck's car. He hadn't hidden it, but it wasn't exactly in plain sight either."

In the back, a map of the island has the beaches farthest from town marked. Scrawled beside them and the marina are four-digit numbers. Sitting at the kitchen table, I take a notepad and pen from my inside pocket. Within a few minutes, I've copied the numbers:

Beaches	Marina
6041	*7041*
4050	*5050*
2052	*3052*
3061	*4061*
0063	*1070*
7072	*8072*
0081	*1081*
9082	*0083*
7091	*8091*
3100	*4100*
0102	*1102*
7110	*8110*

Maryann leans over my shoulder, smoke curling from the cigarette. "That's as far as Walter got. He's worried that we can't solve it without Chuck."

I pull a face. Edwards wouldn't have hidden it if his code was unbreakable. I suspect Collins lacks the imagination required.

The kitchen clock ticks useless minutes away. Maybe the deputy isn't the only idiot.

A deep drag provides no further inspiration, so I shove my chair back to stare at the map.

"What comes in four-digit sequences?"

Mother and son sigh in unison. Maryann sits opposite me. "They're not coordinates, because the values would repeat. And they can't be dates or times."

A shadow of an idea forms. I glance at Chase. "Were you out the night your old man was killed?"

A nod.

"Where?"

Brow knitted, he points. Two numbers, 2052 and 7091. I turn them over in my mind, but there's no pattern I can see. "What about the night before?"

Again, two numbers: 7072 and 7110. The second sequence turns my blood to ice. "They *are* dates," I whisper, turning the notebook to show them. They lean closer. "Chuck died on November eighth, which means Chase and his friends were at this beach on November seventh." As I speak, I write the date: *11-07*.

The widow's mouth forms a cavernous O. "Chuck moved the last digit to the start."

"Simple." Smoke carries the word into the air above me.

Tension bleeds from her in a ragged sigh. "Why didn't we see that earlier?"

Because loss latches onto people, drags them into darkness like some vast squid, and squeezes the life from them until it's all they can do to survive. Everything falls away in those deep waters, including how to see what's right in front of us. I don't blame them for failing to spot Edwards's pattern.

With the code cracked, solving the rest is the work of seconds. Each marina date corresponds to the day after the beaches'. Did Edwards see something? The same boat, perhaps? A question for the harbor master in the morning.

That thought draws my attention back to the clock. Nearly three hours to solve a dead man's puzzle. Time I left his family in peace. I say my good-byes, dust off the condolences again, and head back to Collins's heap.

The Franklin Hotel dominates the corner of Main and Beach, four blocks from the marina. As I haul my luggage into reception, William MacArthur breezes out of the lounge, Hawaiian shirt open to his sternum. The air shimmers with his cologne. He leans an elbow on the counter and snatches my room key from the desk clerk.

"How're you finding our little piece of paradise, Rivers?"

"It's pretty. Good beaches. Plenty of quiet places to commit murder." I stick a cigarette in my mouth, don't offer the pack.

"We should put that on the tourist information posters. Rename Fairfield Point to Homicide Cove." His smile has all the humor of a starving shark.

"I'd say that was in poor taste, but so's your shirt."

Eyes narrow to obsidian slits. "Edwards thought he was funny, too."

"The badge comes with a sense of humor. Did you get along with Edwards?"

"He liked sticking his nose places. Maybe that comes with the badge, too." He drops my key to the countertop and makes for the door.

I let him swagger to the exit before calling his name. "When'd you last see him?"

He pauses, a hand splayed on the door, and glowers back. "Ask my lawyer."

And then he's gone.

I've got a good view of the marina from my third-floor room. The reflection of my cigarette tip is another starburst among the lights of the *Faithfulness*. After a few minutes, a barrel in a God-awful shirt mounts the gangplank. He turns at the top, and I imagine he's staring right at me. I finish my smoke, close the curtains, and place my pistol on the nightstand.

***

Collins finds me in the hotel restaurant nursing a coffee for breakfast. With all the grace of a tugboat, he weaves through the sea of empty tables. I motion to the waiter—similar enough in age and features to be the desk clerk's brother—for another coffee.

The deputy wrings his hat, smooths his lip fuzz. "Listen," he says to the centerpiece, "I want to apologize for last night."

"This job tests everyone's limits." I sip my brew and watch him over the rim.

He nods, his gaze reaching as high as my tie knot. His coffee arrives, and by the time we're nearly finished, I've relayed my findings.

The chair creaks as he sits back. "I can't believe I didn't see it."

I swirl the dregs and drain the cup. "C'mon, I want to talk to the harbor master."

Collins insists on driving the short distance. He parks on the same gravel lot where we met yesterday and points at an octagonal shack overlooking the seafront. A weather-beaten sign declares this to be the *MacArthur Port Authority*.

I knock. A hacking cough answers, followed by inaudible muttering. The narrow door swings open to reveal a wild-haired pirate. Collins handles the introductions, and without a word, the harbor master waves us inside.

He settles back in a torn leather chair behind a desk surmounted by stacks of paper. "What do you want?" he asks, voice strained around another cough.

"You keep a logbook of marina traffic?" I tap out a smoke, wait for him to nod before tossing him the pack. "I'm interested in a few dates."

"Which?" He lights a match with a thumbnail and turns to his desk to consult an open ledger.

I start with the most recent and work my way back. For each, he reads the entries aloud: first the incoming, then the outgoing. I know what Edwards hit on before we're halfway through. As we enter the summer months, the same names crop up again and again, but only one is featured every time: the *Faithfulness*, arriving in San Adiutor.

Collins gawks through the windows at the great yacht. "MacArthur's a piece of work, but you don't think he had anything to do with Chuck's death, do you?"

I've got opinions, but I keep them to myself. "MacArthur say where he was coming from on any of those trips?"

The pirate shakes his head, coughing into a stained handkerchief.

My mind races to connect dots. Even money would say that Edwards noticed the *Faithfulness* in the bay where his son surfed, then saw it in harbor the next morning. Maybe he saw them transporting the snow either from the yacht or onto it. He followed them to the hideout at Fairfield Point a few times, just to be sure. Then he confronted them, wound up dead on the beach.

But how to prove any of that?

"Chase."

Collins looks round. "What about him?"

I check the time. Approaching midmorning. "Will he be out yet?"

The deputy shrugs. "Let's find out."

The trip to the Edwards place is fruitless. Both vehicles gone. We spend the next couple of hours driving the coast road until, with clouds gathering like guilty thoughts, Collins cries, "There!" and careens us down a rough path.

Half a dozen figures slalom atop slivers of color along steely swells. Maryann stands beside a row of cars on the sandbar. She twists to peer over her shoulder.

I'm out the prowler before the engine dies. "I need to talk to Chase!"

Maryann doesn't argue or ask questions. Instead, she faces the sea and waves both arms over her head.

Her son leads the exodus from the water. Within a few minutes, Collins and I are the center of a semicircle of youths. Several affect boredom, curling their toes in the sand or rolling their eyes. The others, like kids in a classroom, wait in near silence for me to speak.

I look from Maryann to Chase, then around the group. "I need you all to think very carefully: the night before Chuck Edwards died, you were surfing at…"

"East Beach," Chase supplies.

"East Beach," I repeat, nodding my thanks. "Were there any boats in the bay?"

The boys exchange sidelong glances. A couple of halfhearted shrugs. Chase scratches an ear as he tries to remember.

A fair-haired boy, younger than the others, chews his lip. "I think so. A big white boat."

Chase's eyes widen. "That's right. It was Mr. MacArthur's."

"You're sure?" I ask the pair of them. Nods. Good enough.

Maryann catches my arm. "You think he had something to do with Chuck's murder?" she hisses.

False hope is worse than none. "I don't know yet."

Twice on the ride to town Collins asks what my plan is. Twice I ignore him. He gets the hint. We hit Main in focused silence. Stony-faced locals leap aside, hurling insults at the prowler's tail pipe. Collins skids onto Beach and guns for the marina parking lot. Gravel chips rattle against the undercarriage.

I check the pistol nestled in my armpit as Collins kills the engine. The deputy sets his jaw, reaches into the footwell behind my seat, and hefts a shotgun in his shaky grip. Together, we stalk toward the *Faithfulness.*

Aboard, I grab the first deckhand who presents himself. "Where's MacArthur?" The gaunt young man examines the badge I thrust in his face and beckons for us to follow him. The lacquered deck squeaks beneath our feet.

He ushers us into a well-appointed lounge in the stern. Square windows and muted paintings provide relief from expensive wood paneling. A chandelier disguised as an astrolabe hangs above a low-backed settee. In a pair of wing chairs flanking the couch sits William MacArthur and Henry Bleeker. They pause midconversation as we file in.

MacArthur, dressed in a different but equally horrid shirt, dismisses the crewman with a savage chop of his hand. "I told you," he growls at me, rising from his seat, "I wouldn't speak without my lawyer present."

"Then you'd best go get him." I lean against a side table. "I'm here to talk about Chuck Edwards's murder."

Bleeker frowns. "You can't be serious, Matthew."

"Me and heart attacks." I turn to Collins. "Search the ship for any of that snow."

The deputy slings the shotgun over his shoulder but waits for a sharp nod from MacArthur, who adds, "Do what you must."

Collins trudges to the nearest stairwell and disappears below deck.

The marina owner lowers himself back into his chair. "Anything he finds will be inadmissible as evidence. Unless, of course, you've got a warrant."

I shake a cigarette loose. "A warrant won't matter if I link you to Edwards's murder, not to mention cocaine smuggling."

He acknowledges my words with a slight shrug.

Bleeker reaches for a half-finished glass of whiskey, drains it, and stares at MacArthur. "Tell me you're not involved, William." The withering look he receives in reply is answer enough. "Oh, Christ."

MacArthur lounges like a proud lion. "Where did you think any of the donations I gave you came from?"

I pause, cigarette halfway to my lips. "What happened to waiting for your lawyer?" The question is out before I realize I already know. He's talking because I'm not going to be an issue much longer.

A large shadow passes a window. Gray daylight runs along a double-barrel. I dive as the shotgun fires. Wood splinters shower me. Collins rushes back into the room, weapon trained on me.

Cursing myself for buying his dummy routine, I lift my head. "You killed Edwards," I snarl. "And Jamieson."

The deputy braces his gun. "Phil saw us that night." He aims his eyebrows at MacArthur. "A bit of late-night fishing. He promised not say anything, but we couldn't risk it."

Bleeker, now kneeling on the floor, takes his hands off his ears. "What now?" he whines, all professional composure lost.

"Now," I say to rob MacArthur of the satisfaction, "they kill me. In return for your silence, that son of a bitch will keep funding you. But you'll belong to him forever."

MacArthur finishes his drink. "You make it sound so dirty. Chuck was the same. That come with the badge, too?"

As he talks, I meet Bleeker's eye and look to his empty glass. He follows, comprehension stealing what little color remains in his cheeks. With a shaky hand, he reaches.

Collins shifts his stance. "Bleeker, don't…"

I draw. Too late, the deputy realizes his mistake. Three slugs turn the wall behind him red. He stumbles into the doorframe, coughing blood into his mustache, and topples like a redwood.

His death rattle is lost beneath the sound of a safety clicking. I roll. MacArthur's first shot chews the deck. I scrabble behind another couch. Every nerve screams for me to keep going, right out the door, but I'd never make it. Bullets tear through the upholstery and seat backing, parting my hair.

Glass smashes. I press my face to the floor, cover my head.

But MacArthur is screaming. He fires again, but not at me.

Kneeling, I look over the sofa. Bleeker clutches his gut, blood turning his pale suit black. MacArthur bleeds from a temple gash, slivers of Bleeker's tumbler lodged in the wound.

Our eyes lock.

Time becomes meaningless.

MacArthur rounds on me, moving as if through silt.

I take a deep breath, and as his gun points at me, I fire.

No fanfare, no final words. A bullet through the throat. The marina owner drops in a puff of sickening cologne. I hate myself for breathing so much of it as adrenaline ebbs.

Bleeker coughs. I rush to his side, pressing my hands to his wound. Meaningless reassurances tumble from numb lips as I fight to keep the mayor alive. He grips my wrist, wincing as he pulls himself up to whisper in my ear: "Need help."

From the intensity in his watering eyes, he's not talking about himself.

I glance back at the dead. Bleeker's right: MacArthur's smuggling operation might be over, but whoever he was working with is still out there. They might pay a visit to find out what happened to their investment.

Someone should be here to tell them.

I'll write to my captain in the morning, let him know I'm staying for a while. Maybe I'll include a review: *If traveling in the off-season, beware of November snow.*

Ewan A. Dougall was born and raised in Glasgow, Scotland, which is probably why his stories are full of rain. He's always been a fan of the stylized worlds of Raymond Chandler and Philip Kerr, and stories of knights in tarnished armor who lose more often than they win. He's working on a noir novel, numerous short stories, and dabbles in other genres. Most recently, he's contributed to the noir anthologies *Summer Bludgeon* (Unsettling Reads) and *The Astronaut Always Rings Twice* (Tyche Books). Ewan is supported by his wife and his two cats and, when not writing, works in clinical research. He can be glimpsed on most social media platforms. @EwanDougall (Twitter) | @ewandougall (Instagram)

The Rolex

David Zimmerle

The fullness of late summer had faded, and it was now clearly fall. Evenings less high-contrast red, more and more vanilla dusk preceding night. Furtive, cold winds sliding down from the north and into the dry high pressure that still lingered. Everything dripping in autumn gold—tilted by its perennial crispness and the low glow of forthcoming standard time. Still enough heat to delight in though. Cool water with no trace of the chill. Offshore winds and orange blips in the surf forecast had felt like they'd never end. Waves that ran the southern coast for a chunk of the workweek. Memorable enough, where the parking lot banter at Salt Creek centered on how it was all a setup for a powerful winter. It was time. It was long overdue. *It always feels like that*, Xander Cantwell thought.

But the last two weeks were flat. Lake Pacific. A sheet glass spell. Gutless shin-high dribblers. Still trunkable though with Halloween a week in the rearview, which was crazy. X finding no use in a board, often recoiling at the thought of riding a log—even in these conditions. Instead he opted for old fins from his sponger days, and late afternoon swims along the rocky points and coves of South Laguna. Work was a farce after two in the afternoon, anyway. And he needed to move. Needed the plunge. Needed the water for him to stay sane. Wishing for things to wake back up and for Creek to reel like it did. Like the old poster of Point throwing miracle tubes over Boneyards in the surf shop. But that would only be a distraction to his utter desperation. He had a job to leave, clients to poach, and a gigantic twenty-one-thousand student loan collections bill to pay.

Alone on PCH after his swim, X dried off and stared into the open trunk of his old Civic. Spellbound almost. Lost in streaks of sand that never failed to make it into the trunk. Lost in a few old, empty cans of Monster energy drinks from work. Lost in the faded-gray interior. He was avoiding the severity of the cardboard file box in the trunk's corner, which contained all those loan files rife with the important, discretionary documentation of his home-refinance clients, which he'd copied and smuggled from the office. Addresses. Socials. Paystubs. Home titles. Everything he ever would need to service their rapport and seal those future deals when he landed somewhere else.

Headlights crested toward him, rolling up brighter with dark closing in. All X wanted was to leave this whole situation and never come back. Exhaust his savings, pay the bill, and never look back. And this time it would be for good. Fuck law school. Fuck grad school. Fuck any and all institutions. The world was just too big, and everything about the full-time humdrum too precarious even with the possibility of finding his niche amid the moneyed prescription everywhere. He'd had enough of South Orange County, perfect evenings like this one somehow tinged with more and more regret. Like he was wasting his time on a super lame version of paradise.

Paradise definitely was not here. Paradise was out there somewhere beyond the sun's hot dip. *Uluwatu barrels and Indo escape. Maybe Australia.* And X was stuck. *Stuccoed in?* Stuck here. Feeling stuck forever. Lying to himself and those others on the phone. Conning them into the deals. Conned them on the cold calls and false promise of financial freedom through home ownership. Through refis and a nice dose of cashing in. *The home is your bank. You've earned it.* Pushed the shadiest of shady loans as his only reasonable option out. His back against the wall, the whole thing a forced concept he fell into after Creek was firing, and post-surf beers with his best bud, Brian, and the bright idea that X still had time to cash in. Brian had the world by the taint. A different girl every few weeks. Total smoke shows. A BMW M3. A condo in Dana Point. Didn't have to prove income nor assets to get it, either. Spent as he went, and he didn't go to college.

"Get on the gravy train with me," Brian had said, all bleary-eyed, nine beers deep. "Easy money, X-bro. Fucking easy dough. These past four years filling your head, man. You've been missing out. You should be filling your fucking bank account."

But that was nearly ten months and twenty-three closed loans ago. The whole thing was off the rails now, ready to fly off the cliff into a river of lava. The news a constant blur of bad news and total financial collapse.

X shut the Civic's trunk on the lives in the box, startled by the sound of feet suddenly padding up behind him at a slow jog. A slight defensive urge quickly surged through him until he realized it was just the older man in from the swim. The one X had passed just south of Ninth Street. His stroke totally trash. No strong slice. No grace in his glide through the slight chop. X, the shark at his side, who passed him in as long as it took to sing half the chorus to "Badfish." Barely enough light left to really see the man, but enough where X could still make out the blue dial of the Submariner stark at his thick, hairy wrist. Enough patina to know it was vintage. X seeing the man's potbelly as he passed by and hoping it never came to that. The man's dismissive scowl so insufferable, too, which was becoming more and more the theme among older men around here. Older men with all the money. X watching the man walk up to a garage a hundred feet ahead, type a code at a keypad, and walk in. X knowing fundamentally at his core that would never be his life no matter how many loans he conned.

***

"The *fucking* points—you see this shit!?" Diego barked from his office two doors down. Diego always rolled up the daily rate sheet and used it like a soft brush drumstick against his desk when the calls weren't happening. He must have rolled it up tighter to make it sound like that, a harder smack to convey his frustration. Like he was questioning not just all of them, but the entire loan operation. His voice somehow sounding dry between sips of fresh orange juice they all liked to get from the bagel shop a few lights down. Looking itchy in his new Macy's slacks at that morning's huddle. His look balanced, though, by slick black hair.

"Why even call the leads, Scagetti? Fuck, why buy them!?" Diego's voice growing louder so Skegs could hear. "No one's getting prime-ass watches if this is the new norm. We're totally in for the shit now. Buckle up, bitch boys."

Incredulous. It was all ending just as X was getting started. It was in the steady rate upticks. It was in the points they were losing on each loan. It was in the cash flow; people suddenly didn't have it to pay their mortgages. It was the way banks were falling over and failing, straight seizing up. It was the way Brian's cube hadn't smelled like stale jizz in more than a month since he now spent his free time jacking off in the bathroom instead of all hurried and into the wastebin between calls behind his desk. The party was ending.

When X had joined the loan crew, that was Skegs's big fucking play. The Rolex on his wrist. Twenty grand. They were all going to get rich enough where buying expensive watches was just a way of life.

"I've got five more," Skeg had said in the conference room a week into X starting the job. It was impossible for X or any of the other guys to look away from the watch's sterling finish. Its aesthetic of known austerity. "They're like markers of all the shit you did to earn. And you don't get them unless you close. And only winners close. It's in the movies for a reason, boys. Time fucking immemorial."

Soon after, Skegs was taping Breitling ads above the copier. Images of Patek Philippe adorned the crude space above the urinals. TAG Heuer cutouts in the laughably small break room. But it was the vintage Submariner at the back of Skegs's Rolex catalog that held X's eyes captive. That someday, if he ever got out of this fucking thing and had the dough, that would be it. The one. Fucking Bond status. Just a cool hundred fifty large and no big deal.

X had been at it almost a year and led everyone in sales that whole last summer, stringing together the most closed loans for three consecutive months. He even packaged and sold four option ARMs—the riskiest ones with the biggest payouts. The ones the government had just ended. And he did so with a little help from his Wite-Out roller. X was really good. Best in Skegs's small crew of five loan officers. Won the summer grand prize of a weekend getaway in Cabo with all expenses paid. Skegs's way of keeping them engaged through competition with everything in destructo mode. Whether Skegs would keep his word was another thing entirely, since he had yet to produce plane tickets or the overall itinerary.

"I don't welch," Skegs said when X asked about it after work in his boss's corner office. "By New Year's you'll be sipping margaritas and tapping strange down there. I'm just making sure to pick the right one."

That was three weeks ago. Fucking Scagetti. Saying he was Youngstown, Ohio's craziest white boy—crazier than the Black kids he would get into vicious dogfights with while growing up in the hood. That he was forged in fire. That it all led to his great becoming: the perfect

Army Ranger. The assassin. The fucking killer. It wasn't like X was going to push it.

It all had become more than an increasing annoyance for X, but he made the calls anyway, focused on the exponential gut-sick annoyance that he was going to soon part with so much money. Way more than he'd won in Vegas, which had essentially started this whole thing, if he had to pin it. Twenty-five grand and change—even with the hefty cut Skegs took off the top of every loan, they all closed—all saved up. Most of which he'd hand over to finally bring his student loan out of collections and clear his name. Fucking Scagetti making boatloads as the main broker from the ninja salesboys he trained from nothing. Building a fiefdom in a randomly quaint and bland, brand-new corporate office in Aliso. It had felt like a big deal for X. Made him feel important at first. Made him feel disgusted with himself all the same. Reasoning it was all just a minor inconvenience to make some real money fast and get out of the mess he had made, and do it quickly.

X tapped another number on his desk phone. It was the dinner hour, and Skegs drilled them that this was when the deals often blossomed. He listened to the line ring and ring and ring. Nobody was picking up like they used to. Goddamn, how he'd fucked up on that student loan, he thought. Big time. Pretty much right out of undergrad, too: Finally back home from San Francisco. Parents freshly divorced. Living from boxes in his old room. That small track home he grew up in on the hill was looking more and more the worse for wear. His younger brother—by accident—failing eighth grade and on a steady diet of mac and cheese. It was a wonder X even made it out the way he had. Coming home was so unceremonious. All too familiar, and yet so different than when he'd left four years ago. The default sparking an entirely new direction, lettering X another statistic in a growing bell curve of failures just like him. It was his fault. Sure. He spent that whole first year in denial that he had to pay it all back. That he had to figure it out alone and get a real job. That he'd even signed the papers. No one was bailing him out though. There was no college fund. Real life was just too much, and his English degree not enough to warrant any kind of calculated career direction. No fucking contacts to network whatsoever. He thought he liked newspapers and magazines, but all that was dying anyway.

It didn't help running smack fucking dab into the unrequited lust that was Sophie Taylor outside the post office in Laguna at the end of that first summer back home. God, they hadn't seen each other in years. Four years. Ten minutes prior he had been asked to leave one of town's more exquisite restaurants, the owner gruff and arrogant about not giving unscheduled interviews especially for some local fledgling internet news site that X was peddling. The pay was shit, and X was looking for experience in what was fast becoming the digital age. His resignation, bruised ego, and general sense of helplessness felt more pronounced. But as he walked into the post office to mail off a crucial postgraduate form for his student loan servicer, all the bad things he felt were totally and suddenly poof-gone with Sophie Taylor from high school in front of him and now in the promise of her supple twenties. Both of them wildly compelled in that instant to explore the unknown they'd only flirted with during class and that one time he asked her to homecoming junior year.

Though there had been a natural magnetism between them, Sophie ultimately decided a week after the dance that it wasn't going to work with X, and instead gave all of herself to Rob Lennay for the rest of high school, whose family had money just like hers. It didn't hurt X too much back then, because nothing had really happened except for how good it felt to hold her close, his hand against the small of her back, and the lights low in the gym. There had been other girls. Good girls and bad girls, but generally not-as-rich-as-Sophie-Taylor girls. The thought of her and what to ever make of her and him together always lingered though. It didn't help that she called him two years after their high school graduation, while he was all the way up in San Francisco, out of her gourd on cocaine and racking lines alone in her USC dorm, wondering if he was around.

"How'd you get my number?" X asked. Hewas floored.

"I called your house," she said, her inflection rapid and clipped. Roiled in excitement. "Your mom gave it to me!"

She'd hoped the city's cold, uncompromising gray was finally enough for him to come home and take her out now that she and Rob had split up and he was with some other girl in LA tossing seeds and sowing oats. They ended that conversation with plans to meet when he was home for winter break. Plans that never came to fruition. X would get flashing thoughts of Sophie at a frequent clip after that, her hazy blonde hair tied back and those wide green eyes, especially for the brief time he dated Brooke, who was going to school at state. He had met Brooke at a party in the Richmond at the beginning of his senior year. The NorCal Indian summer in full effect. Brooke, speedy and charged by the stuff. Brooke, too, a mix of blonde and green but with bird shot freckles. Brooke, who gave X his first major taste of good cocaine, and the fast nights that followed, racing the iron crossbars of the Bay Bridge in her Acura at 2:00 a.m. to track it down from her dealer on Treasure Island. Brooke, who just loved the hunt and the sex that followed. After three months of Hurricane Brooke and his grades nearing the point of no return, X took the bus to her apartment in the Sunset, ready to break up. The whole weight of it easier to release when he found the door ajar and her fucking the dealer in the bedroom. They didn't hear him—the techno music was too loud. Didn't see him, either, in their throes. But he'd seen enough to never call her again.

It didn't help that after his chance encounter with Sophie Taylor at the post office in Laguna Beach, X won the five grand at the Vegas slots playing Wheel of Fortune on a weekend whim with Brian in Vegas. X figuring it was his cue to bail. His time now. Bail on the whole fucking thing. A career could wait. He hadn't seen that much money in his account at once, not ever.

So he bailed for Mex. He bailed with Sophie for Mex, soaking in all that time away, not only from her, but the gold-light waters of home after all that cold time in the city. He bailed with an eight ball of cocaine with Sophie for Mex and a wild week that spilled into two, surfing epic beach breaks and clubbing from Rosarito to Ensenada. Hotels on the credit card Sophie's parents supplied and food with X's cash. Drinks. Lines. Sweat and sheets. He would grasp for her soft naked side in the night and burrow in, tempered by how fleeting the whole thing felt. The weird déjà vu of something he thought he'd put well behind him a year prior. Coming home unscathed with the coke gone and then going to Hawaii with Sophie on a lark. That was unexpected.

It consisted of resort living for almost three months and partying the strip on Oahu. X couldn't believe how quickly life had become a dream. Amid the endless fresh pineapple boats and shrimp cocktails they ordered to the rooms, they also dabbled with some meth that X had gotten from Big Braddah in an overgrown, abandoned gravel lot, doing enough to feel some edge of ill heaven between new bags of coke whose taste and composition hit all the senses as being sketchier on the island.

"Makes my whole mind swirl, you know?" he said to Sophie about the meth. He was in the middle of snorting a bump off his knuckle in the bathroom stall of what had become their go-to bar for warm-up drinks. "Like I should shower, but I'm already clean."

"Yeah, like, I just have too much to say. At once!" Her eyes burned right into him. "I couldn't do this stuff, like, all the time."

"Yeah, nah. Me either. But the cocaine?"

"Oh, yes." She sighed. "The *good* cocaine."

She leaned in as he did, and they stayed in the stall, the sidewalls shaking until both had extinguished that illicit moment of fire.

They each knew their physical limits with the stuff. With all of it. Any of it. Even with the weed. But what was weed anymore anyway? It was all for the good times and to enhance their freewheeling spirits, not consume them. Not enough to become the skin-picking freaks shown at D.A.R.E. week way back in the day. They honored their bodies with breathtaking hikes and supplemented with juices, eating well into night. X surfed several times a day. He'd become wolf lean. Gold-tan shredded. But that third month, though, nearing Thanksgiving and X down to his last hundred dollars, that's when Sophie's card was declined at the front desk.

"Dad says I gotta go," she said while they watched a final volcanic sunset. "They're making me go to Newport for rehab. That's the deal. Otherwise I'm cut off. Nothing."

"I don't have enough to fly back right now."

"Then surf, X. Just surf. It was good. Like that Christmas break I wanted with you but way better."

"But all this?"

He motioned back and forth with his hand at the space between them.

"They'd never approve. Like, ever, X. I'll see you, I guess."

Sophie stood outside the hotel room door, her things haphazardly tossed into her big suitcase except for the teal bikini they'd lost after she decided to change at the beach with the tide rushing and the shoreline pounding on that weekend hike in Kauai. She'd coaxed a feral calico kitty and play stuffed him into her bag two miles into the hike, both of them laughing and daring each other to smuggle back the poor thing—all claws anyway—only to suddenly notice her treasured two-piece gone. A victim swallowed by high tide for sure by now. But at least they had made it all the way to the waterfall, kissing while submerged under its heavy rain.

Sophie pecked him on the cheek, but it felt like good-bye defeat. Gone that electric, freewheeling charge. What he knew, whether feigned or not, was lost. And he knew this had run its course. And he knew he might see her again, further off. Maybe in five years. Maybe with Rob, all clean and prim in the cush life he would afford her. Sophie and Rob with two kids and an actual home in Laguna. Maybe one more kid on the way. Maybe he'd never see her again. But most definitely not anytime soon.

X spent three weeks coming down. Fighting tremors in his hands and hell in his veins. He washed dishes at a Hawaiian food joint and ran a few parking lot scores for Big Braddah, who set X up in a pup tent with holes in his family's backyard that bordered old sugarcane. Eventually saving up to buy his one-way ticket back to Orange County. When he walked in the door just before Christmas, his mother took one look at him and said he was no good.

"You can have your room back, but that's it. That's all you're getting."

She sat at the kitchen table and thumbed at the *Pennysaver*. Smoked her Marlboro Light cigarette and didn't even look up. Finally met his eyes when she sipped her wineglass.

"Don't ask for nothing else, because there is nothing else," she said. "I left your mail on your bed. You're fucked. *Pfff.* But at least you're tan. And still young enough. Merry Christmas."

Fucked indeed. All that mail. A pile of it. Between the credit card offers and seasonal surf stuff catalogs, all those notices. The red-letter type on the envelopes indicating emergency. *YOU'RE LATE. YOU'RE OVERDUE. FINAL WARNING. NO REALLY, YOUR FINAL WARNING.* Blowing right past any kind of grace period. Any kind of phone call at the end of a month to explain his position. That he just didn't have it in him to do anything related to real work or a real career. And could he just have an extra week, or a month, or six, or forever to figure it out? After New Year's was when Creek had just fired and the beers with Brian and with it his decision to work loans. And now, the decision to give almost everything he'd made over to what had become so far the biggest mistake of his life.

***

"I'm sorry, Mr. Cantwell, there's really nothing else I can say. You didn't account for *our* servicing portion of interest. It's a fine payment really, but there's still twelve thousand dollars owed."

X wanted to become fire. He wanted to become ash. He wanted to self-immolate. He stood there at Creek's overlook, watching the sun melt into Lake Pacific. Still no waves. He wanted to become the sun and burn.

"Robin, I can't hear that right now, man," X yelled into his flip phone. Realizing his voice had startled a Stepford-looking passerby and her two Pomeranians on the leash, he lowered his voice. He was about to cry.

"It's not the response, Robin. It's not the *fucking* answer. The original loan I took out was almost eleven thousand. I'm paying more than double! I gave you the payment. You took the *fucking* payment. The whole $21,291.12 that drafted from my *fucking* bank account to your *fucking* institution three days ago. Nothing about your interest. I sent it. I don't have anything anymore. It's all gone—to you."

Robin was his collections liaison. He'd been, so far, a mix of smarmy and charming. His English accent disarming, yet never failing to apply the pressure that X had money due. That X was the one who had messed up, not World Corp Collections. Robin was simply doing his job.

"It's *simply* not what our records indicate as the full amount, Mr. Cantwell. We'll take this sum and apply it, certainly. I advise you connect with us later when you have the additional amount. We can easily set you up on a payment plan again. But the interest still applies."

"You can't be serious."

"I'm sorry, Mr. Cantwell, but I am," Robin said. "I must be going. I don't know what else to say. You still owe us—and, in turn, you still owe your university."

X hurled his phone into the rocks and reeds below. He clutched the rail at his waist and squatted. He felt the vomitous tickle in his throat and choked it back down so it wouldn't come rushing out all over his slacks and dress shoes. *Unbelievable. Un-fucking-believable.* None of the other guys in the office knew about X's default. It was none of their business.

The plan for the evening was to meet them for drinks in Laguna. An extended happy hour. A few more final toasts to what had been quite the run with everything now falling apart everywhere. X planned to buy the boys a few rounds and celebrate his accomplishment in secret. He'd even been thinking about quitting the whole racket by the end of the week and use the pittance that was left over to purchase the flight to Indo. He'd figure it all out from there. Give America some time. Things were about to get real messy. He was all set to be free. Now the plan was simple and borderline reductionist—get blackout drunk.

***

A parched mouth and sour spit woke him with the cold feeling in his lap and underneath that he'd pissed himself; cold early morning, too, and the reality of having passed out and slept through the night in the back seat of the Civic. Pain racked every crevice inside his skull. Images of the night sparked his memory like electric whips—shots at the Saloon, more shots and cocktails at the Marine Room, more shots and dance-floor neon shots on Main Street, brewery beers and… He lost track after that. *How did I get here?* He felt poisoned. Thinking just made him hurt more. Knowing he was broke all over again—that the money was gone and he still owed more—made him throw up on the floorboard. He imagined strangling a man that could look like Robin until his eyes bulged.

He sat up and remembered the loose half-full bottle of water in the trunk. His thoughts then turned from slaking his thirst to the springsuit he also had stashed back there, too. But it was Catalina's jagged beauty out the windshield that really pierced him—its outline shadowed yet discernible on the foggy horizon. He felt a flash of shame for being here and trying to drive home, and recalled the numb feeling of how his body hadn't worked behind the wheel, grateful for his better angels leading him to put the car in park in an empty spot on a neighborhood street. He settled by a big bush line in front of a remodeled Craftsman just up the hill from PCH—two blocks away, where he had been parking for his recent cove swims. It was always hangover moments like this where the ocean offered salve. A cleanse. How revived he felt after a night of hard drinking from a mellow surf. A nice, cool dip. How Brian would say that it cleaned your taint so good, you didn't have to put on old underwear from the night before. X painfully exited the car, where he wrapped a towel around his waist, peeled off his soiled clothes, slipped into the wetsuit, and walked barefoot toward the ocean with fins in hand.

The chipped concrete stairs led to a desolate beach, and X saw that the flat conditions of the last few weeks had changed. The water was in flux. Something out there beginning to pulse and rise, the visible build of swell ever so slight. Clean, waist-high green-gray tubes broke on the reefs, and X felt an energized chill at his ankles. He knew it inside, the tangible pull that waves were coming. One more big south with a little northwest crossed in likely this time. One more run of swell to end this hell of a fall.

X skimmed along the seafloor, going with the current's pull. A human torpedo. Arms at his side with an easy dolphin kick. Sand and silt tracing along his un-suited skin and through his hair. He felt the blood in his eyes begin to slow, and the ice pick headache dissipate into a dull thrum. Powerful enough, still, to remind him that his hangover was far from over. He surfaced for a breath and sliced through a set, making his way outside where he could swim parallel to the coast unencumbered.

He floated on his back and kicked, fixed on the foggy nothingness of the marine layer above and what it would take to conjure those additional funds in this house-of-cards economy. He switched to a side crawl. He switched to a lazy backstroke again when his side ached, content with nobody around. Still somehow awestruck by the beauty of it all despite his awful position. The crags and nooks along the shore. Their starts and stops, broken here and there by lush, soft, white sand beachheads. Narrow, sloping sandstone cliffs and bumpy corners that worked as foundation for the few quiet, empty-looking homes scattered along them. He thought of Skegs and the boys, and the sad conundrum of having to go back to them later that morning for the back half of the workweek. That sadness driven to darker, more sorrowful depths as he knew how much more of himself—and others—he would have to sell to make it through this terrible life while on this terrible track.

He felt the soft brush of kelp below and did not ignore his flagrant wish that it could somehow entangle him and take him into the deep. But then a fleshy knock against his head startled him. He reached above in a panic and grazed bare skin with his palm.

"Help me."

The voice was almost a whisper. X flipped onto his stomach and started to tread water. In the gray-green of that morning, all he could see above the surface was a face suspended. It took a moment, but then he knew—it was the older man who lived nearby. The one with the sour look who swam, too. He was clutching a handful of his breast below the water.

"I...I th-think I-I'm ha-having a heart attack. Please...I need help."

He was pale and on the verge of turning light blue. X went to raise his arms and signal for help, but nobody was around to see it. Nobody around, and just around the rocky bend was another empty beachhead. The older man lifted his hand toward X with what fleeting strength he had left, and in that moment, X saw the Rolex dull against the gray sky, confirming it had all the esoteric markings of the vintage Submariner from Skegs's catalog.

Part of him didn't want instinct to take over. He instead wanted to grip the older man's thick, hairy wrist. He wanted to unfasten the watch and take it. Slip it off while the old man quietly slipped under. But the dying light and shock of horror in the old man's eyes was too much.

"C'mon, guy!" X yelled. "We're getting you help! We're going in! Hold on!"

X shot his arm under the old man's armpit and pulled their bodies close. He felt the stubble of the man's cheek against his own. He used his free arm and legs to swim them to shore. But the waves had grown. A substantial set had begun to swing in, complicated by the fact that they were beginning to sink. They missed the maw of the first wave as it pushed them into the second wave's impact zone. Cresting together in its lip, the two fell through the air headfirst. X rolled over at the last second and tried to flatten them both out but took the ocean floor with his shoulder while the turbulent explosion ripped the old man from X's grip.

In the blurry moments after the set had passed, X surfaced and found his breath. He found his legs and stood up in shin-deep water. He scoured the outside first for the old man and then turned around when he didn't see him. X found him facedown in the wet sand. A rag doll in the shore's foam. X dragged him to the soft sand by his arms, trying to recall compression-to-breath ratios he'd seen illustrated on laminated poolside signs more times than he could count. But when he turned the old man on his back, it was too late. The old man's head twisted in such a way to suggest his neck had snapped from the free fall.

X searched once again for help, remembering how the lifeguards were never fully around after Labor Day. He searched for someone to call 9-1-1, wishing to land his sight on someone, anyone—even a Stepford-looking wife walking her Pomeranians on the beach. There was no one. Just empty beach and sand in his teeth. He put two fingers to the old man's throat and palpated around bones to find a pulse, just to be sure. There was none. And so, he closed the old man's dead eyes. And after he did, his vision landed on the unmistakable metal glint at the old man's wrist. Part of him didn't want instinct to take over. He unclasped the Rolex and held it in his hands, admiring its weight. On its case back, an inscription: *For Every Win.* Suddenly X's entire future rolled out before him like a movie reel: a fast drive to LA, a visit to one of the premier watch brokers advertising in back of the catalogs, *then* on a plane to Indo.

David Zimmerle lives with his wife and two young children in the rural Southern California town of Fallbrook and grew up in South Orange County. He publishes frequently in *The Surfer's Journal,* has published poetry in the *99 Poems for the 99 Percent* anthology, and is working on a debut novel.

Undertow

Shannon Hollinger

Another drink might kill him. Despite that, he stares down into the bottom of his empty glass, willing another sip to appear. But much like his life, nothing's there.

His throat still burns from the last shot. Stomach acid scalds his esophagus. His hearing's gone fuzzy, his vision blurry. He knows he drinks too much. Another one might kill him. But it just might save him, too.

He signals the bartender. She quirks an eyebrow, her gaze shifting from the hundred he laid on the bar top when he sat to the computer screen where his tab is running. He watches her do the math. Satisfied that there's still plenty left for a decent tip, she obediently fills the glass.

His hand trembles as he lifts the drink, hoping this one will be the one. He anticipates the sweet salvation of oblivion. The tumbler is halfway to his mouth when he's jostled from behind, amber liquor sloshing over the rim.

"My bad, bro." A heavy hand clasps his shoulder, weighing him down as the owner uses it to steady himself while he slides onto the next barstool. "Let me buy you another one. What's your . . . Reggie?"

He looks up sharply, body tensing, hands sliding across the sticky bar, curling into fists in his lap.

"Dude, how's it going? I haven't seen you in forever. You still live around here?"

Reggie squints through the haze clouding his vision, vaguely recognizing the voice from a previous life, back before . . . "Scottie?"

"Yeah, man, s'up?"

Reggie's fists unfurl. He shakes some sobriety back into his head. "Not much, just—" He gestures at the bar around them. "How about you?"

"Awesome, bro. Seriously. Couldn't be better. Just landed a gnarly new deal. Actually, we were just celebrating."

"Yeah, I heard you were killing it. You started your own company, right? Wetsuits?"

"Yup. Always said I'd find a way to work while I play. And how about you? Didn't you end up with Julie Ungers? Damn, she was hot. You two married yet?"

Before he can answer, Scottie continues. "And I heard that you sold out? Became a cop? What's up with that?" he teases, his white grin popping against his tan skin.

Trust Scottie to not have seen a news headline in the last year. "Nah, man. Not anymore."

"Dude, did you go private? That's excellent. I totally got a job for you, you gotta take it." Scottie jerks his head toward a group of rowdy surfers gathered around a pool table in the back. "Wanna join us?"

"Thanks, but I've got an early morning. I should really get going." Reggie slides the hundred across the bar, nodding as he catches the bartender's eyes.

"Another time, then. But seriously, bro." Scottie slides off the barstool and pulls his wallet from his back pocket. Slipping a business card out, he hands it to Reggie, his face suddenly serious. He glances over his shoulder, making sure his pals are out of hearing distance, then says, "I've got something I really need your help with. I can't trust just anyone with this. Don't get me wrong, it's totally legit, it's just—it's personal. It would mean so much if you'd do this for me, bro. Promise me you'll stop by, at least hear me out."

Reggie looks down at the card in his hand.

Epic Enterprises
Shredding Surf Gear
Scottie Scoley
Head Honcho

"Can I count on seeing you tomorrow?"

He has a busy day of drowning his sorrows planned but supposes he can put off that first drink until noon. "Yeah, I'll stop by before lunch."

"Epic. Thanks, man. It means a lot." Scottie shakes a shaka at him and turns to rejoin his friends.

"Yeah." Reggie watches him go, then tosses back his drink, not sure what he just agreed to, or why. Maybe it was friendship. Or nostalgia. Or just plain old desperation.

***

It's almost noon when Reggie walks through the swinging glass door in the glorified warehouse where Epic Enterprises is located. He instantly feels out of place, wishing he hadn't worked so hard to shower and find something cleanish to wear—he's the only one not in a state of undress. Everywhere he looks, he sees bare feet, bronzed chests, a girl with no pants and barely a bikini bottom. Dreadlocks, stringy hair, salt-crusted tresses—it's like a time warp back to his youth.

"Dude, you made it!"

Scottie jogs down a spiral staircase leading from a windowed office up above. He, at least, is fully dressed, as long as you count flip-flops as shoes. He grabs Reggie's hand, pumps it a few times, then ushers him toward the steps.

"Oooh, somebody's in trooouble."

Reggie's pace quickens, trying to distance himself from the mocking whispers below. The stairs wobble unsteadily as they climb.

"Dude is definitely a nark."

Scottie closes the door behind them, cutting off the taunts and jeers. "Sorry about that." He gestures for Reggie to take a seat in one of the nylon folding beach chairs set before his desk while he settles onto a balance ball. "Dude, it really means a lot that you came."

Reggie nods, still not entirely sure why he did come. This morning, once he'd slept off the night before and his thoughts had cleared, he remembered that he'd never really liked Scottie that much. They'd never really been friends. Their crowds overlapped, and they'd gathered around the same bonfire or keg plenty of times, but Reggie had always felt there was something off about the other guy. Something shady.

"Can I get you a drink or something?"

"Nah, I'm good."

"I gotta tell you, when I first saw you last night, felt like I was tripping or something. Like, *whoa, blast from the past* and all that."

Reggie nods. He glances at the clock behind Scottie's head, a hula girl marking the time with her hands. He's already wishing that he hadn't come. That he'd found somewhere dark, seedy, and with a liquor license instead. Five minutes. Five minutes, and he'll have fulfilled any obligation owed a high school acquaintance.

"And it was just such stellar timing, you know?"

"Actually, I don't."

"You, huh?" Scottie's head tilts to the side like a confused parrot.

"You never told me. Why you asked me here."

"Dude, my bad, bro. Thought I had. Guess I had more to drink last night than I—well, anyways. The reason I asked you here is 'cause I need you to do a job."

"Looks like you've got plenty of people working for you already."

"Yeah, they're cool, man, but not for this." Scottie rubs the back of his neck and looks away.

Reggie stares, waiting for him to elaborate.

"It's just, it pains me to say this. And I wouldn't want anyone to find out. But I need someone to watch my old lady."

"Your old lady?"

"Yeah. My wife. It's not like she's stepping out or anything, nothing like that. It's just, she's been . . . unwell."

"Unwell?"

"Dude, stop saying everything I say, it's making me nervous."

"I'm going to need you to explain."

"About why it makes me nervous?"

"What? No. About your wife. Her illness."

"Oh. Yeah. Well, about a month ago she was totally shredding this honker when she wiped out bad, man. Board bonked her on the head something good."

"Did she get medical attention?"

"Well, not at the time, no. But she has since. For something else. But I think it's related."

Reggie pinches the bridge of his nose, squeezing his eyes shut. The hula girl has counted down three minutes. Only two left. "Speak plainly, Scottie. I can't help you if you don't level with me."

"She's been different, ever since she took the hit. She—" His voice hitches. "She tried to off herself. Pills. I came home early, in the middle of the day to check on her 'cause I had a strange feeling. If I hadn't got there when I did, well, she wouldn't be here now."

Reggie sits straighter in his chair. His fingers drum against his kneecaps. "When was this?"

"'Bout ten days ago. I've been doing my best to keep my eyes on her since, but I've got a business to run. Her parents are gone. She has a sister around somewhere, but she's no help. Her friend's been staying with us the last few days, but she's leaving tonight."

"And what exactly is it that you want me to do?"

"I don't know, man. Keep her safe. Whatever it takes."

"You mean like around-the-clock surveillance?"

"I know it isn't going to be cheap. But I don't care about the money. I just want her to be all right."

Reggie bites the inside of his cheek, grinding the pinched skin between his molars. "She's bound to notice some stranger stalking her."

"I already thought about that. That's why it's so perfect that it's you. You'll stay with us."

"I'll what?"

"Move in. Just for a while, until she's better. She's a tough chick, she'll pull out of it soon enough. Until then I'll tell her you're a friend from high school down on his luck, staying with us for a while. Ask her to try to cheer you up."

"And you think she'll go for that?"

Scottie shrugs. "It's worth a try."

Reggie watches the hula girl's arm pass another minute. He only has another week until the sheriff's office forces his eviction. He's been trying to think of a way to avoid the awkward reunion with his former co-workers, one that is sure to make him an even bigger joke around the force than he already is, but besides paying his rent, which he can't afford, he keeps drawing blanks.

And downing shots. Because when he's by himself—and everyone has long since turned their backs on him—all there is to do is think about how badly he's screwed everything up. And he's only found one way to turn off the thoughts.

But maybe now he's found another. One that will also help him get back on his feet. Maybe he'll even make enough to move somewhere new, buy himself a fresh start.

"What do you say, bro? Tell me you'll do it."

Tearing his eyes from the hula girl, he gives Scottie a nod. "I'll do it."

***

Perhaps Reggie should have known that it wouldn't go as planned. And he should probably feel bad about what's happened. But he doesn't. Not at all.

Because it's impossible to believe that something that feels so right could possibly be wrong.

He runs his hand down her bare back, making her shiver. "Tell me about your family."

They'd put up a good fight, resisting each other for weeks, but he knew from the moment he saw Trish, from his first look into her eyes, the same warm brown as his favorite baseball mitt had been, that they were destined for this. To become lovers.

"It's just me and my sister now. My parents passed away right after I graduated high school."

"I'm sorry."

She shrugs. He leans forward, brushing his lips against hers, kissing the pain away.

"And your sister?"

"Irish twins. She's eleven months younger."

"Are you close?"

Her blonde hair sways as she shakes her head. Her eyes darken. "No. Not anymore."

"What happened?"

"Nothing. Everything. It was silly really. Not worth talking about."

"Do you miss her?"

Her face turns red, lips trembling as she nods.

"Come here." He wraps her in his arms, holds tight as her tears dampen his shoulder. "I bet she feels the exact same way. You should look her up."

Her muffled voice cracks against his chest. "I'm afraid it's too late for that."

They both freeze at the sound of voices outside the front door. They untangle from each other, gathering their clothes as a key slides into the lock. Their lips meet again briefly; then they hurry to their respective rooms to get dressed, the bolt turning behind their naked backs.

Laughter carries down the hall as he pulls his jeans on. Reggie rolls his eyes. It's no wonder Trish was desperate to get away from this place any way she could. Scottie is continually bringing people home—never any of their friends or people she knows, just whichever random stray he picked up over the course of the day. The endless introductory small talk is exhausting.

He takes his time. Tugs a shirt over his head and runs a hand through his hair. Looks around the bedroom longingly, reluctant to meet the human flavor of the day until he can't put it off any longer. He gets to the kitchen just in time to hear Trish say, "Reggie and I were getting ready to take a walk down the pier if you want to come with?"

Scottie gives him a lopsided grin, one eyebrow arched as he pops a beer. He passes a second bottle to a skinny blonde guy covered in freckles. "Nope. I think we're good here. You two go on without us."

Trish smiles and gives him a kiss on the cheek.

"Enjoy yourselves."

They're almost free when Scottie calls to him. "Hey, Reg?"

Reggie fixes a blank look on his face and forces himself to turn around. "Yeah?"

"You take care of her."

"Of course."

He doesn't take another breath until he feels the late-day sun warm against his face. "That was close," he says.

"Too close."

"We have to be more careful."

"It's your fault."

"How's that?"

"For being so damn irresistible." She bites her lip, punctuating a smile that makes his legs feel weak. "How'd you ever wind up single?"

He breaks her gaze, eyes dropping to his feet. "I'm not the catch you think I am."

"Oh, please. Why? Because you're going through a rough patch? Women don't care about money, Reggie. Not the right ones, at least."

He shakes his head, both dying to tell her and dreading it at the same time. "I wish it were that simple."

"Tell me." Her cool palm catches his. Her head tilts as she gives his hand a squeeze. "Come on. Please? You know you can trust me. It's not going to change the way I feel about you. Promise."

"You're not going to like it."

"Tell me anyways."

Their steps thump hollowly as they step onto the pier. The smell of salt air wraps around them on a warm breeze. A trio of seagulls caw as they ride the downdraft to the shore. Reggie licks his dry lips with a dryer tongue. His heart beats double time, straining against the walls of his chest.

"I was a cop."

Trish laughs. "You?"

"Uh-huh. Me." He squints out over the water, the waves choppy, the sea rough. "But not a very good one."

"Oh, I doubt that."

"No. It's true."

The scent of grilled meat makes his stomach queasy as they pass the restaurants. The smell of booze calls to him like a pair of comforting arms. And he knows if he can't do it, if he can't be honest with this woman right here by his side, then that's the only comfort he'll ever deserve. "I got some kids killed."

Her hand tightens on his.

"Guy ripped off a convenience store. I was tailing him, lights and siren going." He swallows hard against the lump in his throat. "My CO told me to stand down. Let him go. It was the wrong type of area for a car pursuit. Too much traffic. But I followed him anyways."

They reach the end of the pier. She faces him, leaning her back against the railing. He risks a glance. The tears in her eyes sparkle with the rays of the setting sun. Her skin has gone pale, her hand slick with sweat.

"Guy slammed right into a minivan on the way home from a Little League game. Five kids. They never stood a chance, not with me calling myself one of the good guys."

Her palm slips from his. Her chin trembles. Shiny trails streak her cheeks. "I'm so sorry."

"I lost everything. My job. My fiancée. My self-respect. And, until I met you, my will to go on."

Her voice wavers. "I'm so very, very sorry."

She lifts her fingertips to his face and shivers. Her hand drops, bracing against the railing behind her. Then she's gone.

"Trish!" Reggie leaps forward, grasping the rough wood, splinters spearing his flesh as he leans over, searching for a glimpse of her. "Call 911," he shouts, kicking his shoes off. Strong hands seize his arms. "Get off me."

"You can't do it. The riptide will kill you."

"Get the hell off me."

He thrashes, struggling to get free, clawing at the railing, but he's dragged away. A crowd gathers, murmuring as they peer into the sea below. Sirens sound in the distance. Three birds, perhaps the same as before, soar past, beaks open. But the only thing Reggie hears is Scottie's voice as they left, telling him to take care of her.

***

Reggie rolls over, tipping a half-empty bottle of booze. "Motherf—" He snatches it up, the wetness spreading on the sleeve of his already yellowed shirt, and downs what's left as he struggles into a sitting position.

His back is stiff from the hard floor. He looks around, rubbing his bleary eyes, but it doesn't help. He hasn't seen straight in months. And that's how he likes it. At least then he doesn't have to see the face that would reflect back to him in a mirror.

His joints pop as he pushes himself to his feet. He wobbles, tripping over empties, sending bottles rolling across the floor. Something furry skitters in the shadows. He checks his arms, making sure he doesn't have any fresh rat bites, then stumbles to the corner and takes a piss.

He smells rank. The inside of his mouth tastes like kitty litter; his hair so greasy, it feels wet. Dead roach bodies crunch under his shoes as he crosses to the window and peers out through the broken glass. It's already nighttime. Or it's still nighttime. No way to know for sure, since he can't remember what it was when he passed out.

He slaps his pockets even though he knows they're empty. His tongue shifts inside his foul mouth as he eyes the plywood that covers the door. He doesn't want to go out there, not among the people. Not when he's becoming something different, something other, a thing that makes noses wrinkle and eyes dart, footsteps rushing away in haste.

But he's out of supplies, and there's only one way to erase her face from his mind. Or maybe he should just let it stay this time, let her brown eyes haunt him until his madness brings an end to this pitiful existence. Only, he's too weak for that and he knows it.

Reggie lies on the floor, squeezing his way under the board guarding the threshold, the jagged end of the plywood scraping his chest, reopening old scabs and creating fresh scratches as he shimmies past. On the other side, he blinks against the moonlight, flicking a roach carcass from his arm hair. Standing, he sniffs the air like a dog.

The faint pulse of music throbs in the distance. Someone laughs. A woman shrieks. He doesn't want to head that direction, but his feet lead him anyway. It's the best chance he has to beg enough money to quickly dull the pain. No one wants a reminder of what can happen, the perilous nature of the human condition, not when they're busy having fun.

He wanders toward the pier, promising himself he'll pass right by, that he won't stumble down to the beach, weave around the pilings, wet sand clinging to his pants as he futilely searches the murky water. But he can't help himself. As far as he knows, they never found her body.

In the first days that followed, he had slept on the sand, waiting for her to emerge from the sea, hoping for a miracle, or a fairy tale, maybe a mermaid granted her human legs. When local police patrols made him stop, he stole discarded newspapers off bus benches and bistro tables, pouring over the pages for articles about Trish. That ended when Scottie's smiling face was smeared across the cover accompanying a goodwill piece on how his company was injecting fresh money into the local economy.

He didn't get it. How Scottie could go on living, smiling, *profiting* after Trish's death, when Reggie himself could barely manage to draw his next breath. Good fortunes and times were a thing of the past. Now his future bore only the raw pain of loss.

He winces against the lights as they grow brighter, the noise louder, bruising his ears as he approaches the crowds. His nose burns with the sharp scent of mingled perfumes, colognes, and soaps, the acrid stench of cigarette smoke, the smells of the living. Just a few bucks, and he can retreat. Enough for a bottle, and he can go back to his darkness, be alone with his despair.

He keeps his head down as he extends his hand, knowing the revelers would prefer to not actually have to look at him. The sight of a dirty palm makes for easier dreams than the memory of tormented eyes. He lifts his gaze just enough to scan the crowd for a likely mark; they snag on a familiar face.

His knees lock, refusing to carry him forward. His ankles threaten to buckle. His lungs won't work, trapping the air from his last breath inside. A choking sensation builds, his eyes bulging, a cough finally erupting from between his chapped lips.

"Ew, gross."

A cluster of women sidestep him on their way past. He braces his hands against his legs as his lungs purge. After each round of hacking, he lifts his head, searching until he finds him again.

Scottie. Scottie, mouth opened wide, laughing. Scottie, his arm tight around the waist of an underdressed girl, whom he kisses. Scottie, free of grief.

But how can that be?

Reggie retreats, backing into the shadows as Scottie and his group enter a club. He watches. And he waits.

***

Sobriety hurts. Reggie wishes he could have a nip of something, just to take the edge off, but he can't. Because he has a purpose. And that purpose involves staying sharp.

He exits the shower at the shelter and redresses as quickly as possible. He hates to take the risk, to take his eyes off the prize for that long, but it's a necessary evil. He needs to blend in. For that, he needs to be able to pass among them.

He hurries past the cots where he never sleeps, past the food line where he never eats, and past the pamphlets that he never reads, until he feels the heat of the day wrap around him. He jogs down the road, weaving through the other pedestrians, slowing only when he reaches the sidewalk leading to the Epic Enterprises warehouse. Glancing around to make sure no one is watching, he slips into the narrow alley across the street.

Day after day it's the same thing. He's lost track of how many weeks he's spent sneaking from the scrubby bushes in the empty lot down the street from Scottie's house, silently darting between shadows as he follows him to work. Once he feels Scottie's settled, he rushes to the shelter for a quick shower, then heads back here, to the alley, where he forages in the trash cans for scraps and waits for Scottie to reappear.

He follows him to the grocery store, to the gym, to the beach, to the clubs, always watching, always waiting, but he doesn't know for what. Not yet. It's not to see Scottie's girlfriend trip her way into Trish's house every night. Not to know she's sleeping in Trish's bed. It's not even for the opportunity that presents itself the night Scottie passes out on the front porch, when it would be so easy for Reggie to tiptoe over, wrap his hands around Scottie's neck, and put an end to it all.

His gut, that little sliver of cop instinct that inspired him to join the force what seems like not just one lifetime, but several lives ago, tells him to wait. That there's something more. Something that he needs to know first.

Reggie is pulling the cheese off a moldy stub of bread, the stale remnants of another man's lunch, when he glances up and sees Scottie walking through the swinging glass door across the street. He drops the food, his hunger forgotten, and steps out onto the sidewalk in pursuit. Something's up.

Scottie usually doesn't leave his office in the middle of the day. And there's something wrong with his posture. His normal obliviousness has been replaced with a sudden awareness, his head swiveling on his neck as he looks around, like he knows he's being watched. Or he's about to do something he doesn't want anyone else to see.

Reggie slows, lagging as far behind as he can force himself, practically running in place to expel the energy that longs to propel him forward. His hand curls around the crumpled five-dollar bill in his pocket, an unexpected prize scavenged from the trash, someone's change forgotten in the bottom of their take-out bag. That five dollars could buy him so many things. Things that he needs. Things that he wants.

Instead, careful to keep his face turned to the front, he passes it to the driver as he gets on the same bus Scottie boards. He ducks into the first seat, glancing from the corners of his eyes to make sure there's no rear exit. Then he does what he's come to do best. He waits.

It's been a long time since he's been in a vehicle, and the bumps and starts of the bus make him glad for his empty stomach. But that's not the only reason his nerves are on edge. He fingers a hole in his jeans, worrying the edges until he's doubled its size. He stares out the window at the changing landscape, bungalows and condos giving way to businesses, then houses, and finally a run-down mix of apartments and seedy shops. From his peripheral vision, he catches Scottie pulling the cord to signal his stop.

He waits until Scottie has completely disembarked, until the bus is already back in gear, to hop up. "This is my stop. Sorry, sorry." He avoids the annoyed eyes of the driver, the angry stares of the passengers as he hurries down the metal stairs, finding himself on a pockmarked sidewalk, weeds squeezing through the cracks.

Reggie feels a momentary jolt of panic, then glimpses Scottie's back disappearing through the door of an apartment complex down the street. He feels hollow as he dashes up the stairs and into the building, worried about losing Scottie, what he'll do if they get separated by an elevator, how he'll make it back home without bus fare. He's so wrapped in his thoughts that he almost blows his cover, passing within feet of the man as his former acquaintance knocks on the door of a ground-floor unit just inside.

The complex isn't nice enough to have a formal lobby, just an empty space the depth of a small apartment, leading to a stairwell and an elevator on the far wall. Reggie stands before the closed lift, pretending to push a button, watching Scottie's reflection in the dull metal surface as the door he knocked on opens a crack. He gets only a quick glimpse of the face before Scottie pushes his way inside, but it's enough.

His head feels like it's spinning, the room dipping and swaying around him like he's had too much to drink. He sinks to the floor, his palm on something sticky, his breath coming too quickly. He's overheated, on fire, the sweat suddenly springing from his pores barely enough to fight the flames burning beneath his skin.

He's stunned. And confused. Betrayed. But most of all, Reggie is angry.

***

Reggie makes no move to follow Scottie when he emerges from the apartment a short while later. It hasn't been long, but he's done a lot of thinking, or maybe remembering is a better term for it. He's recalled what it feels like to hold his head high, to be able to face himself in the mirror. The way his uniform felt when he put it on, the sense of pride he had when he reported to duty. The elation he felt when his ex-fiancée had said yes when he'd proposed.

You may think it takes a lot to ruin a man, but sometimes, it only takes one thing, a single straw to break the camel's back, so to speak. If it were you, and you were given the choice, what would you do to the straw that broke you?

He takes several deep breaths as he watches Scottie leave; then he exits the stairwell, crosses the lobby, and steps into the hall, stopping before unit 1B. A muscle in his shoulder spasms as he knocks. His pulse drums against the underside of his skin like a hungry woodpecker—tap, tap, tap, tap, tap.

The door opens. Even though he knows what to expect, he stumbles back a step in surprise. Up close, he sees that the time has been no kinder to her than it has to him.

Sharp bones protrude through flesh thinned by . . . by what? Drugs? Hunger? Grief? Or guilt? Her eyes look too big in her gaunt face. He feels them feeding hungrily on him, his skin simultaneously crawling and yearning for her touch.

"Reggie."

She stands back, allowing him inside. He hesitates for only a second before stepping over the threshold, into the shadows beyond. The door is barely closed before she throws her arms around him, squeezing tightly.

He pulls from her embrace, taking a step back. Not trusting her. Not trusting himself.

"Trish."

She shakes her head, lips trembling as tears spill down her cheeks. "No," she whispers.

"Yes."

"No. I was never. I'm Caitlyn."

He feels his mouth curl in a sneer. Realizing he should have expected this, some kind of trick, a trap. "And who's Caitlyn?"

"Trish's sister." She wraps her arms around herself, looking ill. "I never—" She gulps. "I never meant to hurt you. You have to believe me. That's not what was supposed to happen."

Reggie props himself against the back of the couch, feeling light-headed. Weak, woozy, confused. His voice is low as he asks, "What *was* supposed to happen?"

"You were only supposed to be a witness. Someone to confirm that the woman you knew as Trish went over the pier."

The woman he knew as Trish. He thinks back to the random visitors Scottie brought over to the house, not friends, but people he'd just met. To the night Scottie ran into him at the bar. Scottie had known exactly where Reggie would be, what had happened, how down he'd been on his luck. How desperate he'd be for the money he'd make doing what— watching the supposedly suicidal wife of a friend? A woman he didn't know. It all seems so obvious now.

He'd been the perfect mark.

"And your sister? The real Trish?"

"Scottie said there'd been an accident. A blow to the head when she was surfing, that she'd refused to go to the doctor, had said she was fine, but that the next day…" She shakes her head. "She never woke up."

"And you believed him?"

"I did at the time. He seemed so upset. So sincere. Said he'd panicked, that he was afraid they'd blame him for not getting her help, so he'd . . . he'd hidden her body. He told me my sister had provided for me in her will, but since he'd messed up, since there was no way to prove she was dead without him incriminating himself, that we'd have to wait seven years to have her declared dead before I could have it. He said he wanted to make things right, to help me get what was mine."

"But she was your sister."

"Don't you think I know that! I wasn't thinking. All I could hear was that she was already dead, and that she'd left me money, enough so that I could get out of here. Maybe even do something with my life. I was so young when our parents passed, so foolish. I squandered my inheritance in a couple years. But Trish. To find out she'd saved hers, and left part of it to me? It felt like it all happened to give me a second chance. At least, that's what I wanted to believe at the time."

She holds out a hand to him, her eyes begging him to take it. He can barely hear her voice when she says, "I went looking for you, after. I tried to find you, to tell you the truth. And when I couldn't, I thought I'd lost you. Please don't let that be true."

They stare at each other for a long minute. He wants to believe her. He's suffered so much already. They both have. He takes her hand and pulls her to him.

His shirt grows damp as she sobs against his chest. Tears of his own trickle down his cheeks into her hair. It's not until the shadows around them have grown into darkness that either of them pulls away.

Caitlyn leans back just enough to see Reggie's eyes through the gloom. Her voice is hoarse; it wavers as she says, "I think Scottie killed my sister."

The coals inside Reggie blaze a little hotter. It feels like his entire life has been leading to this moment. He tightens his grip around her waist. "What do you want to do about it?"

"I want to make him pay. And I want to bring her home."

***

Reggie hurries through the crowd, head turned, watching over his shoulder. In his haste, he bounces off anyone in his way, seemingly oblivious to the complaints around him. He looks spooked, like a man being chased. Or haunted.

He gives a startled "Oof!" as he knocks into the man in his path. "Sorry," he says, releasing his grip from where he caught himself on the man's arm. He takes a step to the side, reluctantly drags his eyes forward as he apologizes again. "Sorry."

"Reggie?"

Reggie stumbles back a step, eyes widening with recognition, though the man before him is barely recognizable. "You."

Scottie's gaze is wary, his eyes drawn deep into skin the color of a bruised banana. He laughs nervously, runs a hand through his hair, leaving it standing on end. "Bro. Where've you been hiding yourself, man?" He glances at his companions, licks his chapped lips. "I've been wanting to talk to you. Wanted you to know there's no hard feelings."

He takes Reggie by the elbow, leads him several yards away from his group. His new girlfriend rolls her eyes, her laugh a cruel bark that bites through the night air. Scottie's shoulders hunch at the sound of it. He doesn't see the look she gives the man beside her, the way their arms brush against each other's as they stroll away, leaving him behind like a punch line. "Listen, I, um . . ."

Reggie's attention once again drifts behind him, wide eyes searching the sea of faces.

"I gotta ask, dude. Have you been experiencing anything weird?"

Reggie's head jerks forward. His sharp stare pins Scottie like a shirt collar. His words spill out fast. "What do you mean?"

Scottie forces a chuckle. "Nothing, man. I'm just…Nothing. Been working too hard, I guess. Long hours have me seeing things."

Reggie seizes Scottie roughly by the shoulders. "You've seen her, too, haven't you?"

"Whoa." Scottie takes a step back, severing their connection. "Dude, chill." He draws a palm across the waxen skin that's replaced his tan, glancing around, checking to see if anyone's overheard as he says, "Don't know what you're talking about, bro."

Reggie digs in his pocket with one hand. The other strikes like a snake, grabbing Scottie by the wrist. He forces a small item into Scottie's palm.

Scottie stares down at the charm, mouth working like an empty Pez dispenser, gaze bouncing between the tiny silver surfer and Reggie's face. He swallows so loud, Reggie can hear it. His voice wavers as he says, "Where'd you get this? Huh? Where?"

"She told me to give this to you. Now I'm done, man. I'm out." Reggie backs away, wild eyes flashing, movements skittish and jerky. "Do you hear that?" he calls loudly, earning curious looks from the crowd around him. "I'm done. It's over. Now leave me alone." He spins, darts through the milling bodies, vanishing into the night.

***

Reggie slinks into the dark alley. Leans against the side of a building, wiping sweat from his face as he catches his breath. A phone buzzes softly from the shadows beside him.

"Hello?"

"Where are you?"

"My apartment. Why?" Caitlyn gives him a thumbs-up as Scottie's voice continues to rumble at her through the phone.

"We need to meet."

"No. Uh-uh. You're the one who said it was too risky for us to be seen together."

A frustrated growl echoes through the line. "Fine. Listen. You know that necklace your sister always used to wear?"

"The one with the surfer charm on it?"

"Yeah, that one."

"What about it?"

Reggie shoots a sharp look at the crackle of static to his left, draws a finger across his throat to signal silence.

"You had one just like it, right?" Scottie's tone sounds pleading now, like a child begging for something he knows he can't have.

"No. Trish was the surfer. I never got the hang of it, but I loved swimming, so our parents got me a mermaid charm instead. Why?"

There's no answer, just a string of curses before the call ends. Caitlyn frowns at the phone in her hand, then raises her eyes to Reggie's hopefully. "Do you think . . .?"

The radio murmurs with another transmission. A low voice behind them says, "He's on the move."

Reggie pulls her close, nodding as he kisses the top of her head. "Yeah. I do."

***

It feels good, having a purpose again. Being in pursuit. Even if the case isn't his, if he never sees active duty again, the chance to right a wrong is a small victory in the long battle to forgive himself.

It had been a last-minute decision to bring the police in on their plan, but a vital one. It meant forfeiting control, but if this evening played out the way he suspected, a man would be charged with murder by the end of the night.

It had been Caitlyn's idea. A spritz of her sister's perfume in the house when Scottie was gone. Her shoes left out on the floor for him to stumble over when he woke in the morning. Images of Trish taken from pictures, projected against the windows and mirrors of Scottie's house for him to see when no one else was around.

After weeks of gaslighting Scottie, of slowly breaking him down, transforming the man into a ghost of his former cocky self, Reggie knew that he was finally ready to crack. Which is why tonight they played their coup de grâce—a replica of the necklace Trish always wore, a gift from her parents that she never took off, that she was never without, and, from the look on Scottie's face—that she must have been wearing when she died.

They sit in the back of the unmarked car, holding hands. Reminding each other with gentle squeezes to breathe. That the moment they've waited for is close at hand.

Garbled voices carry through the radio, relaying instructions, locations. The car they're in turns the corner, rolls slowly down the street like a cat stalking its prey. Outside, they hear shouting. The radio transmissions become louder, a frenzied melee of individuals struggling to be heard. Caitlyn moans, covering her face with her hands.

Reggie stares out the window, head cocked as he listens to the confusion. His knuckles blanch as his fingers tighten into fists. His eyes narrow, head craning forward as he searches the shadows beyond the glass. He throws the door open, springing from the vehicle.

Caitlyn gasps his name. The officer behind the wheel yells it.

But it's too late. His legs pump, long strides eating up the sidewalk as he races down the street. He skids around the corner, struggling to maintain speed and balance. The car engine grumbles as it follows him.

Reggie darts into an alley, squeezing into the dark space between two houses. He draws to a stop, falling silent. Holds his breath. Raises an arm in front of his face, elbow out. Braces himself. Staggers from the contact but remains standing.

"Been wanting to do that since high school."

The comment falls on deaf ears. Scottie is flat on his back before him, out cold.

***

Reggie watches the hula girl's hands shift. Her hips sway, a dance to celebrate the changing of the hour. He shimmies in his seat, joining her. Time no longer feels like a threat mocking him.

"Should I be jealous?"

He turns, grins as Caitlyn enters the room. "Nah. It's strictly professional. Nothing more."

She smirks, eyebrow arching. "Mmhmm. Sure."

"Seriously." He jumps up, does his best hula dance for her. "I'm going pro. Gonna turn it into a full-time gig."

Laughing, she closes the distance between them, loops her arms around his neck. "I like this side of you. And the midday visit. What's the occasion?"

"We're celebrating."

"We are?"

"Yep. Thought I might be able to convince you to play hooky so we could get an early start on it."

Caitlyn tilts her head to give him the side-eye. "I've got a few more hours of work here. But . . . ." She purses her lips, gives him a coy look.

"But," he prods.

"But there are some perks to being the boss. Tell you what. Why don't you go pull the car around? I'll meet you downstairs in five."

Reggie punches the air, does a victory dance like a rowdy teenager as she shoos him out the door with a giggle. He'll do anything to make her laugh, to earn a smile. There'd been a dark stretch of months that he'd feared she wouldn't pull out of after Scottie had led them to her sister's body. The unequivocal proof found by the medical examiner that her sister had been murdered had almost broken her, even after Scottie had been banished behind bars.

When the courts had awarded her sole ownership of Epic Enterprises, a company built with her sister's money to manufacture Trish's—not Scottie's—innovative wetsuit design, she'd thrown herself into running the business, almost losing herself to her desire to build

Trish's legacy. He'd walked a tightrope as he supported her success while also encouraging her to take time for herself, to grieve and heal, and yes, even enjoy life. A work-fun balance had seemed like a betrayal to Caitlyn, and he was the bad influence.

But he'd dedicated himself to supporting her, and now things weren't just good. They were great. And with the woman he loves in a good place, the time has finally come for him to move forward.

He steps out into the bright day, thinking of the job offer he accepted earlier that afternoon. There'd been a time when a full reinstatement of his duties as a police officer had seemed beyond his wildest dreams, but after he'd apprehended Scottie, his former superiors had opened the lines of communication. He'd known the offer was coming for a while, and now that it has, well, now he can proceed with his real reason to celebrate. He pats the small square box in his pocket, thinks of his future, and smiles.

Shannon Hollinger - With degrees in crime scene technology and physical anthropology, this Florida author hasn't just seen the dark side of humanity—she's been elbow deep inside of it! Her short fiction has appeared in *Suspense Magazine*, *The Saturday Evening Post*, and *Mystery Magazine*. Her debut novel, the psychological thriller *Best Friends Forever*, will be released in January 2023 and is the first of a five-book deal with publisher Bookouture.

To see where you can find more of her work, check out **www.shannonhollinger.com**.

Seal Colony

Brian Asman

Hey, kids. Here's the deal.

If you've got a fake ID and wanna have a good time in Pacific Beach, there's a couple things to keep in mind.

First, you don't go to any of the upscale bars, the joints with so much to lose, they scan everybody's ID, no matter how old. You go to a place like the Electric Otter—cheap beer, worn carpets, shitty lighting. There's no DJ, but there is a juke, a couple pool tables, and some heavy goddamn pours. It's a good time, and with no scanner at the door, that's one less thing to worry about.

What you *do* have to worry about is Darren.

He's the guy on the stool, in the black *SECURITY* shirt, short beard and shaved head, tattoos up and down his arms. Three inches under six feet, but the way that black shirt bulges, the way those gray eyes glower at you, his height's the last thing you're thinking about. Darren's got the final say on whether you're going to have a good time, a bad time, or go home and drink box wine out of the fridge.

Which could be a good time or a bad time or something in between, depending.

If you want to get past Darren, there's two things you can try. You could roll up to the door, ID already in hand and a smile on your face, make things easy on him, and maybe he'll appreciate that and not give you shit about the fact that the kid in the picture's got a different nose, different jaw, whatever. Or you could leave the ID in your wallet, throw a strut in your step, act like you belong, and hope that peach fuzz on your chin answers his questions in advance.

Darren's no dummy, and since he actually gives a shit about his job, it's probably not going to work anyway, but the odd nineteen-year-old frat boy's been known to slip past.

What you definitely *don't* want to do is drop your ID while you're handing it to him, then fall on your ass when you go to pick it up.

"Careful," Darren says mildly, while the teenage polo-shirted body-spray addict crawls around on his hands and knees, looking for his older brother's driver's license.

The kid finds it, peels it off the floor with some grody black gunk smeared across the name and address, and shoves it in Darren's general direction. He's at least three feet off the mark.

Darren eyes the kid, a look that's usually enough to end all further inquiries. "Not happening. Go get yourself a hot dog." He nods at the sidewalk. The hot dog man's spooning relish onto a foot-long.

The kid sways his way to his feet, leans on the doorframe. "Come on. I was in here earlier."

Darren's been on since four, helping Giselle set up the bar. If the kid was in earlier, he was drinking with the Rudolphs—red-noses, the folks who drink the day away and clear out when the college kids pour through the doors.

Not that it matters.

Darren slides a foot off his stool.

The kid's drunk, but the gesture doesn't go unnoticed. He backs away, slips his ID in his pocket.

"Make sure you clean that shit off before you try it again," Darren calls after him.

Technically he's supposed to *take* the IDs, but the license never actually made it into his hand, so Darren figures it's not his problem. Besides, he was young once.

"Hey, D!" Giselle yells from the bar. Her tone says she's yelled a couple times already, but it's loud as shit inside; Axl's wailing and scatting from every speaker.

Darren swivels, looks across the room. Still early, maybe half-full of sunburned surfers and assorted beach rats. The bar runs down the right side of the joint, pool tables and dart boards to the left, bathrooms in the back.

Giselle's standing behind the bar, a jigger in her hand and three shot glasses lined up for three dudes with backwards hats. She points with the jigger at an old guy slumped on the bar, face down on a forearm, his shaggy gray Caesar cut glowing bluish under all the neon. His wallet's lying open on the bar top next to him, a half-empty rocks glass next to that.

One of the regulars—Murph. Kind of guy doesn't know when to close out.

For a minute Darren wonders if he's dead. Unlikely, but one old drunk busted a sprocket in the bathroom at his girl Jessica's bar a couple years back—went out just like Elvis, minus the peanut butter sandwich because they sure as shit don't fuck with outside food or drink at the Driftwood.

You never really know.

Giselle's shaking the jigger at him, mouthing something that gets lost under Axl's sweet *chi-yi-yi-yild*s and *my-yi-yi-yine*s, but her intent's obvious. Nothing ruins a good time like a passed-out old man, some Ghost of Christmas Future reminding everybody else the party doesn't last forever.

And then there's the health department.

Darren slides off his stool, cruises on over to the bar. He pats Murph on the shoulder. "Hey."

Nothing.

He grabs his shoulder, but Murph just slides back into place.

Darren picks up his wallet, yells to Giselle, "He pay his tab?"

She gives a thumbs-up, so Darren shoves the wallet in Murph's back pocket.

Murph doesn't notice.

Maybe he really is *dead,* Darren thinks, then pulls him away from the bar.

Murph's head lolls back, his mouth falls open, saliva running freely; then he's shoving Darren away. He tries to make a break for it, trips, catches the bar, and keeps himself upright, which is more than Darren can say for the kid with the fake ID outside.

Even accounting for posture, he's still a couple inches south of Darren, and Darren, he's not the kind of guy who can get by on his height.

Down there, clutching the bar, Murph looks small, pathetic.

Work the room long enough, you realize pathetic and harmless aren't the same thing, not by a long shot.

"Yo, Murph. Time to go."

Murph looks at him, blinks a couple times. "I'm okay."

"How many times do I have to tell you? No sleeping at the bar."

"Wasn't sleeping."

Darren points at the security camera. "You want to check the tape?"

"Yeah?"

"No, you fucking don't. Let's go."

"My wallet."

"Back pocket."

Murph blinks again, reaches around back. Pat-pat. He nods. "Thanks."

"Sure. Now—"

Murph lunges for the half-finished drink on the bar, but Giselle's faster; she snags it and dumps it out in the sink.

"*No mas,*" she says, shaking the empty glass at him.

"Come on, just one more."

Crash!

Breaking glass, over by the pool tables. Darren whips his head around—Choy and a couple of his buddies laughing. One of them's staring at a busted bottle of Longboard Lager at his feet, a pool cue in his hand. Doesn't take CSI to figure he set it on the rail, against Darren's repeated instructions, and knocked it off, trying to make some dumbass trick shot.

Choy and the boys always bring some bullshit with them, but not every patron's created equal. The owner's a surf nut, creams himself over the fact that Choy had a spread in the July 1998 issue of *Surfer.* Never mind he hasn't done much since but throw rocks at lawyers who try to paddle out at *his* break, but that's none of Darren's business.

A guy like Murph can't handle his booze, he gets kicked out. Choy and the boys? Darren gets the mop.

"Let's go, I got shit to do," Darren says, grabbing Murph by the arm and muscling him toward the door.

Murph wrenches away, marches out himself.

At the door he turns and jabs a finger at Darren. "You can't fucking do this to me. I was a Navy SEAL!"

Place like PB, Navy SEALs are a dime a dozen. Or rather guys who *say* they're Navy SEALs. It's like a goddamn SEAL colony.

"Get home safe," Darren says, and goes to get the mop.

***

Murph comes back.

Shit's winding down in the Otter, the evening crowd making their way west on Garnet, toward the more upscale bars. Reason they call it "pregaming" and not "game-gaming." Darren doesn't get offended.

The Otter is what it is.

He gets the broken bottle cleaned up, clears glasses off a high-top, intercepts some kids at the door who turn out to be in their thirties (with valid ID, even), changes a Bud Light keg for Giselle, fights the urge to unplug the juke when somebody plays Garth fucking Brooks, counts his blessings when "Brilliant Disguise" comes up next, cracks his knuckles, cracks his neck, turns down an offer to join Choy and the boys in a game of Punch Me in the Dick, surveys the bar and likes what he sees, then sits down on his stool again, digging the hot dog–scented breeze through the doorway.

Something he's still not sick of, even after half a decade of sharing space with the hot dog guy.

Whose name, no bullshit, is Frank.

A couple kids stream out the door, including Choy—who feints a sack tap in Darren's direction but isn't quite dumb enough to let it connect—and his idiot friends, the guy who broke the bottle babbling about some trick shot he made, and some other jackass telling him it didn't count because the toe of his Vans left the floor, and Darren thinks maybe with a running start he could push the whole cluster of dick-knocking dipshits in front a passing car all at once.

Even with the noise from the juke (deep cuts from Tupac, the *Makaveli* album) he hears Frank go, "Hey, put that shit back!"

Then Murph lurches into the doorway. Both hands holding a ketchup bottle, pointing right at Darren.

Murph screams something and squeezes.

Ketchup splurts, sails through the air.

Darren stumbles back; it lands on his stool. He stares at Murph.

"Did you just shoot ketchup at me?"

Murph squeezes the bottle again; another splotch lands on his own shoes. "Oh, fuck."

Darren's got nothing. Guys have come at him with pool cues, barstools, knucks. More than one woman has taken off her shoe and tried to whup him with it. Fools throw drinks at him. A lot.

Nobody's ever tried to squirt him with ketchup before.

"Gimme that shit back," Frank says, appearing in the doorway behind Murph.

Murph turns, gingerly holds it out to him.

Frank snatches the bottle. "Ketchup's for customers, asshole."

If some twentysomething douchebag tried that, you'd better believe Darren would lay him the fuck out.

Maybe it's Frank, snatching the bottle away. Maybe it's Murph, already stumbling down the sidewalk with ketchup all over his shoes, head held low.

Whatever it is, Darren goes and gets himself a roll of paper towels and the 409.

***

He goes home to Jessica. She's already in bed, scrolling through her phone. Delilah, their pit bull, is curled up at her feet.

"Good night?" he asks.

"Slow. They cut me around eleven, I walked with about one-fifty."

The Driftwood, the Otter, they're like counterweights. Old-school dives holding down PB from the freeway to the boardwalk. Similar clientele, although the Drift's got more windows, so people tend to go there for fun, not for medicine.

Jessica puts her phone on the nightstand. "How was yours?"

"You know. The usual."

"You've got something on your shirt. Ew, is that blood?"

Darren looks down—the white *S* in *SECURITY* is spattered with red.

"Ketchup," he says. "Just ketchup."

***

Murph doesn't show for a few days. Then he doesn't show for a few more. Darren only notices because none of the bartenders ask him to kick Murph out.

It's a good thing—Darren's decided Murph is banned. He tells the day bartender, Allegra. She doesn't object.

He tells the other bartenders, the other door guy. Nobody's got a problem. They've banned people before—Donny Piss-Pants being the most notable example—and even one of Choy's boys is permanently eighty-sixed for bringing a gun to a bar fight.

(Not that he *pulled* it on anyone; rather it fell out of his sweatpants while he was running *away* from a fight between Choy and some Marine).

With Murph gone, Darren's surprised to see nobody else picks up the slack. None of the regulars dial up their own behavior to supplement the sad, drunk-ass energy Murph brought to the place, and fate doesn't see fit to drop a clutch of HAs or Sin-Eaters or Dirty Water Crips at their doorstep. The Marines respectfully crush cans of Busch Light against their wide foreheads. Choy and his boys don't let their games of grab-ass leak out of their own circle.

Everybody's cool.

Almost like Murph was the cause of every headache, conflict, whatever, and now he's gone, shit's just peaceful.

Every night, Giselle looks bored, sitting there twirling strands of Targaryen-blonde hair around an index finger.

One day she calls him over. "Can you see my roots?"

Darren makes a show of looming over her, inspecting the part in her hair. *Not in this light,* he thinks—she's blonde already, but not blonde enough in her own estimation. "Looks okay," he says.

"Just okay?" She's mooning at him, lips pouting.

Darren shrugs and goes back to his stool. Giselle's not bad to look at, but he's got Jessica.

A fact that wouldn't stop most of the bouncers he knows, and most he doesn't.

But Darren's not them.

Darren's Darren.

***

Murph shows.

Four fifteen on a Wednesday. Nobody's around, so Darren's vacuuming under the pool table; somebody says, "Hey," and it's Murph, standing in the doorway with his hat literally in his hand. He's shaved, got a haircut, a clean shirt. Eyes that look like they see you.

Murph gestures with his hat. "Can I come in?"

Darren looks down at the *S* on his shirt, slightly off-color from the other letters. It's just a shirt. He nods and says, "Yeah."

Murph sits.

Giselle's in the can, doing her makeup, so Darren goes behind the bar. "You want something?"

"Look, the other night—"

Darren points to the *SECURITY* across his shirt. "Technically, I'm not supposed to serve drinks. So I'm definitely not playing psychiatrist."

"Fair." Murph eyes the row of bottles behind the cash register and says, "The usual."

Darren waits.

"Scotch, rocks," Murphy says.

Darren nods. He pulls a glass, tosses in some ice, grabs the Glenfiddich.

"Uh, well scotch. Please."

Darren looks him in the eye—other than the broken blood vessels, he looks good. All there.

"Told you I'm not a bartender," he says, and pours. "First one's on the house."

Murph takes the glass, sniffs it, puts it back down. Maybe he's doing that thing drunks do, they sit there eyeing their first drink long as they can, fifteen, twenty minutes, and then they take that first sip and the drink's gone, they're gone, it's all gone.

Giselle's still not back yet.

Murph finally sips. Puts it back down. Walks over to the juke and feeds it a couple bucks. Takes his time, picking songs.

The Boss comes on, "Tunnel of Love," and when Murph finally sits back down, he says, "I know you don't want to hear it, but I'm sorry. Other night? I got it under control now."

Darren's heard it a million times. They've always got it under control. They're always getting it under control. It was just a bad night, never mind all the other bad nights.

Giselle comes out, gives him a weird look, but she doesn't say anything—kicking guys out is Darren's gig.

Darren finishes vacuuming, hits the ice machine, fills up the caddy behind the bar.

Murph's still on his first drink.

Then the happy hour crowd rolls in, and Darren gets caught up with the usual. Frank pulls up at the curb in his truck, unloads his hot dog cart. A stream of kids come and go; the smell of grilled wieners fills the air.

Nobody squirts ketchup at Darren, or mustard, or even fucking mayonnaise.

Murph's back, and it's quiet.

Later on he leaves. He gives Darren a nod, and his eyes?

They're still seeing him.

***

Sunday afternoon.

Football's on, and even though the Chargers pulled up stakes and moved to a city that doesn't want them, the Otter is *packed*. Everybody in PB's from somewhere else anyway, as the sea of Lions and Bengals and Bears jerseys attest, and nobody's going to drink a fucking craft cocktail with a sprig of thyme or some shit while they're screaming at the goddamn linebacker to get in Pat Mahomes's face. The Otter's got the dish, the cheap drinks; it's the perfect place to kick back with the boys and get mad about shit you can't do a thing about.

Days like these, Darren spends half his time directing traffic—all the delivery guys coming in to drop off pizza or whatever, since they've got no on-site grub. Frank the Hot Dog Man is really Frank the Hot Dog God, and on Sundays the Hot Dog God rests.

They've got two bartenders on, Giselle plus this guy Parker. Darren doesn't really know him, but he stays out of Darren's way, so that's cool.

Murph comes in, wearing a Dolphins hat. Looks about as straight as he did the last time. They nod; Murph grabs a stool.

"ID?" Darren says to the kid walking in behind him.

The kid stops, looks confused for a second, then smiles. "Sorry. Been a minute since I've been carded."

Darren knows it's a fake before the kid's got his wallet halfway out his pocket.

Darren eyes the license, eyes the kid, who turns his head slightly sidewise (smart trick—give 'em a partial profile instead of the full-face DMV shot, play down any differences). Thing is, this is either a really good fake, or the kid's got a doppelgänger a couple years older. The possibility that the kid in front of him really is Steven Lombard of 2988 Diamond Ave never crosses his mind.

If he had a scanner, he'd know for sure, but he doesn't, so Darren asks, "What's your driver's license number?"

The kid blinks. "Why would I know that?"

Right answer. Darren doesn't know his own DL number.

Worst thing you can do is memorize everything.

"Have fun," he says, handing the license back. The kid tucks it back into his wallet and saunters into the bar, no rush at all.

He still thinks no way that kid is twenty-one. But he's smart enough to be, and out of professional courtesy, Darren's not going to jack him up any further.

Darren's a door guy. He questions people. But sometimes, well, it's not even easier, per se, but it's *nicer* to take them at their word. Assume they're exactly who they say they are.

Some lies, we can live with.

Skate wheels screech on cement. Choy and his boys roll up. One of the other dudes can't get stopped and slams into the fire hydrant, board going one way, him going the other. His legs cartwheel in the air; he does a full backflip and lands on his ass.

Laughing the laugh of the extremely fucking wasted.

Darren realizes he's wincing for the guy (*fucking* tailbone, *bro),* but Choy's over there, helping him up; the other dude comes back with his board—"Almost went down the sewer, bro"—so maybe Fall Guy's going to be all right.

The three of them try to stow their boards by the door, Choy and the other guy leaning their wheels against the brick, but Fall Guy Pee-wee Hermans it, knocking all three over.

And they laugh.

And they laugh.

Funniest shit ever. Fall Guy's bent over at the waist; he picks up all three boards and leans them against the wall, but Choy gives him a sack tap from the back, and he goes down, hard like he should have when he hit the fucking fire hydrant, and all the boards go flying.

Fall Guy's falling-down drunk. His other buddy's braying like a donkey.

And Choy?

Choy's watching it all go down, working that jaw like a typewriter, *clacka-lacka-lack*. He rubs his nostril with a knuckle. Then he smooths out his jeans, right where the pocket descends, runs his thumb over a little rectangular outline that sure as fuck looks like a two-milliliter plastic baggie.

He does it again. Pats it. Sticks a hand in his pocket.

Whole time, he's rocking back and forth on his heels, jaw going.

Darren knows the move. He's done it himself.

Coke turns everybody OCD.

The boards fall down again. Choy shoves his idiot friends out of the way, goes to take care of business himself.

There's a knife in his back pocket.

There's also an *ABSOLUTELY NO WEAPONS* sign above the ATM.

Not like there's a metal detector, and Darren doesn't have X-ray vision, so there's probably a half dozen or so guys in the bar, packing an edge of some kind. Most are harmless, a little something to make them feel better on the stumble home.

But you can't flaunt it. You do?

Anyone else, he'd say, not today, *ese*.

But Choy's got Riccardo's number in his cell. And Riccardo thinks it's very, very cool that Choy had a spread in the July 1998 issue of *Surfer*.

And yeah, he hasn't done nothing except chuck rocks at kooks since, but try telling Riccardo that—a pro surfer's good for the bar's image.

Boards are stacked and staying. Choy backs away, exaggerated slow, hands up. Fall Guy starts to say something but Choy shushes him.

Such a fucking production.

Darren doesn't check their IDs, since they're regulars, but he does move to block the door.

Choy looks at him like *What the fuck?* His buddies don't clock it; Fall Guy walks right into the other guy's back, who turns and pushes him.

"What gives?"

Darren puts a hand out. "The knife," he says. "I'll hold on to it for you."

"It's my knife."

Choy doesn't *really* need to be a dick—not like Darren's asking for his blow. But asking Choy not to be a dick is like asking nachos not to be delicious.

Darren points to the sign above the ATM. When Choy doesn't look, he says, "No weapons."

"Come on, I'm in here all the time. You never hassled me before."

"I never saw it before." Darren's hand is still out. He flexes his palm.

"Yo, I think I see Jade," Fall Guy says, looking over Darren's shoulder. He's dancing from one foot to the other. "Oh yeah, Lydia's with her too."

"Lydia?" Other Dude says. "Damn, she's—" He cuts himself off, starts humping the air, turns to Fall Guy, and pretend humps his leg.

Or actually humps his leg.

"Knife?" Darren says again.

Choy looks from Other Dude to Fall Guy, back to Darren, face screwed up. But he reaches in his pocket, pulls the knife, goes to hand it to Darren.

He's laying it in Darren's hand when it pops open.

"Oh, shit!"

Darren yanks his hand back; the knife falls to the ground.

"Sorry," Choy says, and maybe he actually means it, but he's already slipping past Darren into the bar, his two buddies dogging his heels.

Darren picks up the knife, thinking he needs to update his résumé. Find a new boss who's not so impressed by twenty-year-old glossies of a teenage punk shredding Windansea.

He pockets the knife, sits back down on the stool. Hopes Choy doesn't start any shit inside. Knows he's not that lucky. He shoots a look over at the bar—Giselle and Parker are working it, busy but not slammed. Murph's got a scotch, still mostly full; he's glued to one of the many TVs above the bar—Dolphins versus Pats.

Things are humming along nicely until all of a sudden Giselle's shouting in his ear.

"What the fuck?"

"Sorry. It's loud." Giselle's worked up, fiddling with her jewelry. "Look, you have to do something about Choy."

Darren sighs. "You know Riccardo—"

"He's doing coke."

Darren shrugs.

"On the pool table."

Now *that's* some shit.

Darren sticks his head in the door just in time to see Choy ripping rails off the fucking *rail* of the pool table. He tosses his head back, beats his chest, rolled-up dollar-dollar bill y'all still sticking out his nostril.

Fall Guy grabs that dollar bill and rips a line himself. *Très* hygienic.

Half the bar's watching them. The other half's got money on the game. Young Stevie Lombard sidles over with a Bud longneck and tries to cadge a line. Fall Guy tells him to fuck off.

Darren can't hear anything over the music, the chatter, but working in a loud-ass bar is like half an education in lipreading.

Posture reading, too—Stevie's face flushes; he walks away with a shred of the confidence he came with.

"Coke," Giselle is saying. "*In* the bar. I mean, I like skiing, too, but there's a time and place. A time and place, Darren."

"Yeah," Darren says. "He can't do that shit."

Darren slides off the stool.

Choy and Other Dude are brushing coke dust off the pool table, getting ready to rack 'em up again.

The balls, not the blow.

Fall Guy pushes through the men's room door—maybe that coke's cut with baby laxative, who knows.

Either way, he's out of the picture for the moment.

Darren reaches behind the juke and yanks the power cord. The machine goes dead; the music cuts out.

This isn't a movie. He doesn't need a soundtrack. What he needs is for Choy to hear him.

Everybody's still talking; then the chatter peters out when they realize the music's gone.

Including Choy and his buddy.

"Yo, who killed the tunes?" Other Dude asks.

Choy knows. Choy's staring straight at Darren, watching him cross the room, weave around some guy with an honest-to-god cheddar hat on.

Darren pulls up on the other side of the pool table, crosses his arms. "You need to leave."

Nobody cares about the music anymore. Other than the clink of glasses behind the bar—Parker and Giselle, professional as fuck—all eyes are on the pool table.

What Darren wants, anyway. Egregious as this shit is, there's a chance Riccardo gives him his walking papers. And if that's happening, why the fuck not shine a light on this ass clown?

Try something, a little voice inside Darren says, but he shushes it because honestly he doesn't want to fight three guys, even three guys who are all fucked up. He doesn't really want to fight one guy, unless he has to.

A lot of bouncers do. But Darren?

Choy twirls his pool cue. "We're in the middle of a game."

"Game's over."

Choy smirks. "Nah, I'm gonna play this out. Then maybe we'll head down to Shore Club."

"Choy—"

"We're not leaving until I'm ready. So go take your ass up front and watch my fucking knife. Capisce?"

Bold way to talk to a guy you know's holding a knife, no?

Darren looks from Choy to his goober friend, who's drinking directly out of a pitcher and only half paying attention.

"Last chance," Darren says, even though he knows it's a losing battle.

Choy bends over the pool table, threads the cue through his fingers, and breaks.

Clack!

Darren's around the table. Choy takes a step back, flips the cue so he's holding it with both hands. Eyes wild, he swings at the air, forcing Darren back.

"Fuck you, bitch! You want to fuck with me? You want to fuck with *me?*"

Too fast, breathless.

Darren snatches the cue out of his hands, grabs a fistful of shirt. Drives Choy up against the wall.

The pitcher *donks* him on the side of the head.

Not hard—it's goddamn plastic.

Darren tosses Choy and spins around. Other Dude's there, bouncing on his heels like Muhammad Ali, waving the empty pitcher. Darren slaps it out of his hands; the pitcher goes flying and bounces off the silent juke.

"Are you fucking kidding me?" Darren says, and swings.

Hard.

Other Dude takes it in the jaw, drops like a sack of rotten oranges. Hits his head on the pool table on the way down.

Cries of "Oh shit" echo throughout the bar.

Darren's dimly aware of all the assholes filming on their fucking phones.

Then Choy jumps on his back.

The weight staggers him; a bony arm shoots across his throat. Darren claws at it, gets his fingers between forearm and Adam's apple, then pitches forward.

Slamming Choy on the pool table. Balls go flying.

The eight rolls into the side pocket.

Choy flails, grabs the cue ball, tries to hit Darren, but he's on his back. No leverage. Darren grabs his wrists, yanks him off the table, dumps him on the ground.

Choy tries to get up, but Darren stomps on his chest and leans, hard, every ounce of his two-oh-five applied without a lick of mercy. Choy grabs his ankle, tries to pry him loose, but even with all that coke in his system, he can't do shit.

Darren twists around. "Hey, Parker? Give me a hand with these assholes."

Parker nods and drops his bar rag, then—

Chik-chak.

Fall Guy's back from the bathroom.

With a Glock.

He's holding it sideways, hand shaking with fear and blow, but a scared guy with a gun is still a fucking guy with a gun.

And objectively worse than a *confident* guy with a gun.

"Get the fuck offa him!" Fall Guy screams, wiping at his nose with his sleeve.

Darren's hands go high, but he's not easing up on Choy. He probably should let him go, take a swarm beating if Choy wants some get-back, because—*Holy shit that fucking asshole's got a gun.*

That would be the smart thing.

But Darren's not that kind of guy.

"Come on, put the gun down." He searches his memory banks for the guy's name, but he doesn't have it, not even a wild guess. He leans harder. Choy whines in pain.

"I mean it," Fall Guy says, the barrel waving back and forth. "I'll fucking do it, don't think I—"

"Hey."

The sound's soft, makes no sense for a situation where one guy's got a gun, the other guy's looking down the tube, there's a dude on the floor getting crushed by Doc Martens, and another one lights-out under the pool table.

But it gets their attention.

Fall Guy, Darren, they both turn at the same time, and there's fucking Murph, of all people, easing up on Fall Guy's flank.

He's got his hands up, T-ed out away from his body.

His Dolphins hat's on backwards.

"Hey," he says again, softly, and then the words all come tumbling from his lips like a stream. "Look, you don't want to do this, let's all just take a step back, no reason to get crazy, it's just a bar fight, right? What's your name, anyway? They call me Smurf."

Smurf?

Murph?

"These things happen, but hey, no reason you can't put the gun away, take a walk out the back—"

Fall Guy doesn't notice this; he's looking back and forth between Murph, the harmless old guy, and Darren, the real fucking threat, but Murph?

He's inching closer.

"—and then we all just chalk this one up to 'boys will be boys,' right?"

Fall Guy sees it. Levels the gun at Murph.

A flash.

Scene deleted.

One minute Fall Guy's got the gun, the next it's in Murph's hand, and then the butt smacks against the side of Fall Guy's head, and he goes down.

Hard.

Murph, casual as you please, ejects the clip, racks the slide, dumps the chambered round into his pocket.

Sets the gun on the pool table.

He looks at Darren. "For the ketchup thing."

Murph walks away with the clip, back to the bar. Picks up his drink and takes a sip, maybe a long one, but he's not fucking *chugging* it or anything.

Sets the glass back down.

Spins his Dolphins cap around.

And walks the fuck out.

Six or seven hours later, everybody stops holding their breath, starts chattering:

"Oh, shit!"

"You see that?"

"Fucking badass, bro, fucking badass!"

Darren's pulse is beating a mile a minute.

Choy's still fucking with Darren's ankle, trying to get free.

Darren *really* wants to hit somebody.

Fall Guy's still knocked the fuck out. Same with Other Dude. Choy's the only one who's up and at 'em.

Darren rears back, and for a second, Choy thinks he's letting him up; he gets that kind of hopeful look in his eye like maybe, maybe, Darren's gonna forgive and forget.

Then the boot comes down.

Hard.

***

The cops show. Then the ambulances. Fall Guy and Other Dude get checked out, taken off in the backs of separate squad cars.

Choy goes to the ER with an orbital fracture, a concussion, and a mouthful of broken teeth.

The cops ask a few questions, but they're not surf fans, so for them it's exactly what it looks like. Drugged-out dipshits packing heat, causing trouble. A bouncer doing his job. A Good Samaritan going above and beyond.

They watch a couple videos; everything's confirmed.

Everybody's phone cut off right after Murph made his exit.

Allegedly.

***

Everybody's gone.

Something about a near-death experience, when it's all over? Really sucks the air out of a room. Tabs are settled, drinks left unfinished.

Darren, Giselle, and Parker talk it over. *Shut it down* is the consensus. They draw straws to see who gets to call Riccardo, explain what exactly just happened.

Obviously Darren loses.

He uses the phone behind the bar. He's never used it before, but he figures calling from the bar phone rather than his cell, well, maybe that'll make it seem more official. Shield him from some of the blame that's sure to come.

The phone rings. Once, twice. Goes to voicemail. There's no message, just a beep.

Darren says to call the bar and hangs up.

They stand around, looking at each other. Giselle pours them each a shot. They clink glasses.

The phone rings, like Riccardo can tell they're drinking his fucking booze on the house.

Giselle and Parker look at Darren.

He tosses his shot back and picks up the phone.

"What's going on?" Riccardo asks.

Darren tells him.

Rails of coke. Bar fight gone bad. Everybody running for the exits.

Oh yeah, and cops. Lots of cops.

Darren doesn't say who. Just some guys.

"Holy shit," Riccardo says, "take the night off. All of you. You're okay?"

"Yeah. Nobody got hurt. Except, uh…" And here he's thinking maybe don't say anything, but PB's a small town, word's wending its way to Riccardo's ears as they speak.

So Darren says, "Just so you know. The guy got the worst of it? Choy."

There's a pause on the other line. "Who?"

Giselle and Parker are breaking down the bar, trying to act like they're not listening intently to every single thing he's saying.

"You know," Darren says, "that ex-pro surfer? Thought he was a buddy of yours."

"I have no idea who you're talking about. Lock up and go home, okay?"

"Yeah, okay."

Ten minutes later, they're gone.

***

Darren gets home before Jessica, who's stuck at the Drift until the game's over. He goes into the bathroom, scrubs blood out of his Docs with an old toothbrush from under the sink. After he's done, the bristles are stained pink. He wraps the toothbrush in toilet paper and shoves it in the wastebasket.

He goes out to the living room, gets himself a beer. Flips the game on—he's got no love for Pats nor Fins, but the guy he's playing in fantasy has Brady. Might as well root for some INTs.

Darren sits and feels the knife still folded up in his back pocket. He pulls it out, flips it open. Runs a finger along the serrated edge.

It's a good knife.

The game goes to commercial. It's that Snickers thing, where the guy's not feeling quite like himself until he unwraps three bucks' worth of chocolate peanuts and shoves it in his mouth.

Darren sticks the knife's point under the edge of the beer label, peels it off.

Pretends he's drinking something better until the beer's gone, and it's time to get another one.

Brian Asman is a writer, actor, and producer from San Diego, CA. He's the author of the hit indie novella *Man, Fuck This House* (recently optioned by a major streaming service). His other books include *I'm Not Even Supposed to Be Here Today* from Eraserhead Press and *Nunchuck City* and *Jailbroke* from Mutated Media. A film he co-wrote and produced, *A Haunting in Ravenwood*, is available now on DVD and VOD from Breaking Glass. His short *Reel Trouble* will premiere at Gen Con later this summer. Brian holds an MFA from UC Riverside at Palm Desert. He's represented by Dunham Literary, Inc. Max Booth III is his hype man.

Find him on Instagram or Twitter (@thebrianasman), Facebook (brian.asman.14), or his website www.brianasmanbooks.com.

Lili's Song

Jenny Bhatt

Before the sun climbs above the high-rises, a baby shrieks on the pavement across the street, a mynah scolds from a nearby balcony railing, and a dog howls at the rattling of their hired gold-colored Ford Figo. In an hour or so, all sounds will merge into a cacophonous medley led by the added drone of Mumbai traffic. This India visit has come after a gap of more than a decade, so that—despite Lili being a twenty-one-year-old college junior—every sight, sound, and sensation is a fascinating mirage to her. Her hometown of McKinney, Texas is anylittletown, USA compared to this chaotic, shape-shifting country of her parents.

It was her parents' idea to send Lili to enjoy her Christmas break in India with her cousin. It is this cousin's wish for them to spend most of this break in Goa. And it is the cousin's husband's insistence that they drive the four-hundred mile scenic coastal route from Mumbai to Goa. Even now, as they finish loading the trunk with their bags and cases, Lili hates the sense of always having to shape her life around other people's wants and whims. But she's been doing it for so long that she doesn't even know what she desires instead. What she's gotten good at, though, is asserting herself through small subversive gestures and actions. Like demanding that she get the driver's seat now, at least until the morning commuters swarm the highways.

As Lili settles into place, her cousin turns to her from the front passenger's seat with a pursed-lips-and-side-eyed look, gesturing at her loose white tank top with the too-wide armholes.

"Don't start, Shaluben," Lili replies. The woman is only about twelve years older than Lili, but she acts like she's Lili's mother.

"We're stopping at a temple later. I have a pink kurta in my carry-on. You can wear that."

Exhaling theatrically, Lili notes in the rearview mirror how the muscles tighten on one side of Umeshbhai's neck as he leans forward from the back seat to give her offending bare arms a once-over. By conventional Indian standards, Lili is no beauty with her short highlighted curls, long nose, and thin lips. Yet, during this visit, men—including Umeshbhai, who's breathing heavily now—have been acting like they're seeing bare female skin for the first time. It's the kind of looking that feels like touching, like she's being coated in something greasy and thick and should bathe herself clean right away.

"Are you sure you know how to drive on this side of the road?"

"Umeshbhai! How many times?"

"My dear Lilima, this is not America. Look at how much narrower our roads and streets are. And these people don't have any driving discipline. Tell her, Shalu." His my-dear mansplaining smarm makes Lili press her lips tight so that the unspoken words burn caustic on her tongue.

Shaluben shakes her head and leans back. "What is this need to drive? I don't understand, baba. Just relax and enjoy, na."

Lili stabs at the radio controls, turns up the volume, and then rolls her eyes when Umeshbhai begins to sing along—throatily, off-key, substituting odd words and phrases with a humming.

"'Ankhiyon ke jharokhon se
Maine dekha jo 'hmm-hmm'
Tum door nazar aaye
Badi door nazar aaye .'"

Shaluben interrupts frequently with high-pitched chatter. "I hope you didn't pack the camera in the bigger suitcase. . . Oh, beautiful lyrics, no? 'From the windows of my eyes'—no, 'soul' sounds better, don't you think?—'when I saw you, my love, you seemed to be so far away, so far away'—my God! What is that girl doing? Watch her, Lili!" She grabs and pulls at Lili's arm.

What happens next is both fast and slow at the same time. As if there's one Lili sitting in the car, trying to control it as it bolts forward like lightning, and another Lili floating in the distance somewhere, watching with mouth rounding into a soundless O as a little girl skips right up to the car.

When the vehicle stalls, there is screaming and shouting, but it comes to Lili muffled, as if from great underwater depths. The people making these sounds—her cousin and brother-in-law among them—run to the front. Umeshbhai gestures wildly with both arms in the air. Shaluben drops to a crouch, the whites of her eyes turning to liquid silver. Lili wants to get out and go to them, but there's a heavy weight around her neck, like a tolling bell that won't stop ringing.

When Umeshbhai opens the car door and hauls her out, there's a furious heat radiating from him that makes her flinch. "What is wrong with you? You almost killed the child!"

The words hit her like bullets.

Shaluben snaps, "Umesh. Just take care of this first."

Umeshbhai drags Lili to the small huddle. That's when she notices how this particular street is deserted save for the three of them, another couple, and . . . the girl. Lili stares down, horrified, at the scrawny little body in a shirt that reaches the knees. One bloodied leg won't stop twitching though it's twisted in an impossible angle. The mother is on her haunches, whispering to the unconscious girl. The father stands beside Umeshbhai. There is no terror or fear in their expressions. Just an age-old weary resignation.

After some back and forth, Umeshbhai pulls a bundle of bills from his wallet. Speaking in Marathi, he pushes it into the man's chest. When the man shrinks from the touch, the woman, without even looking up, raises a hand and takes it. Whatever Umeshbhai is telling them in low, soft tones, they're nodding to it all quietly.

Shaluben walks Lili away, pushes her into the back seat, and slams the door. The entire car vibrates like one of those bumper cars at amusement parks.

Lili cannot tell how much time has elapsed when Umeshbhai reverses the car to drive away. They pick up speed once they're on the highway. The traffic around them is thickening. The sun is still low enough in the east to make her face break out into a sheen of perspiration. But she knows it's not the right time to ask them to crank up the air-conditioning. Or ask them anything, really.

"You should not have given them your mobile number, Shalu."

"We should have taken the child to the hospital."

"And get entangled with the police? They'd take one look at your NRI cousin here and demand enough money to fund the weddings of their next two generations. I already handed over plenty. They will probably pocket most of it and take their kid to the government hospital anyway."

"Fine. We'll dump this phone and get me a new one."

"Are you stupid or what? They can track your ID with that number. Your PAN and Aadhaar numbers are linked to it, remember? They could easily send the police after us if they want. I hope you packed the right clothes for a vacation in prison."

"I told you not to let her drive, Umesh! You never listen to me!"

Silence sits like a festering fourth presence in their midst. Lili keeps looking back to check for police cars. A part of her wants to speak, yell, cry, something. Another part of her wants to take the next flight to Texas. No, what she really wants is to turn back the clock and never to have come to this country in the first place. This thought corkscrews itself painfully deep within her, leaving shards of resentment and rage in its wake.

The city falls away soon, and they are on a coastal highway. Unsigned fishing hamlets go by, punctuated by long stretches of mangroves and casuarina groves opening straight into the Arabian Sea. Umeshbhai has switched the air-conditioning off and opened both front windows, letting the fresh, tangy air in. His juddering acceleration around the frequent serpentine bends makes Lili dizzy. When Shaluben's phone rings, everyone stiffens. Lili's hands and feet turn to ice, as if the blood has stopped reaching them. It's just the neighbor checking about their flat keys to water their plants.

"Switch that thing off, for God's sake. I'll get you a new one." Umeshbhai grinds his teeth as he says this.

"Fine!" A white-hot anger makes Shaluben's voice quaver.

Unlike them, Lili cannot even articulate the shifting topography inside her. Yet, it hurts her—like a physical pain along her entire jawline—to keep her mouth shut. And her unshed tears are like stabbing sensations in her eyes.

A little past mid-morning, they stop in the town of Alibag, at the ruins of a seventeenth-century seaside fort. Shaluben has spent days looking up all the landmarks on their planned route. Now, despite everything, she can't help herself. As they go across the pebbly sand, skirting the southern perimeter, some of the fort's history comes spilling out of her. With the waves crashing nearby, she has to almost shout out how it had been built during Shivaji's time to fight against the British, Portuguese, and Siddi Abyssinians. All of these foreigners had been drawn to India's western coast by stories of the country's treasures and beauty. The Muslim-sounding name of the locality had come later—after a rich Jew, Ali, who had owned and farmed much of the land. Coconuts and mangos, mostly.

Umeshbhai smirks. "A Jew called Ali. Made his riches off other people's lands and labor. Shocker. Weren't those Bene Israelis big in the film industry at one time? Of course, they all vanished after Independence, once their British protectors were gone."

Shaluben's earnest tour guide mode and Umeshbhai's condescension embarrass Lili even though she's only half listening.

"Oh, not all. Nadira was one. She lasted a long time. Remember this?" Then, just like that, Shaluben sings a few lines in a voice soft as rain.

> *"'Mudh mudh ke na dekh, mudh mudh ke,*
> *Mudh mudh ke na dekh, mudh mudh ke*
> 'something something something something'
> *duniya usiki hai jo aage dekhe . . .'"*

Without warning, Umeshbhai grabs Lili by the waist. He waltzes her clumsily around a circle, swinging her almost off her feet. And his whisper is rancid steam against her ear, "You understand, my dear Lilima? Like the song says: no looking back. The world belongs to those who look forward."

Shaking herself free, her mouth dry and raw, Lili turns toward the tourists herding behind them. A few feet from her, a young couple giggles into a phone camera as a wet breeze blows their clothes flat against their clutching bodies. Lili has only disdain for all of these self-absorbed pleasure-seekers who show no purpose, no ambition, no courage. That she, too, is now a part of them makes her loathe her own shallowness.

The ancient invaders had come here, to this very spot, with great spirit and audacity, changed landscapes and cultures, and left enduring marks and legacies. They had mattered.

All at once, it is so heartbreaking, so intolerably heartbreaking—the intense blue-black of the pounding sea, the rippled gold-brown of the sand, the earthy mossiness of the rocks, and the musty gray-black of the fort. An ecosystem unlike any in her contained world in North Texas. Feeling completely out of her element, Lili's senses awaken, and she aches for some sign that will help her understand what she should do. As if chasing some invisible enemy, she charges up to the fort gates.

Shaluben catches up outside one of the fort shrines. "Don't run off on your own like that. If something happens to you, what will we say to your parents? You're not a child! Say something."

A wild laughter trembles inside Lili. No, she's not a child, thank goodness. Or they'd probably leave her dying on the road, too, if something happened to her. As Umeshbhai comes round the corner looking for them, Lili smiles like her mouth is filled with bits of broken glass.

After Alibag, the car hugs the coastline, zipping past small, unsigned villages. A few cows amble past and make Umeshbhai swerve so sharply that they almost bounce onto the embankment. Shaluben lets out a little yelp. Lili slides to the other end of the back seat despite the seat belt and, even then, she's unable to say anything. A ramshackle truck goes by, clanging and coughing down the road with colorful tassels swaying, high-piled cargo undulating, deadly smoke fuming. Under the fierce, blinding sun, the psychedelic slogans, symbols, and iconography painted all over it shimmer like an otherworldly vision. Next to it, their car is a dinky toy.

Slowing down, Umeshbhai checks the GPS. "We're near Korlai village. Let's get lunch." He takes a hand off the wheel to pat and stroke Shaluben's clenched fist as if it's a small, injured animal. Lili leans back and closes her eyes, feeling the chasm between her and them widening further. Maybe, she daydreams, when they get to their Goa hotel, she can call for an airport cab while they're sleeping and get the hell away.

The food stop is at a tin shack, where they're the only patrons. In the open kitchen out back, the shirtless owner boils rice and fries freshly caught pomfret. They eat with their fingers, swatting away fat, languid flies, which seem to prefer drowning to death in the thick, spicy gravy. The limp black bodies have to be picked out and tossed aside. The owner smirks at Lili, his dark-brown belly gleaming like a copper pot.

As they finish up, an old woman shuffles by with a grimy, matted straw basket. Her faded-green sari is draped, dhoti style, around each leg. Worn by weather and age, her skin is burnished near black. Shyly, she tips the basket to show variously sized garlands of roses, marigolds, daisies, jasmine, and other flowers Lili does not recognize.

"Will you take a *gazra*?" Her grin is missing several teeth.

The woman loops a dense wreath of blood red rosebuds around Shaluben's bun. Their sweet fragrance mingles with the lingering pungent smell of fish curry. She gives Lili a cracked mirror to hold while she nudges Shaluben's chin sideways to show off the *gazra* adornment.

Then Shaluben, this compact-shaped, eager woman who reminds Lili of a local bank teller back home, blinks at her husband as if to ask, "Do I please you?" And the bespectacled husband, sweat dripping from his brow, misses that entirely as he goggles at Lili's stubbled armpits.

Securing her payment inside her tight blouse, the old woman sits on the floor. Basket in lap, she strings jasmine flowers together without even looking at them and sings a single verse on loop. A remarkably clear voice too.

> *"Maldita Maria Madulena,*
> *maldita firmosa,*
> *ai contra ma ja foi a Madulena,*
> *vastida de mata."*

The shack owner wipes their table and flourishes his dripping mop cloth alternatingly at her and the entrance. She glares and sings louder.

Umeshbhai asks the man in Hindi, the only other Indian language Lili knows besides her own, "Is that a Konkani song?"

"No. Kristi. Some still speak the old mixed Portuguese here. It's about Maria Magdalena, the cursed beautiful one. Covered with leaves, it says. Or flowers, perhaps?"

As they get up to leave, Umeshbhai puts an arm around Lili's shoulders. "Come on, beautiful one."

Shaluben corrects him with a hiss, "Cursed beautiful one," and marches past them to the car, which is a heap of scorching metal and glass now.

For the next few miles, the music on the radio is jangly and jarring, unlike the usual Bollywood love songs. There is no sing-along now, but Lili wishes she had fancier noise-canceling headphones. She considers asking for the volume to be lowered but knows she will be told to "adjust." Her stomach is churning acid. She needs to get off the viciously winding road, out of the car, away from them.

In an hour or so, they stop again. Umeshbhai has, through one of his Juhu Gymkhana club connections, arranged to check out a horror movie shooting at a former palace. It's closed to the public, so this is a special favor by both the owners and the moviemakers. A white-haired man in a rumpled yellow shirt unbuttoned down his chest leads them through the Gothic-Mughal arches of the entryway and brings them to a far, dark corner of the main hall. He explains, in drawling Hinglish, how they have completed blocking and lighting for the shot and are ready to rehearse for the first take. A young princess is to be told about her arranged betrothal to an aging prince.

"How terrifying," groans Umeshbhai.

Shaluben begins sharing her researched trivia: how the present owner of the palace is a descendant of the original nawab who had built it in the 1800s, how many popular horror movies of the 1980s had been shot there by the infamous Ramsay Brothers, how the palace used to be open to the public but was eventually closed off because of vandalism.

There is teeming activity all over the set. At the center, a heavily made-up actress dressed in red and gold finery reclines on a four-poster canopied bed. Several of the people surrounding her are yelling at each other or at other crew members in the periphery. The princess has the fatigued expression of a caged creature who has given up on the possibility of escape. A couple of camera dollies loom nearby, the cameras trained on her like deadly weapons.

As they wait, Lili's irritation engulfs her like a toxic, suffocating fog. What is so special about watching a B movie being shot? Standing in a hot, reeking corner as if they're B-grade people? Waiting in the sidelines of the imagined lives of others?

A megaphone calls for order. When she's sure no one will notice, Lili slips away into cooler shadows and up a dusty marble staircase. On the first landing, a door opens onto a tiny balcony with a glittering view of Murud Beach. A few kilometers into the sea, there is another smaller fort on a rock island. Little black boats drift about as if lazily circling prey. The lapping waves are a welcome respite after the noise below.

"Kasa Fort." Umeshbhai is beside her. "Shivaji built it to take on the Siddis of Janjira." Gripping the balcony railing with both hands, he emphasizes, "The Siddis who were here."

They look ahead as if a big dramatic scene is unfolding. A sea bird glides by, crying out. Another one answers more insistently. Sunlight crisscrosses the frothy blue water like gold-edged darts. A trapped piece of driftwood knocks against a jutting rock as the tide draws in and out.

He clears his throat. "The people of this place have a story about a Siddi princess, maybe as old as you. The night before she was to be married to a prince she had never met, she came to this balcony for a signal from her Maratha warrior lover. He came in a fishing boat at night to steal her away to Padmadurg Fort, as Kasa was known then. But they were caught by the fort chief in the underground pathway connected to another fort, Sindhudurg."

He's so close to her, Lili could count the pores on his face. She listens to his story but hears something else—something more dangerous—under the words.

"Before they executed her, she begged to be brought back to the palace, her home. They agreed and, the same night, left her dead on this beach. In the morning, she was nowhere to be found. It is believed she haunts the palace, coming to this balcony on Amavasya nights—not even a sliver of the moon is visible—singing for her warrior lover. And all the sailors come forward, dash their boats against rocks they cannot see, and die foolishly."

Now, his hand is on the small of her back. She remains still and quiet.

"You're thinking, 'This is so clichéd'" He mimicked her Texan drawl. "I ask you: Isn't life clichéd? We're born; we live; we die."

She wants to spit in his grinning face and tell him that the last bit of his story is kind of stolen from Greek mythology. The sirens were bird-women who enticed sailors to their deaths with their haunting songs. Breathing deep into the salty air, she realizes that she doesn't feel as sad for the dying sailors as for the sirens—sitting, waiting, singing the same lament for Persephone. Their endless punishment for failing to save Persephone from being abducted by Hades. They had no choice, no control. She knows how that feels.

He moves behind her, and his fingertips are like cool daggers as they move up from her hips and slide inside those wide armholes to clasp her breasts. Pressing his hardness fully against her, he rests his chin on her left shoulder, and asks, "Can you sing, Lilima?"

Something in her armor releases like a rusty, old catch. For the first time since the accident, she lets out a sound: a scream with full force.

Until he clamps one hand onto her mouth. "Shut up, shut up!" He pinches a nipple hard with the other hand. "If you know what's good for you. I could turn you into the police, you know. Hit-and-run. You know what they'll do to a pretty young girl like you? They'll eat you alive. Many times over. Maybe you'd like that, though, huh?"

Lili has to force herself to breathe in and out.

"You be good for me, Lilima. And I'll take care of you. All right?"

She moves a hand slowly to her hip pocket and feels for her phone. "What about Shaluben?"

He laughs, his hands now down the front of her pants. "Shalu? Shalu is like one of those cows you saw earlier. Too busy chewing her own cud to notice anything. Don't you worry about her. She's never found out about any of my girls."

For about ten minutes, as Umeshbhai has Lili pinned against the wall, thrusting into her, his mouth whimpering and drooling in the crook of her neck, she thinks of other things. She recalls how, in the past week, Shaluben had Instagrammed and Whatsapped almost every moment of theirs together: eating street food with bare hands in Elco Market, riding helmet   less on the back of a motorbike along Worli Sea Face, smoking hookahs in posh Carter Road bars, celebrity spotting at Film City, drinking fancy coffees in Colaba cafés. When Umeshbhai smashes his lips against hers and shoves his furry tongue into her mouth, Lili wonders what the Siddi princess's siren song might have sounded like. And when Umeshbhai steps away and pulls his pants back up, Lili gazes in the distance as if he's not there. After he wipes his mouth, pats her shoulder, and leaves, Lili pulls out her phone and stares at it for a few minutes. Then, she takes a deep breath of that briny air and hums a few lines of a siren song from an old school play. Funny how memory works.

> "'Come swim across the sea for me,
> I'll sing and dance, love, for thee.
> For a sacrifice must be made,
> a precious price must be paid.'"

Downstairs, they're taking selfies with the actress. Watching her smile at their polite banter, Lili is surprised at how much younger she is than she first appeared. Barely, perhaps, a couple of years older than Lili herself. Did she choose this career, this life? Or is she a modern-day siren: punished and fated to be as others want?

At the car, waiting beside his own enlarged, silhouetted reflection in the curved windows, Umeshbhai looks like a squat, deformed, frowning penguin, like in that Batman movie. For the rest of her life, whenever she will remember this trip, this day, this man, this will be the first image her mind will conjure.

The last part of the day's journey is the longest. The narrow two-lane highway has rough stretches where, during an unexpected, pelting downpour, it's like navigating muddy rapids. Through the rain-soaked mangroves, Lili catches glimpses of the lashing sea. And the tall baobab trees along the roadside contemplate the world like old, benevolent souls.

Shaluben drowses while Umeshbhai plays a zig zagging game with a white BMW that has been tailgating them for some time. The sheer cliff drop on their side does not have any crash barriers. Lili chews her lower lip, carefully observing in the wing mirrors.

Stopping the car on the shoulder, Umeshbhai dodges vehicles from both directions to get to a coconut seller on the other side. After the BMW races past, Lili gets out to look over the cliff's edge and nearly gags. A rotting odor rises from a mess of torn old newspapers, dirty plastic bottles, frayed chunks of tire rubber, maggoty remains of a small animal, glinting pieces of glass. The breeze churning up the silvery-dark Arabian Sea does nothing to soothe her clamminess. There is a harsh cawing all around as birds gather thickly like a cloud overhead, like an omen looming.

When Umeshbhai sprints back with three large coconuts whose tops have been lopped off, Shaluben points out how he is not a young one like Lili. His response is to raise the coconuts high so she has to skip and reach with both arms to get one. She beams at him as she does so and then turns to give Lili a blinding smile too. They drink thirstily with short, flimsy white straws. The warm, metallic taste is like swallowing tears.

At dusk, they reach Ganpatipule. Through the tall brick-red entry archway, the temple complex is a quiet, clean space with coconut trees casting long shadows everywhere. A thin stream of visitors meanders in and around the main building or dissipates onto the beach a few feet away. The temple is both imposing and impressive with endless intricate wall sculptures of glossy red Ganeshas in different poses, substantial pillars on either side, a cream-colored tiered and spired roof, and an elegant brass *kalash* topper.

They stand in the archway, gazing at the ornamental header where the potbellied Ganesha is flanked by his usual companions, the goddesses Saraswati and Lakshmi.

Shaluben mentions the pink kurta again.

Lili gestures a no with her entire body.

They give her the car keys so she can wait while they return.

But the sea thrashes and thrums, calling to her. As a child, it had mostly frightened her—she would run up to the waterline, feet sinking in the wet sand, then start shrieking as the tides surged up to her. Now, she rushes to it, wanting to be deluged, to be swept up along the crests, to be engulfed in the unknown depths.

In the dulling light, the sand is almost white against the waves, which foam black as they tumble forward, then spray invisible mist as they break. She kicks away a limp tangle of seaweed. Colorful shells sparkle like jewels. Seagulls with long wings skim the water serenely, then swoop toward the thunder-purple clouds.

Standing against a moss-covered boulder, Lili pulls wet, green clumps from it. A girl, probably nine or ten years old, walks into her line of sight. About the same size and look as the other girl, the one who lay still on the street with that impossibly twisted leg. She bends to tie something to her ankles: red velvet pads with rows of little brass bells knotted into them—*ghungroo,* the kind that's worn by classical dancers. After making sure they are securely fastened, she takes a few shuffling steps, then begins whirling.

The ringing of nearly a hundred metal bells fills the peaceful evening air as the girl's bare feet fly. Fine sand billows around her thin legs. Forming delicate mudras with her hands, she flings her arms out in emphatic, sweeping arcs. Encrusted with dirt, her skirt swirls and swishes about her slight body. Her hair comes loose and whips across her face. A dervish-like rapture lights up her tiny being.

Though Lili is motionless, she feels like she has been tossed high into the sky. The entire coastline is now aflame from the setting sun, and its heat reaches to soften and ripen something deep inside.

When the girl comes to a gasping, laughing stop, Lili considers saying something—an apology, an appeal for forgiveness—but it is enough to hand the girl Umeshbhai's car keys as she skips away, merging with the dancing golden waves.

Back near the temple entrance, Lili spots Shaluben, shoulders stooped and hands folded, on the *pradakshina* path—a clockwise orbital of the outside of the temple and the small hill behind it. Behind her, Umeshbhai waddles along. Like folklore figures, they seem destined to forever retread the only course known to them.

Taking her phone out of her pocket, Lili taps on Shaluben's new Whatsapp profile photo: a selfie with that blood red *gazra* from the afternoon, which feels like a lifetime ago. Lili sighs as she taps the send icon.

One of the vendors in the parking lot has thin, colorful stoles inscribed with Sanskrit verses. Lili tugs at a fluttering white one with curvy black lettering, pays without the usual haggling, and wraps it around her bare shoulders and arms. With this new protection, she swivels confidently into the temple.

Just inside the temple's entrance, a larger-than-life brass statue of Ganesha's favorite ride—a divine mouse—stands upright on a stone pedestal. She remembers Shaluben's story of how, if a prayer is whispered in the mouse's left ear, he will take it to Ganesha, and it will be granted. Slipping her shoes off for the attendant, Lili approaches and places a hand on the statue's oversized left ear when Shaluben appears on the other side.

"You have to cover his right ear at the same time," Shaluben's voice is tender like a caress.

Lili nods and reaches over with her other hand to do so.

When Lili is done with the prayer ritual, Shaluben's phone rings.

Umeshbhai, standing a few feet away, barks, "I told you to keep your phone switched off, you stupid woman!"

Shaluben looks at Umeshbhai as she answers. After a few seconds, she mouths, "Dead." And, although there are tears now trickling down her face, her voice is firm and clear as she answers the rapid-fire questions from the other end. "Yes, I understand what 'internal injuries' means. Yes, we're in Ganpatipule, at the temple. Yes, my husband was driving the car. Yes, he gave the parents the money. Yes, we'll wait here."

For one never-ending moment, it's as if their world has become an airless, soundless vacuum. Then, Shaluben holds a hand out to Lili. "You want to go look inside? We have time."

Entering the near-empty prayer hall with its elaborate wall carvings, Lili sets the temple bells swinging and pealing. Bits of the day's songs come to her.

Her soul lifts as her feet leap toward the inner sanctum, toward an inner peace.

> *"'Ankhiyon ke jharokhon se . . .*
> *Mudh mudh ke na dekh . . .*
> *Maldita Maria Madulena . . .*
> a precious price must be paid . . .'"

Jenny Bhatt is an Indian American writer, literary translator, and literary critic. She is the author of an award-winning story collection, *Each of Us Killers,* and an award-shortlisted literary translation, *Ratno Dholi: The Best Stories of Dhumketu.* Her latest is a translation, *The Shehnai Virtuoso and Other Stories* by Dhumketu.

The Dead Spot

John Palisano

Seawater sprayed on Kristina's face and arms like a light rain. A perfume of brine, salt, and seaweed encompassed the area. She looked out at the vast sheet of darkness. It rose and fell; the ocean looked like it was breathing.

"You sure we should be doing this?" Kim asked, her smile catching the moonlight.

"We'll be fine," Kristina said. "We've done this a hundred times." She forced a smile. *Only this is the first time I'm helping to break the law. Never even went to detention.*

"Water looks rough," Kim said. "I don't know."

"No one will fault you if you're not comfortable," she said. "It's understandable." She tried to sound natural.

Splashes sounded around them. The other swimmers dove in. The San Quinlan Boat Club crew was off and running. Kristina shrugged. "That's my cue," she said, grateful to end their conversation. The less she spoke, the better.

Launching herself headfirst, she felt the rush of the ice-cold water touch every part of her exposed flesh. She imagined all her pores closing, like millions of microscopic port windows shutting at once. For a moment, she didn't feel cold or hot—just a strange type of numbness.

She exhaled as she reached a natural arc. Bubbling sounds whooshed around her as she fanned her arms backward and made the first small kicks to push herself upward to the surface.

When she broke the surface, it was the same pitch black as below. She blew out what remained of her breath and dog-paddled. The water felt strong. She sensed a current, too, which she hadn't expected. Salt permeated her nose and throat; she smelled it and tasted it.

She listened for several seconds for signs of the others. Nothing. Just the lapping of the waves. No swimming strokes. No breathing. Nothing she identified as another swimmer.

In the dark, she had no landmarks to know where she was or how to get back to the San Quinlan dock. Reaching for her left wrist with her right, she cupped her diving watch, and thanked God it hadn't come off. She lifted her arm out of the water and pressed the top right button, illuminating its face. Seeing the compass built in, she noted she faced a few degrees to the left of the north. Perfect. *If I swim east, I'm going to come upon the dock or land if I get into trouble. It's only forty-five minutes to sunrise, anyway. I'll be able to see more and more soon enough.*

She had little time, though. She had a mission. None of the others knew.

Reaching up to her swim cap, she pressed the right side above her temple. The squishy pack inside was still there. *The ID chips are safe.* She just had to deliver them.

The waves pushed her and were higher than usual, so the paddling already felt labored.

I have to swim right away, or I won't make it.

She went over the plan. She'd had to have pushed off from the dock straight and swam at eighteen degrees, just to the right of due north. David had gone over it with her the night before. "Get your lubber line right on the eighteen and swim straight. That'll lead you right to the buoy. There'll be a small compartment under the flashing light. Put the bag of chips in there. It'll be almost light by the time you make it, so you should have a visual on the dock if you just reverse it on the way back. Easy peasy."

Easy peasy for him. He doesn't have to swim a mile and a half each way.

She checked the bezel and saw it pointed her toward nine degrees. She turned and aimed as best she could for eighteen and began her strokes right away. *The window of time will be short. Can't be seen. No one can know I'm doing this.*

The water fought her right away. There hadn't been a storm forecast. It was supposed to be a cloudless morning. No issues. The sea could change in a moment. It didn't care what forecasters believed. She knew as much.

Kristina thought back to the countless hours she'd spent swimming in the winter, open waters with the crew. They always went out early in the morning. Less chance of encountering boats. The world was theirs. No intrusions.

Don't think about that Zen right now. You've got a job to do.

Her strokes felt stronger; her body went on autopilot. *Good. Separate my body from my mind. Muscles? Do your thing.*

She went into a strong breaststroke and cruised for several minutes. She slowed and went back into a dog paddle. Checked the watch. She was at thirteen degrees. Not bad. She turned and pointed a bit more and resumed swimming.

Was it cold? Warm? She could never tell, because her body fluctuated between the two seconds to one second. *Used to it. Like the sensation. As if I'm suspended and free.*

Her mind wandered as she hit full speed. *How deep is it under me? Where does the continental shelf drop off?* At the dock, the water remained shallow at maybe ten feet deep. For quite a while, the depth fluctuated between thirty and fifty feet deep, give or take. That's what she recalled from what she had seen when they had mapped the journey to the buoy. Things got scary fifty kilometers out where there were drop-offs that could go down a hundred kilometers to over two hundred and sixty kilometers down. Not quite the continental shelf, but that area had the line between the shore waters and the Pacific Ocean proper. Open water. Strong currents. Waves as large as buildings. Not a place for a lone swimmer. She'd be right on the edge of that nowhere zone. The depth chart looked like a peninsula in reverse, with the deep bits reaching in toward shore.

Try not to think about that, dummy. You're going to scare yourself out of this. You'll be fine. Swimming is swimming at the top of the water. You're not diving, after all. You'll be fine. Trust your body. Trust your mind. Stop overthinking this.

She swam onward.

The immense current pushed her. *I'm helpless. Nothing more than another tiny thing in the ocean. It can drown me in a blink, and it'd be meaningless.* She pictured herself pushed under, deeper than she could comprehend.

The water rose, taking her with it. *How high am I going?* It dipped, and she went with it downward. *If it crests over me, I could drown. Even if I dive with it, the pressure of the water on top of me could keep me underwater for too long for me to recover.*

Blackness. She'd be surrounded. Her breath would run out. She'd swim underwater in vain, fighting against the pressure. It'd win.

Don't think about that. Just go with it. Be a part of the water. Don't swim against it. You'll be fine. Tune yourself into it.

She shut her eyes, even though everything was so dark. Just to reset. Just to find her grace.

Swim. Swim. Swim.

Touching her swim cap briefly as she stroked her arm forward, she recognized the distinctive bump underneath.

Cargo's still with me.

Precious cargo. For precious things. They needed her to at least get to the buoy.

Do that much. If you don't get back, at least those eighteen souls will have a chance.

The current and huge waves settled. It might be for a moment. Maybe for good. Maybe they'd return and swallow her. She had to swim fast. Just in case.

Taking the lull to stop at a dog paddle again, she checked her watch and its compass.

Three degrees. I'm off. Damn it. How'd that happen?

But she knew. The vast wave had pushed her. She hadn't a choice. Turning to point as close to eighteen degrees again, she took a deep breath and set off. *Come on. Come on.*

As she swam, she remembered the plan. David Norris had set her up. The organizer of Voovoo Animal Rescue, and one of her favorite people, made a plan. "We need a place where there's no Wi-Fi. No radio signal. No nothing. A place the chips can't be tracked," he'd said. Of course, she knew where he was going with the idea.

"A mile and a half out into the ocean, there's a dead spot for a few kilometers," she said. "You've heard me talk about it. How peaceful it is. How quiet." She had smiled knowingly. "And that's why you thought of it, right?"

His smile could charm the pants off the devil.

"Guilty," he'd said, shrugging. "What can I say? I'm always thinking of a way to save more pups."

Another reason she loved him and everyone at Voovoo. *They're for the voiceless. For the poor animals experimented upon by these damn cosmetics companies. Voiceless like me.*

He'd held up a small bag with little rice-sized capsules inside. "ID chips," he said. "We can change them out at sea. They're live and registered already."

"I think I see where you're going," she said, her heart racing.

"We've got forty here. Preregistered to other animals. Doctor Shannon can take out the chips the testing lab put in and swap these instead. Cut the lab chips in half with clippers and drop them into the sea, never to be found. The pups we rescue will go into the dead zone one dog and come out the other side born again. New lives ahead."

She nodded. Looked around the room. It was just the two of them. "Why me? I don't have a boat."

"You swim," he said, taking her hands in his. "You can get out to a predetermined location with no one seeing you or taking notice. Next time you swim with the group. No one will know."

"Of course, they will," she said. "But maybe…"

"Ah!" he said. "See? You're getting it."

"I can swim out. Hide them on my person. Deliver them. The others never see me once we push off. We go out and back in our own directions. I get it."

He said, "See? You can deliver them and swim back. You'll be in the dead zone. No witnesses. I know we're being tracked. But no one will see anything with you."

"They probably know I'm a member."

"Right? But will they suspect what you're doing? You'll have no outward or obvious place to hide anything."

She tapped her head. "Just under my swim cap." She looked at the bag. "That'll fit. No one will see. I can put them in the stall in the locker room. None of the other swimmers will even guess or be suspicious."

"There's a buoy out in the bay. I'll get you the coordinates. It'll be a straight shot." He raised his hand, showing off his watch. He pressed the button on the side, and the face lit up. "You know how to use a compass, right?”

“Sure,” she said.

“Good. Then this is going to be easy.” He hugged her. “We’re going to save almost fifty souls next week.”

“Next week?”

“Yeah. No time like the present.”

A few days later, fifty turned to thirty-five. Voovoo had only broken that many free, escaping by a decoy van within seconds of being caught from the damned Man Made Cosmetics company’s laboratory. None of the beagles made a sound the entire way. Dead silent. “Years of abuse,” David said. “It’s like they were ghosts or something.”

Once the beagles made it back to Voovoo, they lost several overnight. They weren’t sure why. Fear? Maybe they were on drugs that, when taken away, killed them. No one was sure. Dr. Shannon was up all hours tending to them, trying everything she could to save them. By the time of the operation, they were down to just eighteen dogs.

“Eighteen dogs,” Kristina had said. “Eighteen degrees. Must be a lucky number or something.”

Another wave hit and she rose. She switched to a dog paddle rather than trying to ride with it, sensing it pushing her to the side and off course. She checked the watch and saw that the wave had changed her direction. Once the swell went down, she changed direction and swam again, harder, faster.

Where is that damn buoy? How far out am I, anyway?

What if the light isn’t working on it? What if it shorted out, and I’m just swimming out blindly into the Pacific?

Remember what David and you figured out? Forty-five minutes, give or take. Any more and something’s wrong. Turn back. That’s about how long it’d take. I’m an experienced swimmer. I know how long it takes. Sixteen laps in the big pool at San Quinlan college. Olympic-sized pool. Should be about the same distance as the buoy. We tried to think of everything. Stick to the plan. Worst case? If you miss it, at least you’ll survive. They’ll find another way with the dogs. David was adamant. Safety first. If it works, great. Anything gets in the way? Stop. Turn back.

No. I’m not turning back. I’m doing this. Don’t let fear get the better of you. You can do this. You’ve swum farther. For longer. The water’s a little choppy, but it’s not even as aggressive as it’s been, and you didn’t go in then, did you? You’ve got this, K.

You've got this.

Kristina lifted. The swell of the ocean carried her high and fast. She felt her stomach go hollow. Even though she was going up, she felt like she was falling at the same time. Her instinct kicked in, and she waved her arms in circular motions while in a Jesus Christ pose instead of swimming forward. The water carried her forward, and she felt panic rising. *Oh my god. This is an immense wave. If I were under it, I would drown, that much is for sure. Just glad I can't see how high. I can only feel it. I can't be on it. If it crests, I'll be pushed under. How am I going to fall back?*

She tried to catch her breath and get her bearings. *Is this just a swell? Or is this going to turn into a wave? How do I know I've not been in something this large before? Hope this doesn't mean a storm is coming. Maybe I should turn back after all. Once this stops, maybe this was a terrible idea.* She paddled and did her best to keep her motions steady and sure, not give in to the panic and fear she knew she already had done. The ocean could claim her at any moment; the strength of the water was overwhelming.

Go with the flow. Don't let your mind get the best of you. This will pass, and it's going to be okay. Just get to that buoy and deliver the chips, and it's all going to work out. If this were easy, it wouldn't have been worth it. We would have found it another way. Saving lives isn't for the faint of heart.

Her mind drifted back. "What we're doing is illegal. We're stealing property," David had said. "That's how they see these animals. They don't see them as kind, individual souls. They're just possessions to them. Things. We must be a voice for the voiceless. We need to be brave. It's up to us to be strong. If we're not, they die. It's hard to carry this torch forward, but when they get to the other side, it'll all be worth it. You'll see."

The water crested over her head. She wasn't sure how it happened. She thought she was on top of the wave, but for a moment she saw nothing but black and green. The water went right up her nose and somewhere in her mouth because she was surprised and didn't have a chance to prepare herself for going under.

She flailed her arms and she rose. Again up and out. Enough so her head was above water. She caught her breath and fear set in. *There's no one out here to save me. Only a few people know I'm even doing this. By the time they realized I haven't delivered the chips, it'd be hours. I'll be washed out to sea, gone and lost forever. If anything happens—this was supposed to be safe. There aren't supposed to be waves like these. The ocean is supposed to be relatively still. There's no storm. Why is it so tumultuous out here? Like in the wake of a big boat—maybe there's a cruise ship coming in. And somehow this is just the wake from one of those or a cargo ship or something like that. Something that will go away soon.*

She felt something move past her legs, something large. The water moved differently around her legs. Somehow it seemed to move counter to the large swell. Her mind raced with possibilities. Maybe it was an undertow. Or some sort of opposing force. Maybe this was what they meant when people got swept out to sea. It wasn't the actual waves on top that got them, but the moving of the tides below her. She tried to raise her legs so that she was in a less vulnerable position. But the water gave her no choice.

The swell fell. It seemed to drop ten, twenty, thirty, forty feet in just a moment. She had only the starlight to go by, which wasn't much. She felt the strange twisting pole around her legs again. *Oh my god. Something else is in the water with me.* She knew it had to be a shark. A great white lurking, ready to take her for a midnight dinner, a tiger shark prowling and ready to rip her to shreds, a giant squid wishing to wrap her in its tentacles and drag her to the bottom.

Oh please, why did I do this? This was stupid. Why did I agree with such a thing? We don't swim in deep waters like this. I need to head back right now. Call it off. Be done with this. How am I gonna fight this huge body of water? Am I tired?

She noticed the cold—hadn't paid attention to it before. Every part of her hurt from the freezing water. *It's not warm at all. It's got to be twenty or thirty degrees colder than what we usually swim in closer to shore. Oh God, what am I doing? Get me out of here. Crap. I wish I had my phone or some way to call somebody to come get me. I wish I had even a life preserver. What am I going to do?* She paddled. *Stay calm. Don't panic. Whatever you do, keep your head. Remember that you'll get through this if you're just calm. Use your training, don't think about the possibilities. Think about what's happening. You're swimming. You're to float on top. You're going to be fine. The waters are rough. But you'll get through it.*

Just as fast as the swell had arrived, it dissipated. The water stilled. How could she have just dropped and been part of such a huge swell just for it to vanish?

She looked around, spooked that something was in the water with her. She almost wished the swells would come back. Maybe they would scare away from her whatever was in the water. Maybe whatever it was would go deeper and leave her alone.

Don't think about stuff like that. You can't. Nothing's gonna want to come and bite you or eat you or anything like that. There are just not those kinds of creatures this far out. Pollution is your friend in that regard, isn't it? This was probably just a wake from a big boat. Get on with the mission.

She raised her left hand and found the crown of the watch. Felt for the bezel, but it didn't light up. Probably ran out of its glow-in-the-dark charge, good for only so long.

Now what? If she couldn't see what direction she was headed in, she had a high probability of swimming out into the deep ocean and drowning.

I only have so much energy. I'm not super tired. Yet.

She squinted and tried to see the compass on the watch, but there was not enough moon- or starlight. *Damn it. Maybe if my eyes were younger.*

The ocean pushed and pulled. She swayed. Her throat felt scratchy, she realized. It was the mouth- and lungful of salt water she'd managed when she went under. *Great. Just great.* She tapped the watch again. It didn't bring it back. It wasn't electricity that lit the thing. She wished it had.

It should be light relatively soon. If I just dog-paddle long enough, I should be able to wait it out and see where I am. Heck, I'd probably see land and be able to get there without too much fuss.

Keep your head.

Something brushed against her. It felt large and almost like velvet.

No. I'm imagining it. Just seaweed or something. Not what you think it is. Come on. What would—

Whatever it was, it touched her again. She jumped and acted instinctively.

She swam, her strokes going right into overdrive.

Come on, sun. Come up.

Let me see.

Get me out of this.

She didn't know which direction she was headed. She just wanted to get away from whatever lingered in the water, bumping into her.

Testing her. Trying to see what she was.

Trying to see if she could be food, she was sure. *Why didn't I bring anything I could protect myself with?*

You know why. It would have been suspicious. You're not supposed to be out here. No one can know and no one will find you.

Wait. They could find me. If I don't make the drop-off, they'll be able to track the chips. Yes. That's it. I'll just have to wait. They'll come looking. He even said so. But how long is that? A half hour from now? An hour? Several? Don't know how much energy I have left.

She slowed her strokes, relaxing and feeling the strain on her lungs and limbs.

Clanging.

From her far right.

Could it be?

The buoy. She'd found it. Stumbled upon it, somehow. Divine grace.

She turned her body toward the sound and swam with all she had.

The sound got louder.

Yes.

Finally.

God is good.

Morning light arrived; sunrays arched just over the water's top, providing just a little more detail.

Ahead, she scanned for the source of the sound. Didn't see it. Not immediately, at least. Still, the metallic clanging grew stronger.

Where are you?

A new sound accompanied the clanging. A motor.

Must be the pickup boat. David and the Voovoo team coming for the chips. *I'm too late.*

No.

They're not coming for a few hours. Not them.

She was tired and slowed. Just as soon as she did, the ocean dipped, and she felt a large drop. She rose as fast as she fell. She took a large face of seawater. She shut her mouth and eyes to it, but a good amount still went up her nose, despite her trying to exhale just the right amount of pressure to keep it out. The ocean was too strong.

"Yah, hah." She barked out the words almost by instinct, responding to the water breaching her sinuses. She spit out what she could.

Her hearing went muffled, but she heard the clanging and the motor. Much louder.

A wall rose from the water. An inky, dark monolith. With it, the water rose for a moment. Kristina swam hard to keep up. Her shoulders hurt. Her leg joints hurt. Everything hurt.

No monolith. Is it a whale? Is that what brushed against me?

She squinted and realized she'd come upon a cruise ship.

Oh, God. I'm in the wake.

That was what the sounds were.

How could one be this close to shore?

The water stopped rising. For a moment, she hovered. Dark-orange sunlight rimmed the silhouette of the ship. So massive.

She tried swimming backwards.

Get away. Now.

Pulling opposite, the water dragged downward.

Keep your head. Stay above water. You'll be okay.

Be the sea.

One with it.

Not against.

A sensation of rolling and falling overcame her. She swam, but doing so ended up in vain.

She soared down the wave fast enough to make the break hurt. She leaned her chin down against it. Turned her head to the side to brace her face. It didn't protect her. She tried to keep her strokes but couldn't help but put her hands up over her face. The pressure was too strong.

She only saw dark water. No glimpses of sunrays. No outlines. She only heard the loud rushing of the water.

Then muted silence.

Underwater.

How did this happen so fast? Didn't even feel it.

Bubbling, whooshing sounds filled her ears.

She fanned her arms toward the surface. It felt like she had a hundred pounds of blankets on her back. Two hundred. Five hundred pounds.

Pushing her down. Deep. The same pressure pushed on her arms, and she found it impossible to keep them outstretched.

In response, she curled her legs into her middle and held them with her arms.

I'm an underwater cannonball.

Pushed and rolled and pitched like a piece of debris, she shut her eyes and held her breath.

Hold on. You'll be all right. Smart move there. You'll float up and out once this passes. When you get to the surface, you'll see the sun coming up. You'll know where to swim toward. You'll know.

Something large banged her head and back. She saw lightning behind her eyes, and she endured a loud sound like a truck smashing into a wall.

What was that?

The thing that brushed against me? Something else? The ship? What?

She could see nothing.

All remained pitch-black.

She felt herself sinking. So fast. Like a stone. Her breath was nearly out. Her head felt like it would burst. A headache took root in a second.

Don't open your mouth underwater. Fight the urge. You'll drown.

She went to move her arms, but they didn't respond. Nothing worked. The good thing? Somehow, the urge to catch her breath passed. All was well.

Am I able to breathe underwater? An ancient part of me woke up? From the sea, we came, and to the sea, we shall return. She pictured herself with gills on her neck; her legs became two tails as she sank into the depths.

Darkness.

Nothingness.

Blank.

Quiet.

Still.

***

Gentle waves. Light splashing. Burning eyes. Nose and throat on fire. Head and back throbbing. Gray above. Sky above. Was it drizzle or ocean spray dampening her cheeks?

Something grazed her back. Strong. Powerful. Large.

I am floating on my back. How did this happen?

She ran through the events. Fanned out her arms. They hurt, but they worked. She paddled. Her legs went back under, and she swam upright.

The morning had come. The water looked calm. To her left, far away, she saw the edge of the shore and the structures beyond. To her right, a few meters away, she spotted the buoy.

God was looking out.

She said, "Well, if you write 'God' backward, it spells 'dog,' after all. Makes sense."

Touching her head, she was surprised that the swim cap remained firm. She felt the bump still present where she'd hid the chips.

She swam forward with all she had. *This was a miracle.*

Something watched her. Something swam alongside her. A dorsal fin broke the water, keeping pace, then shooting ahead. *Shark. Great white.*

But no. The fin wasn't quite the same shape as a shark's. It was a dolphin.

The fin went underwater, but she still sensed it swimming alongside her, ushering her toward her goal. She even thought others were supporting her, too. Racing through the water. *They know what I'm doing. There's no law we are breaking, according to the laws of the seas. We're saving animals from people here. That's why they're helping. That's why they saved me.*

She made it. Saw the buoy only a few yards away. The sun sparkled off its metal parts. Its reflectors glowed orange and red. Larger than she expected, a pair of sea lions lounged on its makeshift deck. As she approached, they leaned upward. "Yes. I'm here to help the land versions of you." Kristina swore they smiled. They knew, too, she was sure. They slipped off the deck in fluid, graceful movements, making way for her.

When she finally touched the buoy, a sense of relief overcame her, unlike any she'd ever experienced. Pulling herself up onto the deck, she sat. Her breathing didn't catch up. She steadied herself by putting her hands on its sides. For a moment, she shut her eyes. *I don't even feel like I'm in my body anymore.* She didn't want to give in to the sensation. *Right. All I have to do now is swim back.* Raising her head, she opened her eyes. Everything was lit in golden timbres. The world looked like a dream. The darkness had passed. She panicked. *Did I miss the boat? The drop-off? The pickup?*

Checking the watch, she noticed the second hand didn't move. The watch had frozen at 5:58 a.m. "Lot of good you did," she said. Even the compass no longer worked.

The rescue boat wouldn't be around until late morning. She looked at the vertical rails and spotted the box with the ring latch, there just as David had said. *This has got to be the one. Yes. I did it. We did it.* Unlatching the box, she saw the code number painted inside. Nothing an outsider would understand.

18

Painted in white, the number signified the eighteenth rescue operation David had masterminded.

Reaching up to her swim cap, Kristina lifted the lip from the side of her head. She used the opposite hand to slide up and under and ensure the small baggie of chips didn't fall out and get lost. Finding them, she took them out and stared at them for a good, long moment. Small and shaped just like little bits of rice. She nodded. "All this for you little buggers. You better do your job after all this." She kissed the bag and put it inside the compartment. She shut the door and turned the latch. She pressed the outside to make sure it didn't open. "Well, that's that." She sighed and looked around. Everything was calm. Nothing felt real. Her legs in the water, she realized they were warmer than she'd ever known, like a bath. She spotted the land opposite her, so far away, but not far enough she believed she couldn't make it. The buildings looked different from how she remembered; they were hazier and not quite where she remembered.

Well, I've never seen them from where I'm at now, have I?

She slipped into the water and paddled for a moment. The pain had gone. She felt better. *I feel like I can swim forever.*

She did and never again found the shore.

John Palisano's novels include *Dust of the Dead, Ghost Heart, Nerves,* and *Night of 1,000 Beasts.* His novellas include *Glass House* and *Starlight Drive: Four Halloween Tale*s. His first short fiction collection *All that Withers* celebrates over a decade of short story highlights.

He won the Bram Stoker Award© in short fiction for "Happy Joe's Rest Stop" and Colorado's Yog Soggoth award in 2018. More short stories have appeared in anthologies from *Weird Tales, Cemetery Dance, PS Publishing, Independent Legions, Space & Time, Dim Shores, DarkFuse, Crystal Lake, Terror Tales, Lovecraft eZine, Horror Library, Bizarro Pulp, Written Backwards, Dark Continents, Big Time Books, McFarland Press, Darkscribe, Dark House, Omnium Gatherum*, and more.

Non-fiction pieces have appeared in *Blumhouse Online, Fangoria,* and *Dark Discoveries* magazines and he's been quoted in *Vanity Fair, The Writer* and the *Los Angeles Times.*

You can find out more at: www.johnpalisano.com

Playing Chess

Gary Grace

I had not dreamt of drowning Chester West in a long time. That wasn't always the case. I hadn't seen him in almost twenty years and had worked hard to forget him. A friend request popped up in the right-hand corner of my work monitor. In his profile picture he displayed a mop of long curly hair. Not the buzzcut I remembered. His eyes were squinting slightly in the sun, and his arm was draped around a surfboard. *Lives* in Huntington Beach, California. A beautiful beach filled the backdrop. He looked like a different person. My hands began to tremble at my deskas I thought about them around his throat, draining the color from his face in a shallow pool of water as they had before in my dreams.

***

As a teenager, I had represented Ireland in athletics, winning a silver medal at the European Championships for the four-hundred-meter dash. I accepted a scholarship offer to attend a prep school in North Carolina. This path made a Division I scholarship to an American university an almost certainty, something I'd been dreaming of since I was a little girl. After a breakout performance at my first meet during my junior year, I received letters from several major programs, and my coach said that she was telephoned by over a dozen others. The following week, I tore my ACL. I didn't receive another letter and Coach's phone stopped ringing.

Whatever hope remained was chipped away by "Chess" and jock friends. When asked by our homeroom teacher how I was feeling following the surgery, I answered somewhat positively, expressing faith in the chance that I might be back to one hundred percent for my senior year. Chess openly sniggered in class in response to this while obnoxiously spinning a basketball on his finger as if to say, "Yeah right."

His friends called him Chess, supposedly because he was such a smooth operator. I often imagined him trying to play an actual game of chess with the look of bewilderment I'd seen on his face on my very first day at the school. I suspected this was a nickname he'd given himself in middle school, flexing in his bedroom mirror following some minor sporting victory.

He did always have a rotation of extraordinarily pretty girls though. Taut cheerleaders, lengthy volleyball players, the homecoming queen. Not exactly valedictorian candidates. At the time, I had no sympathy for these vapid debutantes streaking through the hallways, tears streaming down their faces. He was an asshole and that was plain to see. He'd jump from one to another, get what he wanted and then talk shit once he was done with them, revealing embarrassing secrets they'd shared. This was always followed by performative and public denial despite the timely declarations in thick black Sharpie on the boys' bathroom stalls. Some complete with illustrations. Squiggly lines denoting stenches rising from matchstick crotches.

On my first day, however, I had thought he was quite cute. He seemed shy in the math class we shared. It later became obvious that this was because he hadn't a clue and was keeping his mouth shut for obvious reasons. Candice beamed, a full mouth of gleaming braces presented as she placed a dish covered in Saran Wrap on our teacher's desk as the bell rang starting first period.

"That's not pecan pie, is it, Candice?" Mr. Davidson asked with an exaggerated smile."Y'all know that's my favorite."

Candice took the seat in front of me. The back of her T-shirt read *TRACK*. She turned to introduce herself, placed a laminated sheet on my desk. She began relaying a message to me from our coach about meeting her before practice. Mr. Davidson stood up from his desk and began to speak, and Candice spun around to pay attention.

"I'd better eat this on school grounds, Candice," he said, peeling back some of the plastic and taking a sniff, "because we don't want Mrs. Davidson getting jealous now, do we?"

Some of the guys started rolling their eyes in anticipation as Mr.

Davidson put the glass dish down.

"I like to cook, did y'all know that? Bake, grill, fry, whatever. I got inspired recently. Did y'all hear about the statistics professor and a math professor who worked together on a cookbook? They called it…*Pi à la Mode.*"

Everybody, including myself, laughed. All but Chester. After glancing around the room, he began to smirk and chuckle as if he'd gotten the joke. I felt bad for him. As the class went on, his brows furrowed with each simple problem on the board. I began daydreaming about tutoring him in the attic bedroom of my host family. Precalculus pages turned and our faces drawn closer together. We kissed softly, and he held me in his strong arms. The KVA gym bag at his feet in class prompted my daydream to drift onto our school's sun-soaked track, where we'd put in extra hours training together.

After class I introduced myself, extended my hand, and told him my name, Aoife. He noticed the workout schedule Candice had given me.

"Oh, okay, you're that lightning-fast leprechaun the AD told us about."

I actually blushed as he took my hand. "I suppose I am."

Candice had returned to the doorway. "Pssst, Aoife, c'mon, we're going to be late for chemistry."

Chester said, "I'll see you round," and brushed past Candice, who made no effort to move out of his way.

She sighed in disgust and theatrically flipped her braided hair to one side. She put her arm around me and led me the other direction.

"That dumbass is off to some remedial-ass-shit," she said, loud enough for Chester to hear.

We both glanced over our shoulder. Chester did not look back, echoed a loud "Ha!" down the corridor, raised a hand giving the finger, and continued walking. Candice went on to tell me all about Chess. It turned out he wasn't on the track team. All athletes had those bags. He was a three-sport letterman playing basketball, football, and baseball—for the last one, he was the star player of the team.

"He's just a freak of nature," Candice said, "born all brawn and no brains, and he sure as shit don't have the discipline for athletics like we have to. He's a ho, plain and simple. Don't be fooled by those big old blue eyes of his."

I was never explicitly rude to him. I'd just make polite excuses in response to offers he'd make to hang out with him at a friend's party or to do some quiz prep for algebra together, almost as I'd daydreamed about on day one. He never asked me out specifically on a date, playing it safe. Maybe he wasn't so sure of himself as it was obvious that several of the guys on the track team liked me. I didn't think he even really liked me but that I was more of a conquest as the new girl. The track star. I heeded the warning from Candice and the others. No matter how cute he was, my sport came first. I was determined to get recruited by all the top colleges in the state, and my teammates meant more than any boy.

Chester's cynicism in homeroom was warranted however. My ACL was severely torn, and the chances of making a complete recovery were unlikely. Even the surgeon had said as much. I plummeted into a depression like I'd never felt before.

***

We'd had some goths at my school in Ireland. They had scared me a little, if I was totally honest. Soon I was one of them in North Carolina. I'd totally ostracized myself from Candice and my track friends. I'd gained a lot of weight and had given up on rehabbing my ACL. I'd been welcomed into a group of goth kids, all but one of whom went to the local public school. Hillary, from my music class, had introduced me to some new music. She said that I looked sad and that "this" would "cure" me as she handed me a burned CD of the album *Disintegration*. They would make me feel better, she promised.

I'd always thought that it was spooky music that made *them* sad, but it turned out that if you were already depressed, it made you feel at least understood, if not better.

She went by Ophelia and made me promise not to tell the others her real name. She said that my name was cool enough. She had a beat-up old station wagon that she'd hand painted matte black and decorated to look like a hearse. She'd take me to meet the others at the mall, the pool hall, and to gigs in dive bars. I was fascinated that, despite being underage, we could get in simply with the mark of an X on our hands that easily washed off. We spent most of the summer drunk and high, discovering new bands and staring at the stars atop her wonderful death cab.

I maintained to my folks back home that I wanted to stay in the States for the summer to continue to rehab and get ready for my senior season. This pleased them. But all I really wanted to do was hang out with Ophelia and the crew. They had it right, I thought. Nothing mattered.

Over the summer I'd undertaken a complete transformation. Ophelia was more of a cybergoth and had gotten some neon-green dreadlocks stitched in and often wore a gasmask dangling as a necklace. Our school had no dress code and encouraged us to express ourselves. I'd read gothic novels all summer, painted my room bloodred, and adopted a more puffy-dressed Victorian look. My breasts had gotten much bigger, and the corset I wore on the first day of school accentuated them dramatically. Chester and his goons couldn't stop gawking. After a while, I guessed the jocks got used to the new me or simply got bored, and things died down.

Chester started creeping into my DMs on MSN Messenger however, making little apologies for his past behavior, revealing a genuine love of some of the heavier bands I liked. He'd noticed the patches on my book bag separated from left to right, from the more traditional goth music tothe numetal that was prominent at the time. I had stitched a Celtic spiral on the right side of my bag, where each of the three tips was followed by a patch for each of my unholy trinity of favorite nu-metal bands. Sevendust, Static-X, and Slipknot. Chess sent me playlists he'd made as pregame CDs he'd get pumped listening to while warming up. We talked all the time online. He proved to be quite thoughtful, sweet, and not as dumb as I'd previously thought. I kept this communication hidden from Ophelia. I imagined he did the same with his friends. I wished him good luck in his games, and he did likewise for the one recital I took part in. Ophelia had encouraged me to take back up the cello I'd practiced as a child. I was flourishing.

Ophelia seemed horrified when I suggested that we attend the state championship basketball game that our school had advanced to. It was being held at the University of North Carolina, Chapel Hill. I explained my logic. We could "watch the maggots bubble" in the stands and crumble in a probable defeat. They faced the all-Black private powerhouse academy Word of God. I suggested that for good measure, we could cast a spell against our own school. She still wasn't sure, but I was prepared. A band we liked, Mindless Self Indulgence, was playing at the Cat's Cradle later that night, which wasonly a ten-minute drive away from the arena. We could toast their demise, get wasted, and sleep in the hearse. She had beentickled at my devilishness and agreed to drive. I didn't recall much about the concert. All I remembered were the tears in his eyes after they had lost. My heart hadpounded as Ophelia beat on the bathroom stall door, wondering what was taking me so long. I'd been texting him to tell him that I was sorry and that I hoped he'd be okay. I enjoyed my sacred tryst with Chess but never anticipated it being anything more than what it was. A secret. I stood to be disowned just as much as he did. That was why I was shocked when he asked me to prom.

It was the talk of the school for the weeks leading up to the night. Ophelia and I had previously vowed to boycott the senseless display of vanity and idiocy. I came clean about what had been going on between me and Chess. Surprisingly she was understanding. If I was going however, she was, too, so she took our mutual friend Stitches. I refused to take the stretch Hummer limo with Chess's friends. He didn't seem to mind at all riding in the hearse and talked candidly with Stitches in the back seat about the little discussed merits of the band Staind's album *Dysfunction*, prior to obviously sellingout with *Break the Cycle*.

At the dance, his friends were polite to Ophelia and me. We didn't stay clung to them at all and spent much of the night with our nerdy music group. I'd check in with Chess periodically, and when the slow sets began, he was quick to take my hand and openly kissed me for the first time in the center of the dancefloor beneath the most fantastic chandelier. The sheer unlikeliness of our pairing led our classmates voting us prom king and queen. On stage I half expected his friends to start pelting me with rotten fruit or for gallons of pig blood to be dumped over my head from upon high. But nothing like that happened. We posed for pictures, and it was even Ophelia who suggested that we go back to the big party with Chess and his friends. He even extended an invite to our band-geek friends, who declined. Ophelia was drunk, having sneaked in a respectable amount of vodka in a pair of matching garter flasks. It was like the people that we were abandoning our real friends for had not been mean to Ophelia for the past four years.

"It'll be funny," she said. "I bet they'll be beating their chest after each kegstand, and one of those stupid bitches will probably drown in the hot tub."

No one drowned in the hot tub, but I did wake up in a basement spare bed with Chess. He was already dressed and sitting on an empty keg, putting on his shiny shoes. He told me that his older brother was on his way to pick us up and take me home. Ophelia was long gone. The birds' chirping coming through the cracked window made my head ache. The light was blinding, and the stench of stale beer and vomit had me heaving into a trash can. But soon we were gone, and I was safely home in my bed.

On the Monday in school, I was met with waves of laughter, looks of sympathy and even of disappointment. It had been a bet. To take me to prom and "bang" me. The specifics and the odds that Chess had beaten were detailed in fresh black ink in giant lettering on the tallest wall in the boys' bathroom. Chess was not in school so he could not be blamed. It had all gone to plan. He messaged me on MSN later that night, trying to maintain that it had started as a bet and a joke that he had not taken seriously at all but that he had meant all he said and that he really did like me. Final exams were over. I did not respond to him, and I did not return for the final weeks of class. I returned to Ireland and tried never to look back. I often dreamt of drowning him. The dream was always the same. Just as the last bit of life was about to leave him, his face turned into mine. This went on for years.

***

The lust for revenge I had in high school quickly subsided. I wanted to be the bigger person. I had done nothing wrong. But hadn't I? I'd been stupid and naive. I thought moving back to Ireland would distance me from the pain. I could have rehabbed, gotten back into athletics. Maybe done a redshirt year and still been a competitive college athlete. I'd run away because of him. But I'd done my therapy. I was over it. He was just a kid, too, at the time. He didn't really pester me that much. It was just at very specific times the friend requests would come. The year everyone in our class would have graduated from college. Sometimes on my birthday. Our ten-year high school reunion that I obviously didn't travel to attend. But that was the last one before this. I'd always accept for just a minute, hoping that he'd gotten fat, bald, divorced, or all three. He often looked sad. I told myself these attempts to reach out were simply to appease his own guilt and that he didn't give a shit about me. But something felt different. I didn't block him. It only took a moment for the three dots to start dancing. He was coming to Ireland.

I didn't say much at first. I just let him talk. He profusely apologized for the past as I'd expected he would. Technically I'd forgiven him or let go of it all. At least that's what I'd convinced my therapist of before leaving her care a year or so before. Chess had blown out his knee, too, in his sophomore year of college. It wasn't until then that he knuckled down and focused on school. He'd done well in sales for large tech companies up until the previous couple of years. He said he'd had no life. It wasn't until he moved out to California and started surfing daily that he really found himself. He'd used the money he'd made to set up a small but lucrative real estate agency with just a handful of employees. His brother pretty much ran things so Chess could spend most of days on the beach surfing, walking the dogs, and meditating. At first I didn't know if he was joking. But his photo albums and Instagram feed confirmed that he had morphed into a very different kind of douchebag. Kale and other horrible shakes featured prominently.

Chess was coming to Ireland to surf. He didn't go right ahead and say it until the small talk was over and I'd agreed to meet him. He said that there were a million great places to surf in Europe but that he'd never been able to get over what he'd done to me, and if it was the last thing he did, he'd see me and try to make amends. I told him he needed to relax. That it had been a long, long time ago. That we were both adults and could let bygones be bygones.

Relaxing would be the worst thing he could do around me. Had he forgotten I was the girl who cast spells on him and his friends? Had he forgotten that he had ruined my life? I let him know that I was from the west of Ireland, where the best surfing is. We could go on a road trip. It was going to be a trip all right. The tears that had rolled down my cheeks had cooled but still glistened. My work neighbor leaned back in her chair, removed her headset, and asked me if I was okay. I just nodded. And started cackling to myself, picturing his face.

He'd book flights and be there the following month. Plenty of time to plan. For me.

***

I told Chess that once he landed, to get on a bus that would get him to Donegal. He'd done some research and already had ideas for the best-known surfing beaches in the county. I kept my messages suggestive, laden with winking and other likewise moronic emojis. We would visit the big-wave beach he'd identified, but then I would take him to my beautiful county of Mayo. My local knowledge would allow him to avoid the tourist traps. I had very different traps planned.

I was stewing in the week leading up to his arrival but had intricately planned some horror to visit upon him. He would be amazed by the secluded surf spots, the beauty of the landscape, the food, and of course, me. I wasn't the fat goth anymore. I looked like an Olympic runner again, and I knew he would want me.

When Chess got off the bus in Donegal, I embraced him.

"It's really great to see you, Aoife," he said.

"Likewise," I remarked. "You must be starving, I know just the place for some traditional Irish seafood, if you like?"

He seemed relieved by my warmth and leaned back to place a kiss on my cheek. "That would be awesome."

Chess was enamored by the coastal drive. The strength of the wind physically moved my car several times, and the sight of the waves exploding on the cliff sides.

"That view is amazing, Aoife. It must be so cool to be from here."

"They call the long stretch of scenic coastline the Wild Atlantic Way."

Chess went back to his gazing before turning to me excitedly with a request. He asked if he could connect to my Bluetooth. Chess put on a Beach Boys playlist.

"I like to get in the mood, you know."

"Oh I remember," I said, grinning.

The car shook violently again, and I struggled to keep the car steady on the narrow coastal road. There were no road markings, and an enormous truck had been approaching us. I gripped the wheel at the textbook-perfect positioning of "ten and two" and passed the truck with a narrow berth. I sighed with relief.

"I don't want you to die just yet," I said.

Chess laughed and said, "At least these ain't as bad as those dirt roads in North Carolina near school, remember?"

I nodded that I did, a smile breaking across my face, recalling a day we had skipped school together and gone walking in the woods a couple of days before prom. I'd expected him to kiss me that day, but he hadn't. I began to think that maybe he never really was that bad. That maybe he had been telling the truth. That deep down, he was a good guy and that he had liked me. That the anger I'd felt for so long had perhaps been misplaced. Everybody hurts and maybe he truly had, too, after I had gone.

Chess nudged my arm, startling me a little, gave a little "my bad" acknowledging that he had, and carried on, "Check this out, this is you, this is you."

The song that came on was "The Little Old Lady from Pasadena."

Chess no longer had the shy, boyish smile. He'd gone almost red in the face, as if he'd been waiting to drop this bomb of a burn on me for some time. I recalled how he'd driven his Trailblazer back in the day, seat obnoxiously far back, right hand flopped on the wheel and left arm tanning out the window.

"Are you saying I drive like an old lady?"

"Oh come on, girl, you know you do."

The B&B I'd chosen near the beach was connected to a thatched-roof cottage pub that served smoked salmon and Irish soda bread, seafood chowder and enormous local oysters. The bare open brick walls and turf fire on the hearth charmed Chess. Just like the day we first met,I could see the cogs attempting to turn as the waitress reeled off the specials in her Donegal accent. I ordered for us and told him to trust me.

He raised a toast. "To my first but certainly not my last pint of Guinness."

I just let him keep talking and drinking all night, until the fire was reduced to charcoal and glowing embers. The staff was cleaning up.

"Good call on booking a B&B *at* the bar," he said, touching me for the first time bar our initial hug and his playful nudge in the car. His hand on the inside of my thigh remained there only for a second. Chess asked for the bill. The server explained to Chess that he could rent a surfboard and wetsuit down at the beach and that the hut was open early.

I'd booked us adjoining rooms. He thanked me again for a great night and expressed excitement for the day of surfing ahead.

At my door's threshold he gave me a hug, and as we drew away slowly, I could tell he was testing the waters. I preemptively gave him a nose kiss and opened my eyes suggestively as if to say, "Not just…yet."

"We have a long day ahead of us tomorrow," I said, and he smiled.

We turned our keys in unison and entered our respective rooms.

I was having mixed emotions and, scrolling through his various feeds, wondered if he was really any worse than most of the men I'd been with. Did he deserve my wrath? I couldn't sleep. I could hear him snoring. The adjoining doors were unlocked, and as I stood over him, watching him breathe, part of me wanted to slip in beside him. The other part wanted to suffocate him. I softly clicked the door closed behind me, lay down, and tried to breathe.

In the morning he was gone. I paced around his spotless room in a panic. Rushing back through my room, I noticed a postcard on the table. The image on the front was of Bundoran Beach. Chess explained that he had not wanted to disturb me. The best swell was early in the morning, and I should come down whenever I was ready. I was a light sleeper and wondered how he could possibly have been in and out of my room without disturbing me. I'd not been drunk the night before.

The wind was bitter cold, and I shielded my face from the stinging sand, trying to make out which one of the blurs on the horizon was Chess. It had started faintly snowing despite the sun sparking across the sea. In the distance, snowcapped mountains. I walked along the water's edge, looking for Chess. He'd spoken of the sixty-foot waves, but I'd thought he was exaggerating.

Watching surfers wipeout was nerve-racking. Imagining being dragged under water terrified me. I walked the beach and came across his stuff. I recognized his bag. I'd paid attention to the patches from Hawaii, Australia, Portugal, and Thailand. I heard the echo of my name across the water.

Chess emerged atop an enormous wave.I raised my hand in acknowledgment and couldn't help but smile. He looked so happy. A couple of German guys came out of the water, carrying their boards, panting for breath. One tall and muscly, and the other small and slight. They both had freckled noses, peroxide dreadlocks, and a lot of facial piercings.

"*Der Amerikaneristverrückt*," one said, nodding in Chess's direction.

I greeted them and asked, "How crazy?"

"Oh yes, he's a crazy guy for sure," the muscly one said.

The little guy perked up. "Look, he will take this one...*verdammtverrückt*."

His friend looked to me, pointed at Chess, and said, "*Ja*...fucking crazy but he is amazing. This pipeline is quite dangerous but his instinct is impressive. He can read the waves."

The smaller guy said, "We copped a serious pounding out there. We don't have these giant waves at home in Germany," and put his arm around his friend. "But we live to tell the tale of these Irish monsters."

All our eyes were on Chess. I couldn't help but gasp as he climbed the wall. The taller German placed a hand on my shoulder in solidarity, and we all braced ourselves as Chess began free-falling, cutting down the wave at a tremendous speed. The wave was barreling over him, and each moment I thought he might have gone under, the tip of his board would edge out past the collapsing water.

I could feel my heart beating and was glad the Germans were there, feeling that at any moment something bad could happen. The Germans applauded as Chess approached us, and I did likewise. He gave the guys each a little fist bump before jokingly lunging at me for an attempted hug. I hammed up a girlish squeal and pranced off while Chess chased me, shaking his hair out like a shaggy dog. I let him catch me, and I let him kiss me. It started as an innocent tiny peck that he seemed to let go of, accidentally, high on the endorphins, dopamine, and adrenaline. Perhaps feeling he'd overstepped a line too soon, he tried to withdraw, mouthing the beginning of a "Sorry," but I pulled him back into me, moving my warm tongue into his salty mouth.

"I forgot what a great kisser you are," he said.

He didn't push me too much to get in the water. I told him that the place where we were headed next, the island near my childhood home, was a magical place. I would swim there.

"So I'll get to see you in a bikini, right?" he said cheekily.

"If you're lucky," I said, and smacked him on the ass.

***

By the time we reached Mayo that night, it was already dark. My sister had left a bottle of Poitín on the kitchen table with a note saying, *Try not to kill the Yank!*

"What is that, like, moonshine or something?" Chess asked.

I told him that was exactly what it was. "The rare old mountain dew, you know.Are you man enough?"

He'd taken a couple of swigs before his coat was even off.

My sister had left some wood and freshly cut turf out for us. The fire pit out back had been cleaned and was ready to go. Despite it being cold, Chess was eager to sit outside and throw some burgers on the grill. He regaled me with tales of his surfing trips to other parts of the world. He said that he'd wanted to come to Ireland but that he'd felt too weird about it. That he'd only have ever come if we had gotten back on good terms.We clinked beers.

I'd been drinking that family-brewed Poitín since I was a teenager. I knew how strong it was, so I kept my sips to a minimum and poured out my glass whenever Chess was distracted or looking away. I had kissed him a few times throughout the night. I joked about how there was only one bed made up.I *supposed* we had to sleep together once the Poitín was all gone, that was.

"I might not be much use to you after all this fire water."

"Oh I'll find a use for you…" I let him know with a wry smile.

Soon Chess was passed out. The genius had left his phone on the table faceup. A message flashed, and I pulled the phone over to me.

I could read the first line of the message flashing despite the phone being locked.

Have you porked the piggy yet? it said.

It was from his friend Danny, whom I remembered from high school. An even bigger douche than Chess had been. Danny had been a loudmouth, fat-ass football player. Chess stirred a little but soon settled, mouth agape, and some drool leaving the corner of his mouth shone in the fire's light. To unlock his phone, all I needed was his fingerprint. I hunched down beside him and, holding up his hand, pressed his thumb on the bottom of the screen.

Danny had made reference to "The Album" several times and shared a picture of himself in bed with a younger girl, who had rolled over, passed out. There was no way of knowing how old this girl was, but that was what her body looked like, that of a girl. The message accompanying the photo simply stated, *I fucking love Thailand.*

I imagined the sad eyes of a twelve-year-old on the other side of that pillow.

I needed to find "The Album." I looked in his photos, and nothing. Dropbox, email folders, and was beginning to panic as Chess had coughed and moved around a bit. I texted Danny back from Chester's phone,

I'm going to fuck this pig tonight, bro, hoping that I could get some information from him that might lead to it. My message was immediately seen, and he started to type but then stopped. The phone received a notification:

Danny has added a photo to The Album.

In "The Album" were dozens of folders spanning back as far as high school. But there was only one that interested me. What I saw had never occurred to me. I'd thought I'd just been drunk on prom night. There were at least two dozen photos of me. They had put a plastic pig nose on my face, the kind you'd find at a costume store at Halloween. It was kept on by elastic bands hooked around my ears. I'd been put on all fours, spread out over an empty keg. Chess looked like he was laughing, his fingers fishhooking my mouth open. The shadows of other people in the room were cast upon the far wall. Then it was Danny behind me. Then it was Mike. Then Reece. And half the fucking baseball team. I dropped to my hands and knees and vomited in the frozen grass.

My plan had been to take Chess to the deserted island and leave him there for a couple of days to freeze and grow hungry and fear the kind of fear I'd felt. I was going to call the coast guard when he'd suffered enough, and disappear off all platforms. He didn't know where I lived and wouldn't have the audacity to report me, I didn't think.

That would have been too good for him. Rage swept up through my torso, and getting back to my feet, Igot behind Chess. The fire pit blazed, and bending with my knees, Ilifted the back of his chair, dumping him face-first into the flames. The Poitín had totally incapacitated him. He didn't move, and I watched as his jacket began to melt. It took a minute for his body to wake up and react. He rolled over, bubbling unrecognizable. One of his hands reached out to me, and I held on to that flailing image for a moment before gripping his hand and pulling him out.

He was screaming. After patting out the flames, I cradled him in my arms, assuring him that help was on the way, and convinced him to let me rock him. He passed out with pain, and I scrolled through the album's various folders until they got there and the sun was rising.

He'd gotten drunk and fallen in the fire while I'd been in the bathroom, I'd told the emergency responders. The nearest hospital was far away. We got airlifted out in a helicopter. Chess's nose had melted off, as had his upper lip. Noseless and grunting, he looked like the struggling pig. No Halloween mask necessary. He'd look like a pig for the rest of his life. The transparent plastic oxygen mask fogged. He trembled.

I squeezed his hand and squinted in the sunlight glaring through the window. The scene was magnificent as we flew over Clew Bay and Croagh Patrick where Ireland's patron saint is buried.

I smiled and said, "It's a pity you can't see the view from here."

Gary Grace is from Dublin, Ireland. He holds degrees in English literature from Lesley University in Cambridge, Massachusetts and an MFA in creative writing from American College Dublin. His work has appeared in publications both in the US and Ireland. Gary has forthcoming work in the *LEON Literary Review* and an anthology, The Sex Tape Digest. Gary's short story collection, *The Nitelink*, was longlisted for Best of the Bottom Drawer Global Writing Prize.

Follow: Instagram garygrace10 Twitter@ggrace1984

Sometimes They Bite

Lawrence Block

Mowbray had been fishing the lake for better than two hours before he encountered the heavyset man. The lake was supposed to be full of largemouth bass, and that was what he was after. He was using spinning gear, working a variety of plugs and spoons and jigs and plastic worms in all of the spots where a lunker largemouth was likely to be biding his time. He was a good fisherman, adept at dropping his lure right where he wanted it, just alongside a weed bed or at the edge of subsurface structure. And the lures he was using were ideal for late-fall bass. He had everything going for him, he thought, but a fish on the end of his line.

He would fish a particular spot for a while, then move off to his right a little ways, as much for something to do as because he expected the bass to be more cooperative in another location. He was gradually working his way around the western rim of the lake when he stepped from behind some brush into a clearing and saw the other man no more than a dozen yards away.

The man was tall, several inches taller than Mowbray, very broad in the shoulders and trim in the hips and at the waist. He wore a fairly new pair of blue jeans and a poplin windbreaker over a navy flannel shirt. His boots looked identical to Mowbray's, and Mowbray guessed they'd been purchased from the same mail-order outfit in Maine. His gear was a bait-casting outfit, and Mowbray followed his line out with his eyes and saw a red bobber sitting on the water's surface some thirty yards out.

The man's chestnut hair was just barely touched with gray. He had a neatly trimmed mustache and the shadowy beard of someone who had arisen early in the morning. The skin on his hands and face suggested he spent much of his time out of doors. He was certainly around Mowbray's age, which was forty-four, but he was in much better shape than Mowbray was, in better shape, truth to tell, than Mowbray had ever been. Mowbray at once admired and envied him.

The man had nodded at Mowbray's approach, and Mowbray nodded in return, not speaking first, because he was the invader. Then, the man said, "Afternoon. Having any luck?"

"Not a nibble."

"Been fishing long?"

"A couple of hours," Mowbray said. "Must have worked my way halfway around the lake, as much as to keep moving as anything else. If there's a largemouth in the whole lake, you couldn't prove it by me."

The man chuckled. "Oh, there's bass here, all right. It's a fine lake for bass, and a whole lot of other fish as well."

"Maybe I'm using the wrong lures."

The big man shook his head. "Doubtful. They'll bite anything when their dander is up. I think a largemouth would hit a shoelace if he was in the mood, and when he's sulky, he wouldn't take your bait if you threw it in the water with no hook or line attached to it. That's just the way they are. Sometimes they bite and sometimes they don't."

"That's the truth." He nodded in the direction of the floating red bobber. "I don't suppose you're after bass yourself?"

"Not rigged up like this. No, I've been trying to get myself a couple of crappies." He pointed over his shoulder with his thumb, indicating where a campfire was laid. "I've got the skillet and the oil, I've got the meal to roll 'em in, and I've got the fire all laid just waiting for the match. Now all I need is the fish."

"No luck?"

"No more than you're having."

"Which isn't a whole lot," Mowbray said. "You from around here?"

"No. Been through here a good many times, however. I've fished this lake now and again and had good luck more often than not."

"Well," Mowbray said. The man's company was invigorating, but there was a strict code of etiquette governing meetings of this nature. "I think I'll head on around the next bend. It's probably pointless, but I'd like to get a plug in the water."

"You never can tell if it's pointless, can you? Any minute the wind can change, or the temperature can drop a few degrees, and the fish can change their behavior completely. That's what keeps us coming out here year after year, I'd say. The wonderful unpredictability of the whole affair. Say, don't go and take a hike on my account."

"Are you sure?"

The big man nodded, hitched up his trousers. "You can wet a line here as good as further down the bank. Your casting for bass won't make a lot of difference as to whether or not a crappie or a sunnie takes a shine to the shiner on my hook. And, to tell you the truth, I'd be just as glad for the company."

"So would I," Mowbray said, gratefully. "If you're sure you don't mind."

"I wouldn't have said boo if I did."

Mowbray set his aluminum tackle box on the ground, knelt beside it, and rigged his line. He tied on a spoonplug, then got to his feet and dug out a pack of cigarettes from the breast pocket of his corduroy shirt. He said, "Smoke?"

"Gave 'em up a while back. But thanks all the same."

Mowbray smoked his cigarette about halfway down, then dropped the butt and ground it underfoot. He stepped to the water's edge, took a minute or so to read the surface of the lake, then cast his plug a good distance out. For the next fifteen minutes or so, the two men fished in companionable silence. Mowbray had no strikes but expected none and was resigned to it. He was enjoying himself just the same.

"Nibble," the big man announced. A minute or two went by, and he began reeling in. "And a nibble's the extent of it," he said. "I'd better check and see if he left me anything."

The minnow had been bitten neatly in two. The big man had hooked him through the lips, and now his tail was missing. His fingers very deft, the man slipped the shiner of the hook and substituted a live one from his bait pail. Seconds later, the new minnow was in the water, and the red bobber floated on the surface.

"I wonder what did that," Mowbray said.

"Hard to say. Crawdad, most likely. Something ornery."

"I was thinking that a nibble was a good sign, might mean the fish were going to start playing along with us. But if it's just a crawdad, I don't suppose it means very much."

"I wouldn't think so."

"I was wondering," Mowbray said. "You'd think if there's a bass in this lake, you'd be after them instead of crappies."

"I suppose most people figure that way."

"None of my business, of course."

"Oh, that's all right. Hardly a sensitive subject. Happens I like the taste of little panfish better than the larger fish. I'm not a sport fisherman at heart, I'm afraid. I get a kick out of catching 'em, but my main interest is how they're going to taste when I've fried 'em up in the pan. A meat fisherman is what they call my kind, and the sporting fraternity mostly says the phrase with a certain amount of contempt." He exposed large white teeth in a sudden grin. "If they fished as often as I do, they'd probably lose some of their taste for the sporting aspect of it. I fish more days than I don't, you see. I retired ten years ago, had a retail business, and sold it not too long after my wife died. We were never able to have any children, so there was just myself, and I wound up with enough capital to keep me without working if I didn't mind living simply. And I not only don't mind it, I prefer it."

"You're young to be retired."

"I'm fifty-five, I was forty-five when I retired, which may be on the young side, but I was ready for it."

"You look at least ten years younger than you are."

"If that's a fact, I guess retirement agrees with me. Anyway, all I really do is travel around and fish for my supper. And I'd rather catch small fish. I did the other kind of fishing and tired of it in no time at all. The way I see it, I never want to catch more fish than I intend to eat. If I kill something, it goes in that copper skillet over there. Or else I shouldn't have killed it in the first place."

Mowbray was silent for a moment, unsure what to say. Finally, he said, "Well, I guess I just haven't evolved to that stage yet. I have to admit, I still get a kick out of fishing, whether I eat what I catch or not. I usually eat them, but that's not the most important part of it to me. But then I don't go out every other day like yourself. A couple times a year is as much as I can manage."

"Look at us talking," the man said, "and here you're not catching bass while I'm busy not catching crappie. We might as well announce that we're fishing for whales, for all the difference it makes."

A little while later Mowbray retrieved his line and changed lures again, then lit another cigarette. The sun was almost gone. It had vanished behind the tree line and was probably close to the horizon by now. The air was definitely growing cooler. Another hour or so would be the extent of his fishing for the day. Then it would be time to head back to the motel and some cocktails and a steak and baked potato at the restaurant down the road. And then an evening of bourbon and water in front of the motel room's television set, lying on the bed with his feet up and the glass at his elbow and a cigarette burning in the ashtray.

The whole picture was so attractive that he was almost willing to skip the last hour's fishing. But the pleasure of the first sip of the first martini would lose nothing for being deferred an hour, and the pleasure of the big man's company was worth another hour of his time.

And then, a little while later, the big man said, "I have an unusual question to ask you."

"Ask away."

"Have you ever killed a man?"

It *was* an unusual question, and Mowbray took a few extra seconds to think it over. "Well," he said at length, "I guess I have. The odds are pretty good that I have."

"You killed someone without knowing it?"

"That must have sounded odd. You see, I was in the artillery in Korea. Heavy weapons. We never saw what we were shooting at and never knew just what our shells were doing. I was in action for better than a year, stuffing shells down the throat of one big mother of a gun, and I'd hate to think that in all that time, we never hit what we aimed at. So I must have killed men, but I don't suppose that's what you're driving at."

"I mean up close. And not in the service, that's a different proposition entirely."

"Never."

"I was in the service myself. An earlier war than yours, and I was on a supply ship and never heard a shot fired in anger. But about four years ago I killed a man." His hand dropped briefly to the sheath knife at his belt. "With this."

Mowbray didn't know what to say. He busied himself, taking up the slack in his line, and waited for the man to continue.

"I was fishing," the big man said. "All by myself, which is my usual custom. Saltwater though, not fresh like this. I was over in North Carolina on the Outer Banks. Know the place?" Mowbray shook his head. "A chain of barrier islands a good distance out from the mainland. Very remote. Damn fine fishing and not much else. A lot of people fish off the piers or go out on the boats, but I was surf casting. You can do about as well that way as often as not, and that was why I figured to build a fire right there on the beach and cook my catch and eat it on the spot. I'd gathered up the driftwood and laid the fire before I wet a line, same as I did today. That's my usual custom. I had done the same thing the day before, and I caught myself half a dozen Norfolk spots in no time at all, almost before I could properly say I'd been fishing. But this particular day, I didn't have any luck at all in three hours, which shows that saltwater fish are as unpredictable as the freshwater kind. You don't much saltwater fishing?"

"Hardly any."

"I enjoy it about as much as freshwater, and I enjoyed that day on the Banks even without getting a nibble. The sun was warm, and there was a light breeze blowing off the ocean, and you couldn't have asked for a better day. The next best thing to fishing and catching fish is fishing and not catching 'em, which is a thought we can both console ourselves with after today's run of luck."

"I'll have to remember that one."

"Well, I was having a good enough time even if it looked as though I'd wind up buying my dinner, and then I sensed a fellow coming up behind me. He must have come over the dunes, because he was never in my field of vision. I knew he was there—just an instinct, I suppose— and I sent my eyes as far around as they'd go without moving my head, and he wasn't in sight." The big man paused, sighed. "You know," he said, "if the offer still holds, I believe I'll have one of those cigarettes of yours, after all."

"You're welcome to one," Mowbray said, "but I hate to start you off on the habit again. Are you sure you want one?"

The wide grin came again. "I quit smoking about the same time I quit work. I may have had a dozen cigarettes since then, spaced over the ten-year span. Not enough to call a habit."

"Then I can't feel guilty about it." Mowbray shook the pack until a cigarette popped up, then extended it to his companion. After the man helped himself, Mowbray took one as well and lit them both with his lighter.

"Nothing like an interval of a year or so between cigarettes to improve their taste," the big man said. He inhaled a lungful of smoke, pursed his lips to expel it in a stream. "I'll tell you," he said. "I really want to tell you this story if you don't mind hearing it. It's one I don't tell often, but I feel a need to get it out from time to time. It may not leave you thinking very highly of me, but we're strangers, never saw each other before, and as likely will never see each other again. Do you mind listening?

"Well, there I was, knowing I had someone standing behind me. And certain he was up to no good, because no one comes up behind you quiet like that and stands there out of sight with the intention of doing you a favor. I was holding onto my rod, and before I turned around, I propped it in the sand butt end down, the way people will do when they're fishing on a beach. Then I waited a minute, and then I turned around as if not expecting to find anyone there, and there he was, of course.

"He was a young fellow, probably no more than twenty-five. But he wasn't a hippie. No beard, and his hair was no longer than yours or mine. It did look greasy, though, and he didn't look too clean in general. Wore a light-blue T-shirt and a pair of white duck pants. Funny how I remember what he wore, but I can see him clear as day in my mind. Thin lips, sort of a wedge-shaped head, eyes that didn't line up quite right with each other, as though they had minds of their own. Some active pimples and the scars of old ones. He wasn't a prize.

"He had a gun in his hand. What you'd call a belly gun, a little .32-caliber Smith and Wesson with a two-inch barrel. Not good for a single damned thing but killing men at close range, which I'd say is all he ever wanted it for. Of course, I didn't know the make or caliber at the time. I'm not much for guns myself.

"He must have been standing less than two yards away from me. I wouldn't say it took too much instinct to have known he was there, not as close as he was."

The man drew deeply on the cigarette. His eyes narrowed in recollection, and Mowbray saw a short vertical line appear, running from the middle of his forehead almost to the bridge of his nose. Then he blew out smoke, and his face relaxed, and the line was gone.

"Well, we were all alone on the beach," the man continued. "No one within sight in either direction, no boats in close offshore, no one around to lend a helping hand. Just this young fellow with a gun in his hand and me with my hands empty. I began to regret sticking the rod in the sand. I'd done it to have both hands free, but I thought it might be useful to swing at him and try whipping the gun out of his hand.

"He said, 'All right, old man. Take your wallet out of your pocket nice and easy.' He was a Northerner, going by his accent, but the younger people don't have too much of an accent wherever they're from. Television, I suppose, is this cause of it. Makes the whole world smaller.

"Now I looked at those eyes and at the way he was holding that gun, and I knew he wasn't going to take the wallet and wave bye-bye at me. He was going to kill me. In fact, if I hadn't turned around when I did, he might well have shot me in the back. Unless he was the sort who liked to watch a person's face when he did it. There are people like that, I understand."

Mowbray felt a chill. The man's voice was so matter-of-fact, while his words were the stuff nightmares were made of.

"Well, I went into my pocket with my left hand. There was no wallet there. It was in the glove compartment of my car, parked off the road in back of the sand dunes. But I reached in my pocket to keep his eyes on my left hand, and then I brought the hand out empty and went for the gun with it, and at the same time, I was bringing my knife out of the sheath with my right hand. I dropped my shoulder and came in low, and either I must have moved quick, or all the drugs he'd taken over the years had slowed him some, but I slung that gun hand of his up and sent the gun sailing, and at the same time, I got my knife into him and laid him wide open."

He drew the knife from its sheath. It was a filleting knife with a natural wood handle and a thin, slightly curved blade about seven inches long. "This was the knife," he said. "It's a Rapala, made in Finland, and you can't beat it for being stainless steel and yet taking and holding an edge. I use it for filleting and everything else connected with fishing. Bet you've probably got one just like it yourself."

Mowbray shook his head. "I just use a folding knife," he said.

"You ought to get one of these. Can't beat 'em. And they're handy when company comes calling, believe me. I'll tell you, I opened this youngster up the way you open a fish to clean him. Came in low in the abdomen and swept up clear to the bottom of the rib cage, and you'd have thought you were cutting butter as easy as it was." He slid the knife easily back into its sheath.

Mowbray felt a chill. The other man had finished his cigarette, and Mowbray put out his own and immediately selected a fresh one from his pack. He started to return the pack to his pocket, then thought to offer it to the other man.

"Not just now. Try me in nine or ten months, though."

"I'll do that."

The man grinned his wide grin. Then his face went quickly serious. "Well, that young fellow fell down," he said. "Fell right on his back and lay there all opened up. He was moaning and bleeding, and I don't know what else. I don't recall his words, his speech was disjointed, but what he wanted was for me to get him to a doctor.

"Now the nearest doctor was in Manteo. I happened to know this, and I was near Rodanthe, which is a good twenty miles from Manteo, if not more. I saw how he was cut, and I couldn't imagine his living through a half-hour ride in a car. In fact, if there'd been a doctor six feet away from us, I seriously doubt he could have done the boy any good. I'm no doctor myself, but I have to say it was pretty clear to me that the boy was dying.

"And if I tried to get him a doctor, I'd be ruining the interior of my car, for all practical purposes, and making a lot of trouble for myself in the bargain. I didn't expect anybody would seriously try to pin a murder charge on me. It stood to reason that the fellow had a criminal record that would reach clear to the mainland and back, and I've never had worse than a traffic ticket and few enough of those. And the gun had his prints on it and none of my own. But I'd have to answer a few million questions and hang around for a least a week and doubtless longer for a coroner's inquest, and it all amounted to a lot of aggravation for no purpose since he was dying anyway.

"And I'll tell you something else. It wouldn't have been worth the trouble even to save him, because what in the world was he but a robbing, murdering snake. Why, if they stitched him up, he'd be on the street again as soon as he was healthy, and he'd kill someone else in no appreciable time at all. No, I didn't mind the idea of him dying." His eyes engaged Mowbray's "What would you have done?"

Mowbray thought about it. "I don't know," he said. "I honestly can't say. Same as you, probably."

"He was in horrible pain. I saw him lying there, and I looked around again to assure myself we were alone, and we were. I thought that I could grab my pole and frying pan and my few other bits of gear and be in my car in two or three minutes, not leaving a thing behind that could be traced to me. I'd camped out the night before in a tent and sleeping bag and wasn't registered in any motel or campground. In other words, I could be away from the Outer Banks entirely in half an hour with nothing to connect me to the area, much less to the man on the sand. I hadn't even bought gas with a credit card. I was free and clear if I just got up and left. All I had to do was leave this young fellow to a horribly slow and painful death." His eyes locked with Mowbray's again with an intensity that was difficult to bear. "Or," he said, his voice lower and softer, "or I could make things easier for him."

"Oh."

"Yes. And that's just what I did. I took and slipped the knife right into his heart. He went instantly. The life slipped right out of his eyes, and the tension out of his face, and he was gone. And that made it murder."

"Yes, of course."

"Of course," the man echoed. "It might have been an act of mercy, but legally it transformed an act of self-defense into an unquestionable act of criminal homicide." He breathed deeply. "Think I was wrong to do it?"

"No," Mowbray said.

"Do the same thing yourself?"

"I honestly don't know. I hope I would if the alternative was leaving him to suffer.”

“Well, it’s what I did. So I’ve not only killed a man, I’ve literally murdered a man. I left him under about a foot of sand at the edge of the dunes. I don’t know when the body was discovered. I’m sure it didn’t take too long. Those sands shift back and forth all the time. There was no identification on him, but the police could have labeled him from his prints because an upstanding young man like him would have had his prints on file. Nothing on the person at all except for about fifty dollars in cash, which destroys the theory that he was robbing me in order to provide himself with that night’s dinner.” His face relaxed in a half smile. “I took the money,” he said. “Didn’t see as he had any need for it, and I doubted he had much of a real claim to it, as far as that goes.”

“So you not only killed a man but made a profit on it.”

“I did at that. Well, I left the Banks that evening. Drove on inland a good distance, put up for the night in a motel just outside of Fayetteville. I never did look back, never did find out if and when they found him. It’d be on the books as an unsolved homicide if they did. Oh, and I took his gun and flung it halfway to Bermuda. And he didn’t have a car for me to worry about. I suppose he thumbed a ride or came on foot, or else he parked too far away to matter.” Another smile. “Now you know my secret.”

“Maybe you ought to leave out place names,” Mowbray said.

“Why do that?”

“You don’t want to give that much information to a stranger.”

“You may be right, but I can only tell a story in my own way. I know what’s going through your mind right now.”

“You do?”

“Want me to tell you? You’re wondering if what I told you is true or not. You figure if it happened, I probably wouldn’t tell you, and yet it sounds pretty believable in itself. And you halfway hope it’s the truth and halfway hope it isn’t. Am I close?”

“Very close,” Mowbray admitted.

“Well, I’ll tell you something that’ll tip the balance. You’ll really want to believe it’s a pack of lies.” He lowered his eyes. “The fact of the matter is you’ll lose any respect you may have had for me when you hear the next part.”

"Then why tell me?"

"Because I feel the need."

"I don't know if I want to hear this," Mowbray said.

"I want you to. No fish, and it's getting dark. You're probably anxious to get back to where you're staying and have a drink and a meal. Well, this won't take long." He had been reeling in his line. Now the operation was concluded, and he set the rod deliberately on the grass at his feet. Straightening up, he said, "I told you before about my attitude toward fish. Not killing what I'm going to eat. And there this young man was, all laid open, internal organs exposed—"

"Stop."

"I don't know what you'd call it, curiosity or compulsion or some primitive streak. I couldn't say. But what I did, I cut off a small piece of his liver before I buried him. Then after he was under the sand, I lit my cook fire and—well, no need to go into detail."

Thank God for that, Mowbray thought. For small favors. He looked at his hands. The left one was trembling. The right, the one gripping his spinning rod, was white at the knuckles, and the tips of his fingers ached from gripping the butt of the rod so tightly.

"Murder, cannibalism, and robbing the dead," the man said. "That's quite a string for a man who never got worse than a traffic ticket. And all three in considerably less than an hour."

"Please," Mowbray said. His voice was thin and high-pitched. "Please don't tell me anymore."

"Nothing more to tell."

Mowbray took a deep breath, held it. This man was either lying or telling the truth, Mowbray thought, and in either case, he was quite obviously an extremely unusual person. At the very least.

"You shouldn't tell that story to strangers," he said after a moment. "True or false, you shouldn't tell it."

"I feel the need."

"Of course, it's all to the good that I *am* a stranger. After all, I don't know anything about you, not even your name."

"It's Tolliver."

"Or where you live, or—"

"Wallace P. Tolliver. I was in the retail hardware business in Oak Falls, Missouri. That's not far from Joplin."

"Don't tell me anything more," Mowbray said desperately. "I wish you hadn't told me what you did."

"I had to," the big man said. The smile flashed again. "I've told that story three times before today. You're the fourth man ever to hear it."

Mowbray said nothing.

"Three times. Always to strangers who happen to turn up while I'm fishing. Always on a long, lazy afternoon, those afternoons when the fish just don't bite no matter what you do."

Mowbray began to do several things. He began to step backwards, and he began to release his tight hold on his fishing rod, and he began to extend his left arm protectively in front of him.

But the filleting knife had already cleared its sheath.

Lawrence Block is an American crime writer best known for two long-running New York–set series about the recovering alcoholic PI Matthew Scudder and the gentleman burglar Bernie Rhodenbarr. Block was named a Grand Master by the Mystery Writers of America in 1994.